THE MARVELLOUS BEGINNING OF DOCTOR BAGGY SMACKER

Antoine*Antoine* Publishing
www.antoineantoine.com.au

This first edition 2023
Published by Antoine*Antoine* Publishing

Copyright Baggy Smacker 2023

Baggy Smacker asserts the moral right to be identified as the author of this work.

ISBN: 978-0-6457160-0-9 (eBook)
ISBN: 978-0-6457160-3-0 (Paperback)

This novel is a work of fiction loosely based on historical events. The names, characters and incidents portrayed are the product of the author's imagination. Any resemblance to actual persons, living or dead, is entirely coincidental.

Formatted for distribution by Antoine*Antoine* Publishing

Cover illustration by Sian Horrocks
Cover layout design by Thomas Overend

All rights reserved. No part of this publication may be reproduced, stored in a retrieval system, or transmitted, in any form or by any means, electronic, mechanical, photocopying, recording or otherwise, without the prior written permission of the publishers.

PREFACE

I remember passing out of the womb like an omnibus from a Wilts & Dorset terminal - quite late - and greeting the midwife with a firm handshake.

"Good show," I praised her, before offering constructive feedback on her work. Nurse Meredith laughed a great, hearty laugh and together we spent my inaugural eve sipping creme de menthe out of a beaked cup. She was a passionate, fiery lady and our intimacy would last the best part of the week before Merry was cruelly taken from me. On lonesome nights I still, to this day, often weep as I read out her name from the arrest warrant that I keep in my ticket pocket, and think back to those wonderful times we shared. I learnt so early that love at an adolescent age (calculated in this case using a mean average) can be so naive.

My sweet mother died shortly after giving birth to me. Regretfully, the sound of popping corks had drowned out her calls for attention, but the man we paid to take her body away said that there was probably not much we could have done for her, moments after we'd handsomely tipped him. I do believe though that my mother would not have been the sort to put her own health before a celebration. That simply isn't the Smacker way.

My father was a stoic man, due to a fine balancing of determination and watered-down brandy. During his early life, he built the reputation of a hard worker, having spent much of his youth toiling down in the mines. He would often regale me with gruff tales, throbbing with masculinity, of how he would dangerously descend a rickety mine shaft with a dozen other men, plummeting toward hellish silence. The creaking of the pulley mechanism was all one would hear, unless they were that day accompanied by the soft whimpers of a young greenhorn who'd been brought in to replace the last of them to die.

Once they disembarked the mine lift, they would disperse into a network of open-floor cubicles and sell Vacation Ownership products over the phone to pensioners for eleven hours a day. My father's eyes would glisten and his hands would tremble as he told me of the impossibilities of their sales targets and the meagre retainer that kept them locked into servitude for decades and decades. He spoke of how the dusty shadows of the deep mine would tear many away from life with blackened lungs and, for those that survived, dirty their business shirts with a thick layer of soot that eroded the bearings on their washing machines, tragically voiding their warranties.

It was my father who told me of my destiny, on a cold morning within the pews of the spectacularly-appointed Wimborne Minster.

"Baggy," he said. The words puffed from his mouth along with a vapour of cheap whisky. "You do know you're meant for bigger things?"

"What do you mean, Father?"

"You're not gonna work down the mines, like your old man. You're not gonna work in the filth, with scum at your sides, trying to flog a two-bedroom hotel room on the Costa Del Sol across three weeks in February. You're gonna have it better."

He attempted to wipe forming tears from his eyes but missed considerably and instead struck himself in the temple, exacerbating his weeping.

"You're gonna be a big shot. You're gonna save people. You're gonna take these lemons that life gives you, and you're gonna rip 'em in half with your naked hands. And you're gonna stick life to the ground, you're gonna wrestle that vagabond to the ground, and push the lemons into life's eyes. And then when life's screaming in pain and shouting 'For the love of god, no more lemons!' you're gonna pull your trousers down like this..." he pulled his trousers down to illustrate. "And then you're gonna shit right into life's mouth like this. Watch me, my son. Watch me."

Father then proceeded to defecate onto the hassock before him in the pew we were sitting at, careful to mask the sounds of his flatulence beneath the baritone murmur of the Canon's sermon.

Once Father had completed his movement and tidied up to the detriment of a nearby hymnal, he returned to a seated position and looked me in the eye.

"Baggy, my son."

"Yes, Father?"

"You're going to be a *doctor*."

And in a rare moment of foresight, he would be correct. I *would* indeed become a doctor. But what could not be predicted was the unlikely journey that would be required for me to do so. No one could foresee the tapestry of romance, friendship, adversity or wartime ahead and yet, to meet my ambition, I would need to befriend famous artists, form a mutual hatred with a newborn baby, rise as a celebrated star of television and dramatically fall to emotional lows never thought possible. If one were to tell me that the path ahead would involve cunning espionage across central Europe, daring dogfights above the

English Channel, and the brutal killing of a dessert salesman in a wintry Belgian glen, I would have laughed in one's face for several seconds before stopping and worriedly inquiring further as to the last bit.

To preserve this intriguing tale, I have journalised the details of these stories into this first part of my memoirs, in the hope that it might entertain, inspire and spark dreams of the readers' own, and I have done so with all the honesty and accuracy I might muster. So without any more hesitation, please settle into a warm chair with a large drink at your side, and allow me to tell you of what I humbly consider to be The Marvellous Beginning of Doctor Baggy Smacker.

Contents

CHAPTER ONE:

A Shining Debut

The era in which I emerged was a difficult time. Post-war optimism had petered out, rationing was still in effect and, as such, the people of Britain were all being rather inconsiderate to one another. As a means to curtail the countrywide mood, the government elected to offer free courses on 'Repairing the Nation's Self Awareness' but sadly no one felt that they themselves were in need of improvement in that particular area, and so very few enrolled. To further depress matters, all that was left on the wireless was a series of quiz panels hosted by a home-schooled man named Darryl and his constant inaccuracies were encouraging the national murder rate.

In my father's fiftieth year, he established moderate wealth after penning a series of terrifically well-received instructional manuals on the topic of 'How to Run the Perfect Bath'. The entire first act of these volumes consisted of counterfeit prescriptions for heroin, followed by two-to-three-hundred diagrams of taps, but for a brief and colourful couple of weeks prior to the passing of the Dangerous Drugs Act, the works even managed to outsell some of the less-popular bibles of the time.

Father's revolutionary theories thrust him into the upper echelons of society and he even claimed to have lathered up Alexandra of Denmark one night after drinking too much at a Royal Eurovision Party. "My randy Scandy Alexandy," you would hear him ejaculate late at night, often while alone in his study.

Upon this ascent was where I met my first very close friend, the elegant James Ferdinand Bambi; a much-respected fellow who had expertly navigated the razor-edged industry of log flume design.

"I tell you, it's all about the big drop at the end, my boy," he had once revealed to me in a whisper from the tightened corner of his mouth. "Make them drop and the money don't stop. That's what we all say in the flume industry."

Bambi was an eccentric, caring man with soft hands, forever moistened by the juice of the flume. His wife, Mrs Jennifer Bambi, was the product of prestigious breeding and the heiress to a lucrative empire of traffic light window-cleaning franchises. She often proudly declared that her ancestors had pioneered the concept of celibacy and that their immortal chastity was famed throughout the land. Sadly, after employing heraldic detectives to assert these claims at considerable expense, she was later to concede that her own conception meant they were probably just notably unattractive.

The Bambis were in their fifties when we first crossed paths but the chasmic difference in age stood no chance of preventing a wonderful friendship between James and me, in defiance of societal norms.

I recall how bravely he responded to the accusations and the bitter indignation of those who questioned him for mounting a friendship with a mere one-year-old. But Bambi was not a man to be troubled by the status quo, nor the jaded speculation of others.

"You don't get through life by just coasting along lazily and waiting for something to happen!" he would exclaim, before excitedly mentioning that "actually sometimes you do, because that is *precisely* how log flumes operate."

Bambi was kind enough to assist in furnishing me with a well-paying job at a leisure facility owned by a cousin of his, an exuberant war widow named Ms Clara St. Cloud, who had daringly gambled the state-funded compensation for her husband's intriguingly-grotesque death on a horse named 'Stern Willy'. At thirty-five-to-one odds, she'd won enough money to open her first of many theme parks at a local children's hospital. The prized feature was a water ride (of course designed by James Ferdinand Bambi) called Hades' Delight, and it simulated a relaxing float through the bubbling, mystic river Styx before eventually plummeting into the Underworld. It was enchanting, educational and exciting; all that a child in need should need.

Stylistically, the ride was an acclaimed success and the members of the local community were delighted by its inclusion, however several complaints were soon registered with regard to the awkward implicative nature and proximity to the typhoid ward. As more and more parents of terminally-ill children expressed frustration about having to answer tricky questions on the subject of mortality - a task they felt should have been handled by the nursing staff - the enterprise was eventually closed down and replaced with a much-more-easily explained mural depicting the canonisation cycle of the Pope. Bambi mourned the dissolution of both his cousin's hard work and his own artistry, and would recall in regret-soaked tones of how orderlies would continue to profit handsomely off the coins left in the mouths of fresh cadavers by friends and loved ones who had really gotten into the whole thing.

It did not deter Ms St. Cloud, however. In a world frenzied by booming reputations and lines of credit approved on breast size alone, she established what was considered to be the world's first 'petting pond' near Kendal. It was there I worked as a Swan Wrangler for three months of the year, in the quaint summer of Northern England, wading into the chilly waters of Killington Lake to reprimand waterfowl for biting the eyes out of children's faces.

I resided for that time at a guesthouse in a typical north-English hamlet of no more than a dozen stone buildings, nine of which were pubs. Despite succumbing to a fierce Mint Cake addiction and developing trench foot, I look back on those days with a great fondness.

I experienced my first true love on the pebbled shores of Windermere, where I met a teen-aged, freckled lass named

Mortha. She possessed an enigmatic voice that I assumed to be a Glaswegian accent until I discovered, months later, it was the result of her being deaf. Mortha and I shared so much together; experiences, stories, opium-based foot wash and, eventually, the Epstein-Barr virus. We were completely in love by the end of my first summer at the petting pond and had she not been offered a part-time gig as the Shadow Secretary of State for International Trade, I suspect our lives might have followed a very different path.

But some things are not to be.

I returned to London at the end of summer via airship and made a conscious effort to survive the journey; a decision that went against the fashion of the time. With a tidy sum of money in my pocket and a new world ahead of me, I pondered the man I wished to become. My dear friend, James Ferdinand Bambi and his delightful cousin, the entrepreneurial Ms Clara St. Cloud had both seized mighty legacies and I looked to them with the highest respect, but as I strolled through the streets of Chelsea, I considered the ceiling of their dreams. Did I simply wish to pursue a single facet of life and chase it endlessly, like an ambitious greyhound behind a potentially-unreachable mock-rabbit? Or did I wish for something greater? Could I dream bigger and more intelligently, and find a way to encourage the mock-rabbits to instead come to me so I wouldn't risk being shot in the head if I underperformed?

There was much to consider as time poured away, however, my wonderings and wanderings would have to remain at ease for a moment. Life itself was conjuring an agenda upon my behalf.

CHAPTER TWO:

An Arrest in Development

My father became intimately involved with alcohol as the ennui of retirement fermented. He had developed a considerable desire for what he called "the hard stuff". Whether he meant alcoholic spirits or the floorboards of his dining room was hard to define, as his closeness to one would most often follow the other.

His habit began harmlessly enough, with a simple, respectable, occasional vomit from a sleeping state on a Chesterfield in the middle of one of the many soirees he so frequently attended. In the earlier phases of his condition, fellow party-goers would in fact cheer and rejoice now that the bar for debauchery had been set at a stoopable height, and hosts would find delight in the opportunity to get their money's worth from the cleaning staff. But gradually, the reputation of the Smacker dynasty came to rust.

During these fraughtful times, Father only just avoided renown as an outspoken racist by procuring medical documentation assuring observers that his myriad, bigoted, drunken outbursts were simply the result of a toxic reaction to Coltsfoot Rock. In those unenlightened days, decrying continental Europe and expelling bodily fluid to the carpet of an associate's magnificently-appointed manse was considered a niche field of sophistication but, even then, those close to him were surprised that he continued to maintain a facade of prestige for as long as he did. Such was my father's stature and elegance, that he even set something of a fashion among the local youth, and soon enough men of Oxbridge pedigree would gather at high-end establishments to quaff Chartreuse and see if they could impress female wait-staff by burning gastro-acidic holes through each other's coats over the course of a weekend. This delightful competition was almost considered for inclusion in the Highland Games, though its application failed once the poor learnt of its rules and made the whole affair feel a bit common.

But Father's drinking became as frequent as the rising sun, and often synchronised to it. People began to speak his name in muted tones, and the social invites began to peter out. The help found it more manageable to simply list on his calendar the events he had been requested to avoid, and the local community pooled together a sum of money to employ a taxi-cab during special events to drive him several miles out of town where there would be fewer children for him to upset. At the request of the Church, Sunday mornings were immediately blacked out, and altar boys would instead visit on consecutive fortnights to haul away the immense paper bail that served as Father's absentee confessional. Any declarations of a willingness to attend in person were politely met with the insistence that God is everywhere, so the floor of the downstairs toilet was as good as popping in.

As his condition grew worse, Father would come to my house late at night in the company of a mysterious acquaintance; a slender and serious man known to me only as Pipsy. I would awake to boisterous knocking at my door and a cloud of hazed perry, and my father, barely able to stand up, would slur endlessly about his grandiose plans to write a musical based on the Book of Joshua. He would stumble over the pronunciation of the word 'Deuteronomistic' and then the doormat.

"Pipsy shall play Joshua," he would declare, face down on the floor.

"I'm very good," Pipsy would follow. He said so with all the frequency of one who wasn't.

"And I shall play Moses!" Father would say.

When confronted with the issue of Moses' inevitable admission from the work, due to his having died by that biblical chapter, he would hurl a bottle toward me and cry out, "Moses' ghost! You godless boy!" and then pass out in the hallway. Pipsy would then loyally curl into a ball next to my father and growl at me if I came too close. This happened almost every full moon for six months, and I began to worry.

Father's iceberg finally tipped on a fateful day in Saltburn-by-the-Sea, to which I was an attendant. We were there to pay our respects to the late Sir Derek Elrington, who had recently died of shock following the Earl of Zetland's decision to shoot him four times in the chest. His widow had requested a beach funeral, assuring us all that it was what her husband had wanted and that the burial fees were much more reasonable. There were approximately two dozen mourning souls gathered on the shores of the North Sea, and two or three other souls who were taking it all rather well. Elrington's widow had just finished distributing plastic spades to us all following her very moving and distracting series of spoken eulogic limericks, and we stood waiting patiently for the tide to bring the coffin back in.

Father had brought a barely-clad German prostitute named Katrina with him to the funeral. In those more conservative days, such an action was considered to be in poor taste. He was drunk and had been for an impressive while. At the time when his current binge had begun, the recently departed was not so. A chilled ocean breeze rocked my father back and forth and a half-empty bottle of Kentucky bourbon hung from his fingers. Elrington's widow had begun sobbing mournfully as somebody had just handed her a bill for the catering.

In the corner of my eye, I could see Father's empty hand work its way toward Katrina's left buttock, only to be swatted away by the German.

"How much for a little bit of randy in the sandy?" Father rasped and submitted another application to grope her.

"Nein!" Katrina exclaimed, again pushing him away. Father dug into his pocket and began counting out a comically-tired number of shillings.

"Father," I intervened. "Now is not the time to be engaging physically with our prostitutes."

"Nonsense, there is plenty of time." He gestured toward the sea where a small pod of porpoises appeared to be prodding Elrington's coffin toward Norway. The widow appeared to weep more heavily. She was all too aware of Scandinavian customs fees.

Katrina was having none of this, despite Father's attempts to thrust money at her.

"Halt!" she cried, knocking the coins from his hand, but Father refused to relent.

The other attendees were obeying British tradition and stood silently, ignoring the commotion and hoping it would soon pass - a strategy that would become famously military in the coming decades. I was compelled by a sense of family duty to extinguish the brewing tension.

"Father. Please. This is a time of mourning. There will be plenty of time to violate Germans later."

"Don't speak to me in that tone, boy. This is what Derek would have wanted," he lied. Sir Elrington was a devout Catholic and a very prominent member of the germanophobic community; he would be rolling in his grave, given enough assistance from the porpoises.

Katrina's patience finally wore through and she slapped my father's cheek with the might of a thousand Kaisers. She roared what sounded like vulgar obscenity (a police report would later translate it to be German for "The weather's not as bad as forecasted") as my father recoiled. Father was not overjoyed. He immediately retaliated by throwing the bourbon bottle toward Katrina, but his aim was poor and it hit the face of the wife of the Earl of Zetland, who was in attendance as his proxy to apologise to everyone for all the bother.

It had finally become too much for all the mourners and they exorcised their misery as one, by subduing Father and hitting him repeatedly with their spades. Elrington's widow was busy hurriedly scooping nine shillings from the sand, but she stopped briefly to curse our family name.

"Fuck off, Smacker, you drunk cunt!" she suggested.

Eventually, two constables arrived to break up the tiff and they arrested my father for the attempted murder of the wife of the Earl of Zetland. They arrested Katrina also but later released her when it turned out she was an undercover police officer working to infiltrate the North Yorkshire counterfeit rhubarb trade and had mistaken my father for a person of interest because he smelt so heavily of Coltsfoot Rock.

Father was eventually convicted and sentenced to four years of hard labour in HM Wakefield, an experience that would leave him permanently shattered.

Horrifically, this left me with a tarnished surname and in the awkward position of lacking legal guardianship. At my young age, this meant only one thing; an imprisonment of my own in an orphanage. My calm and simple life was set to endure chaos and I feared I was not ready.

CHAPTER THREE:

A Youth Misplaced

Beeston Orphanage was a wretched place, tucked away in an unfashionable borough of Nottingham. The building itself was a historic seventeenth-century poodle farm, from which the kennels had been converted into four-bed dormitories. The dogs had been released into the wild but had fared poorly, and so were returned and trained to prepare a very watery, over-salted macaroni & cheese dish for our every meal. There were approximately fifty of us in attendance, all boys, but only because being female was, at the time, greatly frowned upon.

Beeston had been purchased from the state by a gang of semi-reformed bikies who practised compassion on a strictly part-time basis and moonlighted as a touring men's choir. Of all the staff, the orphanage director, a skin-headed man named Spider, was the most tolerant of his duties. Once a week, each boy would be sent to confession and encouraged to admit their sins, to which Spider would gleefully respond "WRONG!" and whip them around the mouth with a bicycle chain.

For twelve hours per day, six days per week, we were forced to labour away in an onsite sweatshop, developing cryptic crossword puzzles for local newspapers. We would receive two meals each day and a pig's ear if we were cunning enough to develop a flirtatious relationship with one of the poodles. It was an incredibly dark period of time in my life and were it not for the friendships I established I would have no doubt gone insane, as many did.

In my first month at Beeston, I remained wilfully alone and would only converse with the other boys to loudly taunt them with my magnificent collection of pigs ears courtesy of a neutered-yet-incorrigible cocker-spoodle named Preston. But gradually, lonesomeness draped its heavy cape across my shoulders and the need for a meaningful conversation became overbearing. It was here that I became close friends with a pale, delicate young man named Joseph Darkfire, or Chief, as he proudly introduced himself.

"They call me Chief, short for Neckerchief. My late mother once walked in on me masturbating into a neckerchief, so it sort of just stuck," he explained, even though absolutely no one had suggested he do so, and a thousand false anecdotes would have sufficed.

As it happened, Joseph revealed himself to be a man almost flawed by honesty. So startling was his readiness to broadcast his each and every thought to anyone who cared to receive, even Director Spider considered his earnest nature undeserving of his chain and instead only subjected him to a light slapping upon the inner-thigh with a de-thorned rose stem. It was with pride that I assisted Joseph to funnel his natural gift of effortless articulation into the art of poetry, and he immediately began creating the most beautiful sonnets that provided a marvellous escape from reality for all the boys at Beeston.

Years later, I would carry a leaf of paper with Joseph's adoring words scrawled upon it. It read:

> *Hark ringing bells, that toll to herald morning's feast,*
> *Come gather boys for roll, as called by vicious priest,*
> *Leave tongues at loll, for food prepared by curlied beast,*
> *And lay away those dreams of home, for now at least,*
> *And lay away this gruel on which we live,*
> *And lay away his chain with pain to give,*
> *And lay away these hounds' neglect of sieve,*
> *And climb above this all and learn, forgive,*
> *For sunrise kills each night we dread,*
> *Though our brothers will lie around us yawning,*
> *And never we must count our nearly dead,*
> *As we promise to ourselves, 'just one more morning'.*

Joseph had written it for me following a fierce bout of food poisoning I'd suffered amidst an epidemic of kennel cough in the Beeston kitchens, during which I would loudly announce my imminent death every fifteen-to-twenty minutes. In what I assumed to be my final throes, I liquidated my assets and donated them to an already-prospering chartered accountancy firm owned by Spider's mother who, in retrospect, I now realise was simply Spider wearing two poodles as a hat. Against the ensuing regret and the final stages of nausea, Joseph kindly performed for me, and the poem's sweetness assisted in excreting the remainder of the offending instigators from my system.

There were diamonds among the rough as far as the Beeston staff were concerned. While most were bittered and angered by the sleep loss and poor critical reception of their midnight choristry, there were some who offered lifelines to the boys. A particularly understanding night attendant named Dukey would bless us with access to the outside world so long as each temporary refugee promised to pilfer at least fifty pounds worth of goods from local retail outlets. These daring raids were committed to with such a delightful atmosphere of comradery and adventure by all that Dukey was soon able to purchase an island off the coast of Greece and retire. It was hard to hear precisely what he promised on the night he left, as his voice was troubled by the implant of a full upper row of newly implanted emerald teeth, but I assume he departed following an invite to all us boys to one day visit him on his paradisiacal getaway.

My first year at Beeston was relatively incident-free. I remained well-behaved and industrious enough to avoid any sort of scrutiny from the staff, and my initial reservedness was soon scuffed away, allowing me to establish a considerable circle of friends.

There was Joseph, of course, the young master of poetic literature, and then his bunk-mate, Ajak Chol, a dark-skinned hautboist from Mauritius who would serenade us with complicated oboe solos that never strayed too far from being tolerable. Making up the fourth of my tightest ensemble was a chap we called Whippet; an unfortunate fellow who claimed that his parents had dropped him off at the orphanage two years ago whilst the house was being flea-bombed, and would be back for him any day now.

Together, we labelled ourselves the Ramblers, and would stroll together and bask in each other's creativity during our twenty-minute 'free period' between evening meal-time and our nightly Morris Dancing lesson.

One week, following a patch of considerable boredom, we conspired to escape after discovering that Ajak had been silently tunnelling a way out of the orphanage compound at night, concealing his progress during the daytime with a sultry four-by-four poster of Clementine Churchill. We planned our run for freedom during the night of the famous Nottingham Folk Festival, timing our footsteps with the clacking of sticks and the ringing of bells. Ajak was first to crawl through his hole but quickly discovered that the tunnel he'd dug somehow u-turned and reentered on the opposite side of the same room. Rather than give up, we spun-kick the main door of our dormitory complex until it was opened by an inquisitive orderly, who we overwhelmed with slaps to the head and additional spin-kicks. In a glorious tide of adrenaline, we stole a set of keys to a guard's 'hog' and climbed the outside fence to liberty, racing off into the night against the waning drone of a shrill cantata of melodeons and accordions and libertarian rhetoric.

After our ascension to freedom, we fared poorly. Our food reserves dried out by the following Monday so we quickly became cannibalistic and ate Whippet - who had died of impatience the night before - for a late-night pudding. Ajak appeared disgusted by our inhumanity until he tasted a piece of the boy's poached thigh lightly brushed in a dark chocolate fudge sauce. Subsequently, he became enamoured with the taste of human flesh and departed our company to pursue a career in oncology. That left just Joseph and I, huddled against each other in the dark and wintry Nottinghamshire nights, cast away by society in a Godless existence, perched shivering within our makeshift encampment in the corner of a Salvation Army soup kitchen with irritatingly long queues that we refused to commit to.

After a week, Joseph became fevered and ghostly white. His trembling became not that of the cold, but of the frenzied symptoms of a kind of chemical affliction. His sleep became interrupted by ghoulish moanings and twistings and turnings, and each night would a haze of his cold sweat dampen the canvas of our quarters. I would later learn that the bikies had been lacing our mac & cheese dinners with opium - all part of a dastardly plan to numb our memories, affect our artistic interpretations and sell friendship bracelets and pop music lyrics to a black market of slave art - and that this sickness was a symptom of withdrawal, but at the time succeeding our liberty, I took these convulsions to indicate Joseph's imminent death.

When I abandoned Joseph's frailty just five days from our escape and helplessly returned to the only refuge I knew, Beeston's haunting arches glared over me as a soulless eclipse. I trudged through its steel gates and dragged myself to the tattooed feet of Spider, who was still 'coming down' from something he'd ingested at the festival. He spared me his whip and instead gathered the more effete Sopranos from the gang's ranks, and as one they struck me with something more bracing than a mere chain.

"Your father is up for parole," they sang, over and over again, in an off-pitch, screeching falsetto for roughly an hour.

I was aghast. Could it be happening? Could I finally be free? I closed my eyes and willed myself away from the horrendous noise and dreamed of my father.

CHAPTER FOUR:

My Patriarchal Debacle

"Pertaining to Mister Smacker's rehabilitation and psychological well-being, we will now hear the words of our prison psychologist, Doctor Arthur Porter. Doctor Porter, would you please?"

A man rose from one of the several chairs at the front of the room, and, through a thick west country accent, he cleared his throat and spoke.

"Thank you, Mister Swanson. Thank you all, gentlemen. Ahem. I give you my appreciation for making the trip out here today, and offer my gratitude in advance for listening to my testimony. I would like to begin with a few words about Mister Smacker's excellent behaviour, and then there'll be a small interval in which my beautiful wife, Tulip, will perform one of her dances that she does so very well."

I can clearly remember the sight of the peculiar Doctor Arthur Porter, a bespeckled, balding man with a severe hunch and a right leg approximately two feet shorter than his left. He was that day adorned in the most tolerable brown tweed jacket and a pleated pair of, at the time revolutionary, skin-tight denim short-shorts. Porter was not formally educated in the medical practice of psychology - his Doctorate of Visual Merchandising was an honorary title bestowed upon him by the University of Leeds - but he'd provided exemplary moral guidance and analysis to footballers as manager of Doncaster Rovers in the previous season and had signed on loan to HM Prison Wakefield as soon as the transfer window had opened.

My father was ever the charming man, even following his laborious and destructive sentence, and it eventuated that he had cast a considerable spell over Doctor Porter in their sessions together. Their friendship had blossomed into something that Wakefield could not contain, and they even co-directed the male-only prison's yearly production of Romeo & Juliet, for which they gender-swapped all the female roles in a move that would have been lauded as contemporary brilliance, had they remembered to tell the audience.

Father wore a look of intrigue and also trousers. He was, after all, a mere eighteen months into a four-year sentence and despite his apparently meticulous behaviour, such a premature release was virtually unprecedented. In the room were sat a dozen men of various status, including the embittered son of the late Earl of Zetland who had discovered he'd been pushed from the will by his parents and had volunteered to testify as to the brilliance of my father's foresight.

I was in attendance with my esteemed friend, James Ferdinand Bambi, who sat deep in thought alongside me, quietly muttering something about an upcoming flume venture in distant Australia.

"Who would love the thrill of the flume more than the colonials? A flume could provide a wondrous and welcome reminiscence of their epic journey to the Southern Land! Think of it, Baggy!" he ejaculated close to my ear.

I thought about how absolutely correct my dear friend was in his assertion.

"My James, however do you come about these magnificent ideas?"

"Ideas come to me, Baggy, as eggs to the hen."

"Effortlessly?"

"No, Baggy. I mean I produce approximately once a day and it often irritates a vegetarian."

I laughed at Bambi's joke until I took from his glare that he was fiercely serious.

Dr Arthur Porter continued his testimony.

"I'm stood before you today, to talk of the rehabilitation of Mister Whitlock Smacker, and I stand before you as a man lacking in words to describe how beautifully adorned in redemption he most certainly is. For what is there that can be said about Mister Smacker that isn't the most glorious of praise? He is a gentleman of the finest kind and truly a brilliant asset to the population of this here HM Wakefield."

From behind a trestle table supporting the plates of finger food we had all been asked to bring, Dr Porter produced a large, framed painting. It was a portrait of himself and my father, sitting upon the coast of Swanage, both of them stooped toward each other to facilitate the biting into of a single Cornish pasty from opposing ends. The Doctor swallowed loudly and pointed toward the painting.

"Does that look to you like the posture and generosity of a man who doesn't know remorse and compassion and redemption?"

The gathered audience tittered together in the agreement that a man who lacked remorse and compassion and redemption would not have the sort of light in their soul that could conjure the humble abandon required to share a Cornish pasty with another man upon the twinkling and sparkling Jurassic coastline of the seaside town of Swanage.

For several minutes, Dr Arthur Porter proceeded to describe the meticulous facets of my father's disposition, revealing both the closeness of their friendship and their matching tattoos. It appeared, however, that not all were convinced. As Dr Porter seemed to draw towards a dramatic emotional climax, the prison's Chief of Security, a ghastly-looking man named Captain Radley, announced himself in a stern baritone.

"Doctor Porter, you speak as a man touched by an angel. Perhaps you have been. But we know there to be both angels of light and angels of darkness. With that in our minds, I do have some questions to ask. On the seventeenth night of the most recently passed month of May, Prisoner Smacker found himself involved in an altercation with three other inmates in which he was the only survivor. He was found by inspection, standing in a pool of their blood and limbs, in possession of a crudely-improvised scimitar. As the only Caucasian man involved in the incident, he blamed what appears to have been racially-motivated actions on a most-unlikely allergic reaction to Coltsfoot Rock. How does this behaviour align itself with the figure of pristine decency that you would have us believe in?"

A collective wince rippled through those of us emotionally close to my father. He had indeed been involved in an in-house triple-murder not more than six weeks beforehand and I had completely forgotten of it. But upon Radley's recollection, I remembered suddenly the blood-written letter that had been delivered to me, in which Father had declared the wilful nature in which he had carried out his misdeed, and specified his intention to do it more upon his release, over and over and over "until all in this world that dared to stand within a mile of him were chopped up into tiny little pieces as their children and wives watched on". I had dismissed these sentiments as his usual post-Eucharist, conservative rhetoric and discarded the letter without so much as a second thought, but I began to fear that Radley was about to stunt Father's chances at an early reprieve.

"You see, Captain Radley, those men what he killed were a bad sort," Doctor Porter replied.

"Are not all of our inmates, Doctor Porter, in the eyes of the laws of our land, 'bad sorts'?"

Doctor Arthur Porter was in a tight spot. Several of us shuffled awkwardly in our seats. Jennifer Bambi's disdain became palpable, as she had slaved for several hours over a mango cheesecake all for the event and perhaps would have considered something store-bought had she remembered all the murders.

Porter paused for a moment longer. His eyes flickered slightly. He looked over at my father who cupped his hands to his mouth and, with a look of urgency, attempted to whisper something toward HM Wakefield's resident psychologist. Unfortunately, for the past many months, the constant clanging of hammer upon stone - the staple activity of my father's laborious incarceration - had rendered his hearing limited and therefore his perception of volume miscalculated, and so he quite loudly shouted, "*Arthur! Attack his heritage like we practised!*" for all among us to hear. After a moment's hesitation, Doctor Porter returned his gaze to Radley with a renewed look of resolve and spoke.

"You're uh… You're half Irish, are you not, Captain Radley?"

"Now, look here…" Radley began to splutter.

"An Irish… Catholic, if I'm not mistaken?"

"Oh now come on, we just heard Mister Smacker say you've been prac-"

Doctor Porter waved aside his protests and bravely forged ahead.

"Tell me, Captain Radley, if your beloved Catholicism is so wonderful, whatever has drawn you here across the Irish sea, away from your blessed emerald isle? Running from something, are we? Or do you simply believe you have the right to come waltzing into our fine country, criticising the fine people of His Majesty's England? Yes, perhaps this man is responsible for the brutal triple murder of his cellmates. But maybe you'd care to tell us precisely what is so virtuous about yourself, that you have come here as the outspoken, moral arbiter of a religion you have oddly sailed miles to escape from? Has Ireland finally become so flawlessly crime-free that you're all now with such a surplus of expertise that it simply must be exported for fear of going stale? We're all ears, Captain Radley."

"Oh for goodness sake, this is utter madness. Did we all not just hear Mister Smacker quite clearly advertise conspiracy between himself and this alleged psychologist?!" Radley cried, appealing to the crowd for their support against such a ludicrous tactic.

Unfortunately for the Captain, the political climate of the time had proven anti-Irish sentiment to be a thing of considerable trend, and the tide of apprehension surrounding my father's misdoings felt to be heading away from shore. A hibernophobic, protestant murmur began to form and quickly rose to a boil, spurred on by James Ferdinand Bambi crying out things like "Those beasts could not tell their log flume rides from their river rapids rides!" and "I hear that those godless micks steal from their own grandmothers!" and "The difference is in the myriad variations in the design and capacity of the passenger vessel!"

As the tension and noise escalated, Jennifer Bambi frantically dashed to the table with an empty Tupperware container in hand, hell-bent on repossessing her mango cheesecake. Before she could attend to its safety, the prison chaplain rushed forward from among the attendees and shanked her four times in the back with a sharpened crucifix. True chaos was only seconds away.

With the room turning upon a trembling Mister Radley, Doctor Porter skilfully stepped in with strategic grace.

"Now, now, ladies and gentlemen," he gestured calmly with open hands, "Are we not above all this? Is this not exactly what Mister Radley wants to happen? Is this not the goal of the Irish? The will of the Catholics? To divide us. To separate us against one another. To use their puritanical, monochrome perversion of right and wrong to condemn those of us they consider to be unworthy of their acceptance? Those beasts that the good Mister Smacker moved on from this life, they had it coming. One of them stole a dog. Another had made spurious claims on an advertisement for shampoo. The other was convicted of scratch-lottery fraud. They were society's worst. Mister Smacker does not deserve any more humiliation. So he threw a bottle at a woman on a beach. Haven't we all done that at some point in our lives?"

This was met with nods of agreement.

"How would you describe your mother?" Porter questioned, indicating toward the son of the late Earl of Zetland.

"A right terror, Doctor. I fired off a few bottles at her this morning."

"And so I say to the members of the parole board, here before you sits a good man, wrongly incarcerated. A man who knew he did wrong and who has promised not to do anything wrong, ever again. Even for large sums of money. Isn't that right, Mister Smacker?"

"Mostly."

At that moment, Tulip began to do one of her dances whilst Doctor Arthur Porter handed out complimentary Christmas hams to the members of the parole panel.

Father's freedom was unanimously granted.

CHAPTER FIVE:

A Poetic Reunification

ather's emancipation brought a new energy to him, but did not completely rid him of the harm that hard labour had inflicted. Once free of his shackles, he committed dutifully to parole conditions that insisted he remain within yelling distance of Scotland Yard. Each morning he was required to wake at 7am and scream "WHITLOCK SMACKER, REPORTING HIMSELF PRESENT" at his loudest available volume, and then list any illegal or perversely sexual thoughts he'd been having in the same manner. Whilst this placed a strain on the relationship he shared with his Thai neighbours and their beautiful, wheelchair-bound daughter, Father could see a welcoming light at the end of the seemingly endless tunnel.

He had restarted his life in a similar manner to many other former convicts; as a member of a Formula One pit crew. Later, his famed gregariousness meant he would cosy up with some of the corporate sponsors of the international competitions and finally submit his spirited idea for the world's first racing track to include a roundabout; an innovation that lasted three entire seasons and well fewer than a dozen deaths. I was happy for my father's rehabilitation into society, but it would be a lengthy period of time until our paths crossed in any meaningful way.

As for myself, with parental guardianship returned from a legal standpoint, I had finally begun formal education and found myself enrolled in an East London school amongst peers of considerably-lower social class. 'Saint Adjutor's Comprehensive College of Excellence' was a public swimming school that had recently exposed itself to the financial opportunities made available by the introduction of offering standardised state-mandated curriculum. Due to constraining post-war budgeting, only one mountable room was available to an institute that catered to four hundred children - and that was assigned as a staff disco for St Adjutor's three resident teachers - so all junior school courses were taken in the shallow end, with senior electives hosted further down for those who could comfortably tread water for seven consecutive hours. Lunch could be taken in the dressing rooms but was strongly advised against due to the potential for cramping. This didn't stop the slightly more affluent among us to procure pear drops on tuck shop days and deal them as currency in the afternoon classes when the water was at its warmest. By the end of each month, the boiled sweets in our pockets had dissolved enough to add a gelatinous viscosity to the water which meant we were able to doggy-paddle toward the deep end with optimal buoyancy and gawk at the floating corpses of the less athletic senior students who'd not quite made it all the way through their two o'clock home economics study.

Boarding at Saint Adjutor's was out of the question for anyone not in the possession of a houseboat, so with the financial assistance of my dear friend James Ferdinand Bambi, I leased the second story of a multinational pharmaceutical factory in the far-Eastern boroughs of the city. I suggested to Bambi that I might simply borrow a flume and live upon the school's waters, but he insisted upon granting me a proper residence and, despite being a four-hour walk from school, the factory ticked most other boxes. It was a spacious and well-furnished living arrangement though there were many times when I felt quite alone in the sixty-thousand square-foot space and it seemed that all the throw rugs in the world could not fill the void.

Father's imprisonment had hampered my life somewhat, but I felt an incredible surge of optimism throughout my days at Saint Adjutor's. That positivity was locked firmly into place one spring morning when the factory-ran-forge foreman - a satisfactory man, George Poorman - presented me with my mail. Amongst the normal bills and brochures and erotic postcards from Preston the cocker-poodle, there lay a particularly well-presented envelope bearing a return address of a place in

Lincolnshire. I opened it to receive the most beautiful lettering and spectacular prose; all of it wonderfully familiar.

Dearest Baggy

My heart wishes with all its strength that you are well. My head knows that you have found stable perch somewhere in this tumultuous world.

I must first of all seek to absolve you of the wretched guilt that you are no doubt plagued by, following the unforgiving conditions upon which we parted ways at Beeston. Know that I cling to no feelings for you other than the utmost adoration and that I wholly understand what drew you to depart for safety. You will always have my friendship, no matter what.

I write to you, having been informed of your recent liberty, courtesy of our mutual counsel, Spider. He remains in fine health and would like you to know how dearly he misses the sound of rusting metal clashing against your pearl-like teeth.

I would have you know that I now reside in Lincoln, in the shade of her mighty castle. It is a beautiful city. In a fortnight's time, I shall be presenting my poetic works as part of an arts competition, to take place before the altar of Lincoln Cathedral, and I would dearly request, were it possible, for my good friend Baggy Smacker to be in attendance. I understand that this notice is short, but were you to come as my most special guest, it would mean the world to me.

Yours always,

Joseph Darkfire

I warmed inside to the news of Joseph's wellness and I considered his commitment to poetry a personal treasure. Immediately, I made preparations to travel to Lincoln and support my wonderful friend's venture toward fame and greatness.

"George Poorman, the forge foreman!" I ejaculated down a flight of stairs, almost slipping. "Heed a carriage for dawn. I am to ride to Lincoln on the morrow!"

The foreman explained, via a sequence of various four-letter words, that he was not under my employ so I dashed to the nearest telephone box and made my arrangements.

Within a week, I stood at the foot of Steep Hill in the historic city of Lincoln, full of pride. A day and a half later, I stood at the apex of it, full of sweat. The ascent had been a perilous journey; a non-stop weave between the endless avalanche of tumbling, drunken holiday-makers, who would roar past at break-neck speed in a cloud of Roman factoids and replica versions of the Magna Carta. I narrowly avoided death at the hands of a gruesome vagabond following a misunderstanding regarding her asking if I was "wanting to see a naughty red imp". It was only as my hands reached around her neck, did I see the 'Lincoln Tourism' logo upon her lapel.

My progress halted at a midway point of the ascent, in a liquorice shop owned by a mystical and sensual enchantress. A name tag near her suggested that her name was Catherine Wheels and she was priced at two shillings per pound, which seemed a reasonable price for the time. I was immediately drawn by her deeply-etched facial features, her shining, obsidian-black hair and her well-proportioned, lightly-salted all-sorts.

"Fancy a sweet root?" she proffered suggestively.

"No thank you, I'm five years old."

"So many of my customers are."

"You should be ashamed of yourself, you filthy slut."

She brought clarification of her offer with a wave of her hand, toward her displays of confectionery and I apologised for my outburst, noting that beside her candied items was a sign advertising her ability to communicate with the dearly departed.

"You speak with the dead?" I asked.

"Yes, I am very spiritual."

"And they speak back to you?"

"Not often. They find me annoying."

"Why is that?"

"Because I'm very spiritual."

"I see," I replied, slightly disappointed.

"You have many stories within you, young man. I can tell," the crone continued.

"I feel that you might be correct."

"May I tell your fortune?"

I was intrigued. Catherine led me into a conservatory in which row upon row of glycyrrhiza glabra grew in terracotta plantings. The air was thick with a leafy, aniseed odour. Within the centre of the room were a table and two chairs. Upon the former was a book entitled "Disappointing the Children: A History of Liquorice in Great Britain". Ms Wheels cleared it aside and sat me down.

"Are you familiar with the spiritual art of tarocchi?" she asked.

"Ah yes, a wonderful Latin-based form of energy-burning gymnastic dance!" I daringly bluffed.

Once she had finished correcting and mocking me, Catherine laid four cards before me.

"They say that through tarocchi, you can see the destiny of any man."

"Who says that?"

"It's there on the packaging, next to the choking warning."

Catherine turned the first card. I gasped as I looked upon the face of Death himself.

"Fret not, young stranger. The image of Death in the world of tarocchi is not to be feared. It is a sign of great change, of new adventure. Death is to be embraced. Is not each golden dawn subsequent to the decay of yesterday's sun?"

Catherine turned the second card. It was Death again. I gasped once more.

"What did I just tell you? This is simply to say that your future is generously speckled with all manner of journey. The tarocchi realm wishes for you to know of the incredible life you have begun to live."

Catherine turned the third card. It was another Death card, but this had a photograph of my face glued to it, with a message in dried blood at the bottom. I had only a second to glimpse the words 'No, seriously-' before Catherine hurriedly shuffled the cards back into their packet.

"I mean this is all just nonsense anyway so there's no point in dwelling on it."

She immediately ushered me out of the conservatory and pushed me out of her store, onto the cobblestones of Steep Hill. I turned to demand answers, but she had already managed to lock the front door and had hung a 'For Sale' sign in the window. I resigned my protest and reengaged my climb.

Upon the forecourt of the magnificent Lincoln Cathedral, I was reunited with my beautiful friend Joseph Darkfire. He was crouched upon the church steps, writing into a notebook. I approached and announced his name.

"My Joseph. All the angels this structure seeks to worship could not provide as welcome a sight as you writing upon these tiles."

Joseph looked up from his writing, his eyes twinkling with happiness.

"Those angels know only their perfect heaven. They are robbed of the joy of a return to bliss, from the desert."

We continued to exchange convoluted, homoerotic verse until our phrasing had reached a point of total ambiguity, after which we embraced and committed to a circumnavigation of the tremendous cathedral.

"They tell a story of a mischievous imp, here in Lincoln."

"I know of it. I almost murdered a blind, eighty-year-old volunteer due to a miscommunication of it."

"How dreadful."

"Her carer advised that she has before seen worse harm and would be fine."

"It is said, in legend, that there were two such imps sent to the North of England by Lucifer himself, and that they were to cause havoc. They came upon this house of worship and they attempted to destroy it. But their power, driven by evil, was less of that than the power managed by good. They managed to destroy furnishings and assault a bishop, but they could not destroy what this building stood for; the strivance for good. And in response to their hate-wrought dealings, God sent forth an angel who commanded the imps to stop. One imp obeyed and cowered. The other remained belliger-ent. And so the angel condemned the tragic imp to stone and offered refuge for the imp who accepted his request to cease his chaos. They say when the wind howls here in Lincoln, it is the sound of the surviving imp who seeks the redemption of his companion."

Joseph stopped walking and turned to me.

"What part of this story do you feel you would play, if you must choose a role?"

I thought for a moment.

"The bishop, probably. Amongst proceedings but inconsequential."

Joseph chuckled.

"I think that you would play the redeemed imp."

"A charming proposal. And you?" I asked.

"Of course, the angel."

We held a smile between us for a short second, before resuming our amble around the great edifice and passed a group of jealous, insecure masons who were graffiting the exterior walls with sky-blue spray paint to make them appear smaller.

The competition itself was to be hosted within the cathedral's vast nave, which the event designer had planned to adorn in Lincolnshire's county flower, the majestically-purple *viola riviniana*; or 'common dog violet'. However, due to a spelling-error, the pews were instead crowded with several dozen worryingly aggressive cross-bred pitbulls, whose constant barking and growling reverberated through God's House and immediately lowered local property prices. As the hounds began urinating and shitting and biting children, an angel blinked into existence, explained that he had to deal with this sort of thing all the time, and turned two of the dogs into marble bookends. The remaining canine collective appeared to acknowledge this new threat and ceased their disturbances, while the angel explained to the human attendance that he'd be around for a minimum of three hours due to fair-work stipulations in his contract, and checked to see if anyone wanted to "part a red-wine sea" with him at the pub. Approximately half the congregation agreed that that sounded like a lot more fun than an amateur poetry competition and dispersed as the remainder of us settled in for the impending artistic exhibition.

To coincide with the Mayor of Lincoln's shortly-upcoming ninetieth birthday, the key theme of that year's poetry contest was "Impending Death, Any Moment Now", so the air grew thickly macabre in little time. The entrants were, for the most part, unworthy of committing to memory although a confused, elderly lady named Clementine Moorehouse acquired moderate applause with her entry.

> *I, Clementine Norma Moorehouse of 49 Dacombe Drive, Kettlethorpe,*
> *Of the County of Lincolnshire,*
> *Hereby bequeath the following life annuities namely,*
> *To my daughter, Tash Moorehouse, ten pounds,*
> *To my grandson, Lancelot Sophia Rolleston-Moorehouse, ten pounds,*
> *To my son, "Weedy" Trent Moorehouse, seven pounds,*
> *To my loyal dog, Brian Adams, ten pounds,*
> *To my dearest friend, Gruesome Julia, four pounds,*
> *To Sir John "Horn-dog" Rolleston, minus eighty-two pounds,*
> *And to the Royal Institution of Chartered Surveyors,*
> *I leave chapters nine-to-eleven of the black diary,*
> *That I keep beneath a panel in my sock drawer,*
> *And I trust its contents should assure that the above-listed annuities are maintained indefinitely,*
> *Call my bluff, I fucking dare you,*
> *I've made copies.*

After murmuring approval from the gathered crowd, Mrs Whitehouse approached the audience and had them witness, sign and date the bottom of the page to legally ratify proceedings. Her lawyer zipped about the nave in a flurry of non-disclosure agreements and before long, it was Joseph's turn to take the stage.

My dear friend looked utterly resplendent in a new navy blue frock coat, atop a white t-shirt cunningly emblazoned with the words "Got My Kink On In Lincoln" to appeal to local favour. He approached the podium with six well-rehearsed strides and, upon realising he was still half-a-dozen yards from the required position, brilliantly improvised another five. Even the pitbulls appeared impressed.

Joseph Darkfire cleared his throat and let beauty pour from his mouth-hole.

What faint recall for the monument of life,
That one true novel, chaptered by sepia tones,
An existence of endless instance that dwindles,
To a package of pulses, backlit dimly,
Images drawn from poor memory,
Which are then dipped in tea to make them look older,
And are now blurred, and wet,
And smelling a little bit like old tea.

A million smells, tastes, sounds, feelings and visions,
Whittled down to the dozen,
The joyous balanced by the mournful,
The angry countered by the calm,
And quite occasionally, the odd one without explanation,
Like the name of the cat of a member of the shadow ministry.
Biggsy, I believe.

Yet how am I besieged by the fear,
All that I am and will become,
Will be nought but slides in a show,
Fragments of memory between lost chasms of time,
Like a full drunken night of unmentionable leisure in the company of
Dear Inebriation.

For each moment I meet and each recollection I acquire,
I submit two old,

And struggle to remember hymn lyrics,
And all the different types of cheese.

Curse this decay of my thoughts, my mind,
When they cruelly disintegrate,
Leaving me spinning,
Quilted in confusion and misted remembrance,
This small brain can't contend with large conditions,
Yet nothing can stop his work,
So as product pours in, refuse must pour out,
All one can hope for is that,
With one's age grows one's talent,
And one's handwriting gets smaller,
And one's filing becomes better organised,
And one perhaps hires a secretary,
So I could remember where I left my keys,
And die dignified,
Knowing my wife's name.
Thank you.

The applause was enormous. I led the cheers with tears dripping off my cheeks. Female members of the audience had passed out due to the emotional taxation. Men were hurling bouquets of howling terriers toward the stage area. The admiration was palpable. One could easily have palped it.

Joseph bowed and basked in the wonderful reception. The smile on his face was as broad as the breadth of the cathedral's transept. It was hardly hyperbolic to suggest that this was the greatest moment of his life to date.

Sadly, the praise was interrupted by a boisterous entrance, as a heavy-set man in regal attire crashed through the door along with a wine-flavoured gust.

"Your patience for my long abode!" the man slurred. "My affairs have made you wait!"

He managed to stumble successfully upon a pew, and, with great focus, summoned the balance to remain there.

"My judgement is forthcoming. Who's first?"

Confusion swirled. Joseph had made his way down from the podium, and toward it did a man approach; the final entrant. Upon arrival he announced himself, in a thick Scottish accent, as Andrew McGonagall. From his waistcoat pocket, he withdrew a folded piece of paper and after clumsily unfolding it, he committed to recital.

I had a friend,
His name was Ned,
His life did end,
And now he's dead.

There was little reaction from an audience unsure of whether the man had actually finished, and so McGonagall simply shrugged and headed toward his seat.

The gentleman who'd entered moments before suddenly awoke from the small nap he had fallen into. He belched and looked around to ask if there was anyone else due to recite their work.

"No? Right, well then. I pronounce that jock the winner. I'm off if you don't mind. Jophiel's shout. Cheerio," he said, before promptly exiting.

In the ensuing lavish ceremony, Andrew McGonagall received a princely fortune of fifty-thousand pounds in prize money plus a five-book publishing contract and a novelty, cock-shaped fountain pen. As well as earning the title of Poet Laureate of the County of Lincolnshire, he was sent upon an expense-paid world tour of over fifty countries, during which he would acquire all the fame and venereal disease that a man of the age could hope for.

As a token of his participation, Joseph Darkfire received his own novelty cock-shaped fountain pen, a result he would privately tell me was especially irritating because he already had one.

CHAPTER SIX:

Bambi's Eureka

s Joseph Darkfire returned to carry out his final days at Beeston, I resumed my education in London. To suggest that I was a good pupil would be an understatement. My maturity propelled me through year levels (and to a similar extent, *sea* levels) and I left my peers in my wake (again, both figuratively and nautically). I excelled marvellously in English and Latin and partook in all the sports I could. Saint Adjutor's was regionally famous for its water polo team and, despite having to tediously filter the water after we'd gotten the horses out at full-time, playing was a delight that I treasured.

In my second year, I joined the Royal Naval Cadets and broke the county record for the fifty-metre sprint in a two-man corsair, thrashing six competitors by a vast distance and sinking two others. I promptly attained the rank of Able Seaman, and understandably ejaculated my heart out at a ceremony on the Cliffs of Dover.

I harboured my first-ever erection at mid-summer camp; a stirring that was ignited by my high-school crush, Mrs Wendy Beachamp. She was a sixty-year-old, Welsh substitute teacher who was temporarily in residence to replace a male professor whilst he was committed to a lawsuit against the school for giving him a mild batch of dysentery that had ruined his downstairs carpet.

Mrs Beachamp was a stunning, slender figure with astonishing breasts located centrally upon her chest, in between her navel and collarbone. Her long, athletic legs could be found supporting the weight of her bosom, and her thick, brown hair was often draped over her exotic frontal globes. Her left and right arm hung either side of her left and right mammary (respectively), and her dainty, well-manicured hands were attached to the ends of her forearms, ever ready to be promptly dispatched to point at her busty substances. She wore a permanently-etched, wry smile - perhaps a relic of a recent thought about her delicious, upthrusting, chestoid love bumps - and her cheeks were as pronounced as the glamorous squeeze-hams that hung from her collar like sacks of melted Brie from a tie-rack. She had a top speed of thirty-two miles an hour and an acerbic wit that could de-rust old metal, with a nice set of tits to back it up. I cannot recall what subject she had taught.

All in all, I had learned to thoroughly embrace my education and I considered it a nuisance whenever it was interrupted.

On one such day, I was advised in the middle of a wood-craft lesson by Saint Adjutor's headmaster, Reverend Abbott Abbott, to make haste to his desk to receive some urgent news. After unplugging my workstation and towelling myself dry, I made my way to a far-end booth in the tavern next door to the school that served as the headmaster's office.

It was late in the school day so the headmaster was understandably, belligerently drunk as I took my seat.

"Smacker," Abbott Abbott acknowledged as he poured a mojito for me from a nearby jug. "I have just received a telegram from your friend, a Mister James Ferdinand Bambi. He claims to have made a great discovery, and you are to visit him immediately. He refers to something called the Alchemist's Breadstone and he requires your assistance in its presentation to the Church."

"But sir, my studies-" I began.

"To hell with your studies, Smacker!" he roared and slapped me across the face. "Do you hate Great Britain?"

"No, sir!"

"Then why would you undermine her greatness by denying her innovators and entrepreneurs the support they need to catapult Britain forward into the twentieth century?"

"Those are not my wishes, sir, I just thought-"

"Your independent thought will not be required until you are at least eighteen years old, and even then, it will only be politely tolerated until you're in your late thirties. Tell me, Smacker, why do you believe that our empire became the most powerful upon the earth?"

The economic rape of India was almost certainly not the answer that Abbott Abbott was searching for and so I furnished him with a response better suited to his violent state.

"The people, sir."

"The people? Have you *met* the people? Look at that bloated, abhorrent filth," he demanded, pointing to a nearby mirror that he had mistaken for a window. "The majority of the people are insufferable fools, Smacker. No, the answer is our never-ending quest for brilliance, for adventure, for technological superiority, for discovery.

"We're at the edge of the world, here in Britain, we're leading the way. In this great nation, at this profound age, inquisition and curiosity and confidence could take you to the highest peak of humanity's potential. A billion paths are set out before you and so many of them lead to greatness. Yes, many head toward dark places, but you're a smart boy.

"When one or more of these paths is uncovered, embrace it and survey it and see if you can anticipate its destination. Your studies will always be there and they will always be handy. But know that you will leave this institution with the same information as every other boy that graduates. Your education will not be what makes you, it will be the experiences you choose to immerse yourself in. You must first grasp at a branch before you can use it to pull yourself upward. Do you understand me, Smacker?"

"I believe that I do, sir."

Abbott Abbott's stirring speech raised so many hairs upon my person that I hit puberty on the spot, nine years early.

"Now, go," he said, "A carriage awaits to transport you to Sheffield where your friend currently resides. He wishes for you to share the glory of this Alchemist's Breadstone. Go forth and embrace this unique journey."

I rose immediately and made my way outside to the waiting carriage, which was in fact a poorly-assembled rickshaw tied to a stray dog. A brisk wind took to the streets of London, and a mixed spirit of adventure and uncertainty swelled deep within me, like an inspiring-but-invasive uncle. I climbed aboard.

"Make haste, hound, to South Yorkshire!" I declared. The dog died of old age twenty metres later, so I took its wallet and made my way to a train station.

"A return ticket to the City of Steel!" I demanded very rudely to the station clerk, and took to voyage. A week later, standing in the American city of Pittsburgh, I repeated a similar thing with an emphasis on *Britain's* City of Steel, and I finally arrived in the great place of Sheffield, South Yorkshire.

There was sadly not much to note of Bambi's discovery. I found James face down in a puddle of sweat, full of hubris but mostly opium. After slapping him to consciousness, I came to the understanding that he was claiming to have invented the Chicken Kiev.

Despite this anti-climax, I was not disappointed, for Abbott Abbott's words had emboldened a flame inside me. He had made me realise that I could be anything in this world that I chose to be. As he had said, in this Great Empire, all that divided me from wonder was my selection of route. I knew at that moment in Sheffield, I was then to begin the construction of my highway.

But the world does not allow one such a simple task. These early chapters might seem meandering and episodic, like the droning wander of an elderly mind upon an evening of its winter, but I assure you there is no mighty rope that is not made from tiny threads of hair.

It is something that happens in every life. Small, innocuous moments flitter by with each waking second absent of notice, and it is only when they all reprise at once in a miraculous, impossible symphony of wisdom that you acknowledge their worth. When it happens, as it inevitably will, one will enjoy the same euphoria as I have, as all before me have, and all after will.

For now, I pray you bear with me until then as I still have about five more chapters of apparent nonsense to cover.

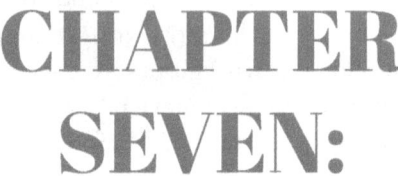

CHAPTER SEVEN:

Released to the World

was, by some margin, the youngest person to have ever graduated from Saint Adjutor's Comprehensive College of Excellence.

Father was in attendance at my passing out ceremony, but only by pure coincidence as he'd been recently dating one of the Naval Cadet Officers. They had met while lost and left for dead in a hedge maze in Wigan; the moans of their desperate, 'pre-starvation' love-making the very thing that signalled their location to a local scout troop and aided their rescue.

Despite his proximity, I had no interaction with my father. To be perfectly transparent, my mind was elsewhere. My thoughts drifted toward my myriad submissions to prominent universities across the land, and how they would alter my trajectory. Obviously Oxford and Cambridge were the shining beacons of educational pedigree, but then also did the more exotic locations such as The Dorchester College of Bread-making and The Royal Cornwall Academy of Pedantry offer the delights of tertiary education, and also relatively exciting pastry options that inflamed my temptations.

Our graduation was celebrated by the introduction of a local celebrity; a gin-soaked ninety-year-old gentleman who had once enjoyed laying claim to an Olympic record for punctuality, before he was eventually revealed to be a drug cheat. He delivered a speech with the precision and clarity of a gin-soaked ninety-year-old man.

"I recall my late father excitedly explaining to me of the coming wave of transformation of the iconic British high street. He was an accomplished architect, my father, known and revered throughout the continent for his beautifully-designed feline scratching posts. His proudest work was a commission from Manuel II of Portugal, for whom he erected a tower over one-hundred and fifty metres tall, on behalf of his two seven-year-old Brazilian shorthairs, Boadicea and Mister Nippy. They took so fondly to it, that they climbed it immediately and disappeared above the clouds, and Manuel followed soon after, and not one of them was ever seen again.

"Yes, their disappearance would go on to cause the dissolution of the Portuguese monarchy, and yes, my father would spend the rest of his days in a prison off the coast of Lisbon, and yes, my dear mother would go bankrupt paying off the fine for neglect he received from the RSPCA, and yes, the heirs to Manuel's throne would hunt down my remaining family members one by one, swearing to avenge the presumed death of their liege and his delightful pets, and not let a night pass in which I might achieve meaningful solace in sleep due to fear pounding upon the door of my soul without respite.

"But I think there is something miraculous to be observed in this story; that my father built with his own two hands a pedestal so great that it could bring down a nation's king. That he could raise two small, furry mammals to allow themselves an ascension to God with nothing but wood and some glue and old bits of carpet that he found in his shed.

"It is the journey *up* that you should all look upon with reverence, and not your downfalls, or your mother's eventual suicide, or the bi-monthly death threat that the Portuguese populace have published toward you in your preferred weekend supplements.

"You all have a pair of young, strong hands with which to assemble your scratching posts. Your greatest objective will not be mixing the glue, or the foraging for the bits of carpet, or chopping down the wood that you build with, nor the height of your post, nor the resale value, nor the ancestral strength of the bloodlines that you decimate, but the sheer quantity of cats that you can launch into God's sapphire field high up above.

"And with that said, I wish you all the best in your lives and declare this medium-sized, family-orientated, regional shopping centre officially open!"

The old man flung his arms in the air to indicate celebration and was promptly hit in the chest by a passing bounty hunter's arrow. We provided a polite parcel of applause and eventually fished his body out of the pool before his oozing blood could worry the hydrotherapy patients over in the shallow end.

I remained aware that I was destined for greatness but still perplexed as to what shape that brilliance would form. Would I become a great entrepreneur such as my revered friend, James Ferdinand Bambi? Or perhaps an acclaimed artist, as Joseph Darkfire was sure to become? Were there still lands to be found upon the earth, that I could discover and attach my name to? Would there be glory attained with victory in future wars? Should I invent a type of low-calorie breakfast muffin?

To cure these lingering questions, I attended a Career Exhibition held at London's glorious Crystal Palace. Within its glass walls were hundreds of booths attended by men and women, each spruiking their line of work as the best among the world's assortment of occupations. Many familiar faces were to be seen.

My own father regaled young men with fantastical stories of his experiences using a makeshift car jack to prop up particularly troublesome front-left tires, downplaying the role of the "superfluous charlatan at the rear-right". James Ferdinand Bambi could be permanently heard above the chatter, detailing his plan to fill a flume ride with the tears of widows as part of a well-meaning but eventually-disgraceful Great War Memorial. Even German Katrina, the detective-disguised-as-a-prostitute who had been in attendance at my father's arrest, was exuding the virtues of plastic anal insertions that were so pleasantly common in her line of work. She was in full dress uniform at the time.

I was dazzled by the possibilities around me, but found myself magnetically pulled toward a particular stand, plastered with grandiose portraits of ancient heroes. A rectangular, clean-looking man stood to attention, splendidly attired in olive-green military dress. His exhibition name tag identified him as Bombardier Dick Womble. He caught my eye and graciously returned it.

"Hallo, sah," he saluted. "Fancy joining the mili'try? We've recently 'ad quite a few vacancies open up, and you look like 'soldier material' to me."

"What are the requirements?"

"'Aving correctly identified which panel of glass is the door to this building tells me that you have already met them, sah."

"I see."

I had not considered myself a military sort, but I was certainly stirred by the epic images surrounding the booth.

"Tell me, Bombardier Womble-"

"Please, sah, call me Bomble."

"Tell me, Bomble Womble, what are the *perks* of joining His Majesty's armed forces?"

"Honour and Glory, sah?"

"Honour and Glory?"

"Yes, sah. It's the brand of cigarettes that comes with rations, sah. Sorry, sah. That's a little joke that we tell in the army, sah."

"Do you often tell jokes in the army?"

"You get one per day with your rations, sah."

"Was that also a joke?"

"No, sah. Deadly serious, sah. Jokes are currently in short supply, sah. We wasted them all on the Germans."

"Hmm. Yes. A notoriously serious people."

There were certainly one or two temptations that military service offered. The powerful illustrations of warriors such as Ajax and Achilles portrayed figures pulsating with masculinity and extraordinary legacy, both of which I desired. However, the romance of conflict was tinged with the prospect of death. Romance, I could thrive in. Conflict, I could manage. Death, I fear I would be poor at.

I inquired with Bombardier Womble as to the rate of pay, but he explained that he'd already used up his joke for the day and couldn't really discuss it. I felt compelled to move on to other areas of the exhibition.

Shortly after, I found myself beckoned toward a gentleman claiming to be a recruiter for the royal family. He declared his intentions in whispers, from within a cream, corduroy jacket. He advertised admission to the monarchy for the reasonable sum of "ten quid" and at first I was enthusiastic, but the man couldn't break a twenty so I abstained. I often recall this moment with deep regret, for following me, with the correct change, was the future Duke of Cornwall who would ascend to greatness.

As I'd begun to abandon hope, my attention was hustled by a theatrical display of salesmanship. A boy of no more than fourteen, in a cobalt-blue felt sports coat and an exceptionally-progressive pair of tight, leather pants, burst from behind a curtain, onto a stage positioned in the centre of the palace. His voice was shrill and quivering. His stance was buck-kneed. His acne was winning a territorial battle on his face.

"'Ello there, my cheeky little chummy chum chums! It is I, Ernie Greenglass, and I am 'ere to tel yew 'bout the wonder of television broadcasting. Yeep yeep yeep yeep yeep!" he cried, and then, in a hushed tone, "*Ernie walks to the centre of stage and does a little spin. The audience rejoices and are won over.*"

The audience did not rejoice and were not won over.

"Yew there, silly boy boy with your lightweight travelling hat and your naughty moustache!" he said, singling out a gentleman in the crowd. "Yew silly little man with your trousers and your 'orrible shoes, what is your jobby job?"

"I am the current Chancellor of the Exchequer," replied the man.

"Ah ha! What a silly jobby job! All the girls must laff at yew! Ah ha ha! *Pauses to allow for audience laughter.*"

The audience did not laugh.

"Don't yew know that the most fanstastical spectastical jobby job for a clever boy with all the sweeties, is not being the counsellor for an ex-cheetah? Oh no, yew naughty little man! *Greenglass skips to the front of stage and bonks the naughty man on his noggin. The audience mutters approvingly.*"

Greenglass skipped to the front of the stage and bonked the man on the noggin. Upon *this* command, the audience *did* mutter approvingly. A recent labour strike was still playing on the people's mind, and the Chancellor of the Exchequer had copped most of the bad press.

"No, no, no! Yew stupid, cheetah-counselling eejit. The most wonderful, clever jobby job in all the whole world is in the sugary and magnificent world of the telly-vizzy-on. Yew there, yew silly man of indeterminable age!"

I was astonished to realise that this strange, hyperactive young salesman was directing his attention toward me.

"Yes," I responded.

"Tell me, my good man, how is it that yew intend to impress all the pretty girls in the playground when yew tell them what yew do?"

"I am yet to decide, strange fellow. To bring clarity to that very query is why I have come here."

"Have yew been on the telly-vizzy, yew silly boy with your flowery waistcoat and last season's sandals?"

"I have not."

"Well that is why the world does not know who yew are! Unlike how the world knows who I, Ernie Greenglass, am and also were and also is and also will be. *Greenglass does a pirouette and woos all the girls in the playground.*"

Ernie Greenglass performed a surprisingly graceful pirouette that would have perhaps impressed girls had any been present. It did, however, disturb the graces of a nearby conservative who would go on to pen an irritated and confused letter to his local parish.

"Do yew want fame, goofy man?" he asked.

I replied that I did.

"Do yew want power?" he asked.

Indeed, I responded.

"Do yew want all the sweeties yew could fit in your pocketses?"

I admitted that confectionery was not atop my list of priorities.

"Gah! Then this is not for yew, yew silly eejit boy! Be gone! *Covers face in aghast gesture, turns and marches to centre stage.*"

The man covered his face, turned one hundred and eighty degrees and marched toward the centre but, with his vision impeded, over-shot his intended position and strode powerfully into a curtain, which engulfed his form. He began to thrash while entangled and his erratic movements eventually resulted in the collapse of a light stand, forcing a small explosion that caused the fabric to spark alight.

All gathered in alarm to witness the growing, twitching fireball that Greenglass had become, and all stood in silent attendance of his screams for help. But none stepped forward to extinguish the man's inferno, partly out of fear and hesitance and awe, and also because he was tremendously annoying.

Thirty minutes later, the audience stood in a wide circle around the smouldering remains of London's historic Crystal Palace, mourning the loss of such an iconic piece of architecture while nevertheless finding small moments to chuckle lightly at the still-flailing Greenglass, who had defiantly survived beneath the resilient cape of stage curtain.

Finally, he fell to the ground and the recently-insulted Chancellor of the Exchequer summoned the humanity to urinate on him until the costume of fire could be whittled to embers.

"Yew rotten swines!" Greenglass called out. "Yew almost deaded me!"

Despite having taken pleasure in the macabre performance, my interest had been piqued. The mystery and attractiveness of this new technology called television was something I found very appealing and so, in a move to salvage this new relationship, I stepped forward to the whimpering young figure and apologised on behalf of the crowd.

"I say, Greenglass. That *was* a spectacle."

He responded with a whimper and asked for someone to call his mother.

"A spectacle..." I paused for effect, "Worthy of *television*?"

Greenglass' despair immediately ceased and his gaze turned, with restored resolve, to meet mine. Trembling lips found steadiness and curled at each end, into what I assumed, beneath horrifying third-degree burns, was a smile.

"Maybe yew are not a silly boy after all. Maybe yew and the telly-vizzy are meant to be."

"Yes, dear man. And you know what? I've developed an appetite for sweeties."

"Ah ha ha, yes. *Greenglass chuckles knowingly before passing out due to smoke inhalation. The rotten swines in the audience weep for him.*"

Glreenglass lost consciousness. The audience cheered.

CHAPTER EIGHT:

Esteem & Decorum in Belfast

rnie Greenglass' impassioned testimony had effectively corralled my thoughts toward dreams of greatness in the burgeoning world of television broadcasting. In exchange for half-a-pound of Dolly Mixture and a Sherbet Fountain, the man had pulled strings to accommodate my entry into one of the few relevant university courses available in the United Kingdom at the time. As with other fledgling technologies, the full potential of television had yet to be embraced universally and opportunities were scarce, but the cunning Greenglass had advised me of the two areas of industry in which mass, one-way broadcast of information to an impressionable, manipulable audience was paramount to the profit-line; sports betting and organised religion.

So it was that I found myself studying a Bachelor of Theology at Queen's University in Belfast, minoring in Evangelical Marketing and Passive-Aggressive Latin. My relationship with Christianity had been, until now, held at a sceptical distance, but the fierce rivalry between Belfast's Catholics and Protestants resulted in some entertainingly violent football games so it became important to choose a side. Like most Englishmen feigning an interest in following an association football team, I simply chose the one that, at the time, had the most money and donned the emerald strip of Catholicism. Upon registering, the coach smiled warmly and assured me that the Vatican insisted on '*developing* youth', although the true meaning behind this statement would not be totally clear until the early noughties.

The participation in football was merely to maintain appearances and stave off polite offers of sodomy from less masculine peers, though despite my predisposition for athletic exploits as exhibited in my days at St Adjutor's, my fullest attention was reserved for the curriculum.

I developed an immediate idolisation for a Professor named Wainwright, who tutored in Back-Handed Compliments of Ancient Texts, Febronianismic Sales Funnelling, and Extreme Quoits. He was a charming man who would task us with non-obligatory but nevertheless compelling extracurricular group objectives relating to our courses. On one occasion, he delivered us the mission to prise from elderly pensioners as much of their weekly grocery budget as we could manage - a traditional and much-celebrated occupation of the church - and I was delighted to be placed in charge of the project.

Our results were hailed by the clergy, as we developed a cunning scheme to replace the stickers on cheap apples with stickers that we'd removed from more fancy tropical fruits such as pineapples and mangoes. We would then paint them in exotic colours and sell them door to door, advertising them to unworldly buyers as well-preserved spoils of the recent war. Not only were point-of-sale profits impressive, but the toxic levels of lead within the paint would send the pensioners just mad enough that they could be visited by charming evangelists who would convince them to leave all their silver cutlery and daughters to the church upon their imminent deaths. Wainwright was so impressed that he sent word to the Vatican who replied with a promise that, were we to successfully avoid legal action, that alone would be considered a valid miracle should we ever seek saintly canonisation.

Outside of my studies, I spent my time as an avid fanatic of the natural world, forever with my head buried in a book on a subject such as the Geoffrey's Marmoset, or attending a travelling exhibition dedicated to the Pygmy Marmoset, or drunkenly brawling at local taverns with those despicable, idiotic Tamarin enthusiasts who knew nothing of the real world and would tout absurd claims about the flexibility of its diet and complexity of its social structures. When calmer and less riled by the dazzling wonders of the Marmoset, I would offer attention to other creations of wonder and pen poems attempting to do justice to their enchantment, while trying to free myself of the insecurity that came with not knowing how to rhyme anything with the word 'Marmoset'.

My first year passed with incredible pace and academic brilliance, but my second term was paused in time by a wonderful reunion as my beautiful fellow, Joseph Darkfire, had been successfully admitted to Queen's University. As an orphan proper, Joseph was not destined for university education and such was the opinion of his situation, that he had already been rejected from three universities - a fair enough result were it not for the fact that he'd only applied for one.

But upon my imploring to both James Ferdinand Bambi and Ernie Greenglass, the necessary resources were mustered to provide him entrance to a five-year Bachelor of Axe-Throwing. It became immediately evident that he bore natural aptitude in the hurling of an axe and, not long after, he found consistent income as a work-from-home lumberjack.

Joseph and I immediately sought arrangements to bunk together and we would spend weeknights listening to the wireless, eating apples re-painted as chocolate oranges and sipping sweet communion wine that we'd procured from a University chaplain who kindly doubled as an off-licence and opium dealer. On the weekend we would abscond to Londonderry via rail and quaff brandy until we could understand the locals. Our expenses were covered courtesy of my pensioner-fruit-fraud enterprise (later to be headlined by the press as "The Awkward Sordid Orchard Scandal: Belfast's Darkest Hour" in a spirited attempt to deflect memory away from the RMS Titanic) and on the occasion that our pockets ceased jingling, Joseph would perform spectacular displays with his axe-work, such as wood-chopping and circumcisions and even occasionally overseeing public executions from an adjacent street, thankfully out of earshot of any potential widows.

During our lectures, we would see little of each other, but we remained ever in our minds, and I would return to our lodgings each night to examine Joseph's thoughts through his daily poetry and, after he'd gotten out of the bath, less impressively via his mouth. We even briefly shared ownership of a calico cat named Progeria Catchmouse that we'd purchased from a homeless man in an alleyway but she sadly soon died of asbestosis, aged only six months according to the supplied birth certificate.

But it must be said, as with any relationship, ours was not without its foibles, and as with any *male* friendship, these would often occur due to the bother of the opposite sex.

I recall one such time, in which Professor Wainwright had requested myself and Joseph to share dinner with him in his quarters. It was not at all unusual for the professors to dine with their more favoured pupils, and the students themselves made no effort to conceal the pride of receiving an invitation. I had brought Joseph to one soiree very early on in my tenure and Wainwright had instantly developed a fondness for his beautiful poetry and his ability to swallow an entire lady-finger banana without chewing.

But on this particular evening, there was a third attendee; an effortlessly charming and remarkably good-looking American girl named Melanie Cuntpurse. Simply upon hearing her name, it was clear that both Joseph and myself were smitten by this girl who appeared to possess as many flaws as she did pensises; presumably zero. In fact, our instantaneous enchantment was apparently so evident and so innocently juvenile that Professor Wainwright saw a chance to toy with us.

At one point in the evening, I had found myself tuned out, entranced by Ms Cuntpurse's glittering eyes, framed so tidily by groomed brows, which grew no more than a yard or two from her perfectly-proportioned up-thrusting bust. I was awakened from my hypnosis by a bellow of laughter from Wainwright and my dear friend Joseph. Melanie smiled and sighed.

"I'll never forget their pleading for mercy," she chuckled, signalling the end of her anecdote.

My daydreaming had deprived me of the details to her story but I saw it wise to feign understanding, and so embarked upon a tide of laughter that lasted for a full fifteen minutes. After I wiped the tears from my eyes and dismissed the doctor that Wainwright had called for, fearing I had succumbed to an onset of psychosis, I commented.

"Oh, Ms Cuntpurse, you do so entertain us with your tales of adventure. Your weaving of a narrative is as glorious as the weaving that binds the silk of that bit of dress near where your breasts are. Just there," I said, pointing with both hands toward where her breasts were.

The cunning Professor Wainwright spotted his time to apply friction to tinder.

"Speaking of glorious narrative, Ms Cuntpurse, are you in possession of a fondness for poetry? For we have before us two accomplished young wordsmiths who I am sure are wont to regale you with their art."

I had been deployed upon unfamiliar terrain, as the quality of my own writings suffered when displayed alongside Darkfire's pristine works, but I did have on my person a notebook containing a large number of verses from my visits to Belfast Zoo. Perhaps there was something within that would appeal to her favour.

"Mister Wainwright, poetry is one of my most beloved pleasures. Would you believe that my father once shared a tequila sunrise with William Wordsworth?"

"Is that so, Ms Cuntpurse?"

"It most certainly is so, Mister Wainwright. They met in a capoeira gymnasium in Cockermouth and came very close to enjoying each other's company."

"That sounds quite wonderful."

"Ultimately, Father did not think so. As he tells it, Wordsworth had deliberately used the straw in such a way so as to consume all of the spirit and grenadine toward the bottom of the drinking vessel, fiendishly leaving my father with only the juice of the orange."

"I'm afraid that even the best of us are not without such scandal, Ms Cuntpurse. I myself, in my more reckless younger days, paid a farmer a small sum for permission to grossly disturb a lamb one night on my way home from a tavern."

"What on earth do you mean by-"

"Boys will be boys, Ms Cuntpurse. Boys will be boys. But now," said Wainwright, his eyes turning back to myself and Joseph, "Which of *these* reckless young men would care to bowl first?"

"Mister Darkfire has the upper hand, I fear, and should therefore play his cards first," I smiled.

Joseph smiled back. I double-smiled, countering his counter-smile, and to counter my counter-counter-smile, he tried to triple-smile at me, but as he was an orphan, he'd never learned how to be *that* happy and he backed down. I had at least tasted *some* victory.

Joseph required no parchment to read from, the sly devil. He looked into Melanie Cuntpurse's eyes and began to recite.

Our hearts chisel words into gesture,
Our eyes dare a gaze, and then away,
Our spines seek to hold a proper posture,
Our lips form to greet and then delay,
Our hands search to perch within some holster,
Our legs recollect the pride we'd planned,
Our hips summon strength enough to bolster,
And tears fall as my Darling takes the stand.

Joseph closed his eyes and breathed in deeply; an orchestra's conductor bracing for applause.

"Mister Darkfire," began Melanie Cuntpurse, "That was the most beautiful verse. So sublime. What is its title?"

"It is entitled 'The Trial of Saucy Jack', part of an anthology that I've been working on, one that tells of the fictional capture of the terror of Whitechapel, Jack the Ripper. It is a tale of sympathy and of a man fighting for justice, and it posits that perhaps those women who became his victims were wearing tight jeans and therefore possibly had all the horrific murders coming to them. Instead of condemnation, the protagonist gets off with a warning on the proviso that he makes a public apology and does really well in an upcoming local sporting event."

"Hmm. A troubling outcome, though I suppose such a thing could only ever happen in the world's unenlightened past," declared Wainwright surprisingly wrongly. "Nevertheless, it is as gorgeous in its prose as it is haunting in its theme. Young Mister Smacker. You were correct to promote Mister Darkfire's abilities. What have you as response?"

Though I have never been one to suffer panic, I must admit that I was mildly flustered by competition, and I fumbled through my book of prose, attempting to find a suitable combatant to Joseph's recital. I wished for something similar, something that could offer sensitivity and the implication of intimacy, but swaddled in enough ambiguity so as to preserve a certain mystique. I sensed the growing awkwardness of my pause and hurriedly settled and cleared my throat.

"Ms Cuntpurse, they say that cream rises to the top, so ready your ears for my cream."

Once I'd apologised to the room for such a wretched sequence of words, I read some from the page in front of me.

Upon some hill, there stands my Queen,
Her beauty so infinite,
Should be her will, then us shall wean,
Twenty-five eggs per minute,
We'll start a war down underground,
And hopefully we'll win it,
And pound by pound, I'll pile her mound,
And store our children in it.

A respectable silence occurred as we all deeply considered the profoundness, or other feelings, that the piece had summoned within each of us. Ms Cuntpurse eventually weighed in.

"That is…. Quite the romance that you've conjured, Mister Smacker. Is there a muse for such… Unusual verse?"

Admittedly, it had been penned whilst observing Belfast Zoo's termite exhibit, but so caught was I in the midst of a buck's charge for dominance I mislaid the truth

"But no, my dear Ms Cuntpurse. This was entirely for you."

Melanie Cuntpurse then lectured me in a stern tone over the course of the next several minutes as to why twenty-five eggs per minute was simply too much for her to accommodate, and also why she possessed no wish to commit to subterranean conflict.

What followed from thereon was a half-hearted back-and-forth between Joseph and me, in tired wit, attempting to wrangle marriage from Ms Cuntpurse. I doubt either of us were sure whether this combative courtship was serious in nature or simply the result of two vibrant young men rubbing their legs together in cricket-like song. The tennis match of testosterone-driven parries subsided almost instantly after Melanie agreed to a matrilineal marriage to Joseph, but only if he would take her surname. For the good of his writing career, he declined.

CHAPTER NINE:

A Letter from Father

HM Prison Barlinnie
Glasgow, Scotland

15th February

My dear son,

It shames me to write to you to tell you that I once again find my-self immorally imprisoned by His Majesty's brutal hand. I assure you, this time it is not due to some ruthless conspiracy set upon me by German law enforcement. No, you will not truly believe the cause of my incarceration. When you hear the terms of my arrest, you will wretch in disgust to the depravity that Lady Justice has bore witness to.

I have been sentenced to ten years because I fell in love.

Don't ponder for one second that perhaps drama has caused me to exaggerate, for I speak the truth. Love takes so many forms. Love can be passed through touch. Love can be delivered by kiss. Love can be in spoken words, it can be in written form. And important-ly, love can conquer distance, moreso than any other force. Love can cross desert. It can traverse jungle. It can navigate the roughest seas.

It is the latter, in which authority seeks to pervert putto's aim, for I am but a man of flesh and blood, and mortality means that we fall so hard in love. Once I laid eyes upon my darling, in her freshly-pressed Navy whites and regimental flippers, Cupid's arrow impaled my insatiable loins.

My darling and I would not let her mobilisation stand between us and our passion. Love conquers all, and we knew it would save us through our separation as she crossed the Atlantic on a military frigate, gone from me for six months. When touch cannot be re-ceived, when kiss cannot be gifted, when words cannot be heard and when letters cannot be delivered, Love will find a way.

We had been sex-morse-coding for three consecutive hours when they struck the iceberg. I will never forget the mechanical tapping

77

and semi-tapping of her erotic cypher. Yes, our deviance had cluttered communications compelling the boat to change course, but is this not what His Majesty's armed forces stand to preserve; the very notion of Great British LOVE?

Sadly, Lady Justice does not see it that way. Apparently God's most beautiful gift of our ability to love one another does not transcend the lost lives of two hundred and fifty enlisted sailors. It disgusts me. Were I in their wet, cold shoes, I would gladly drown in an ocean of salt water to know that a fellow countryman would not suffocate in the torrent of a broken heart.

The good news is that, despite being on trial for manslaughter, I've fallen in love with a gorgeous Samoan dinner lady in the jail canteen, which has really softened the blow of losing a loved one to a firing squad. Even my famous and unfortunate reactions to Coltsfoot Rock cannot divide my adoration for this exotic island beauty. So do not concern yourself greatly with my predicament.

Yours with love,

Your Father (Whitlock Smacker)

P.S - You best not be fucking that Darkfire boy because I will have you shot if I find out you're into that kind of thing. xx

CHAPTER TEN:

The Ascension of Darkfire

By the last year of our education, the sparks of Dark-fire's genius were casting their inevitable flames, ravaging the world of contemporary poetry with an all-engulfing metaphorical inferno that left metaphorical women widowed and metaphorical children orphaned, but nevertheless very impressed with all the clever rhymes. Throughout Northern Ireland, Joseph's notoriety was spreading as quickly as a sexually-transmitted-pandemic, and to a similar demographic.

Such was his growing fame that middle-aged couples would demand meetings in which they would spuriously claim to be his estranged parents and request a twelve-point-five per cent royalty on all proceeds from his work. Still so desperate for a family, Joseph would try to haggle the more attractive ones down to a more equitable eight per cent before negotiations would unfailingly collapse.

I found myself caught in the whirlwind of his success, mesmerised and vulnerable like a suicidal deer watching its sibling bask in the headlights of an oncoming motor vehicle. I struggled to maintain my own lofty goals as Joseph celebrated each milestone in his personal journey toward greatness but I was not at all envious. I supported his achievements and joined with him in each rigorous victory, knowing that my bright days would eventually come, if somewhat later. After all, Joseph had a gift; a magic ability with words that lubricated his ascent. My own would no doubt come after more grit and toil and hoisting myself upward, an accomplishment I trusted would become its own glory.

Joseph's world began to glow in the late weeks of our second year in Northern Ireland, when he was charged with a weekly 'agony aunt' column in the Belfast Telegraph. Through one particular anonymous back-and-forth, Darkfire's calm and well-reasoned responses were so effective in their persuasion that the discourse ultimately led to the brokering and signature of the Kellogg-Briand Pact by over thirty countries, leaving him an assured shoo-in for the Nobel Peace Prize. Unfortunately, his application form was filled in using the wrong-coloured pen, and so the title was given away as a prize in a pub raffle.

Several more opportunities came Joseph's way, including a chance to showcase one of his pieces at the Royal Variety Performance on the stage of the opulent London Palladium. Admittedly, his performance was only part of a technical rehearsal, in front of a riff-raff crowd of degenerates not suitable for broadcast, but as these lesser aristocrats were eventually escorted away to make room for the *actual* Royals, the Earl of Derby momentarily out-manoeuvred the guards and approached Joseph to sing praise and suggest a meeting with an acquainted publisher.

Not more than a fortnight later, Joseph Darkfire was sharing a brandy with Sir Leonard Penguin-Classic, a senior editor of the famous Hutchinson & Co publishing company. During that evening, Penguin-Classic would agonise over the upcoming debut of a promising children's poet from America, and lament the absence of such talent from the home nations. Joseph would grasp this opportunity with both hands, suggesting that he himself had ample work that could be adapted for a younger audience, and could perhaps compete with this stateside tidal force.

Six months after this fortuitous happening, Joseph published his first book, entitled "Darkfire's Pocketbook of Poetic Erections", to moderate critical and commercial success. An excited Sir Leonard Penguin-Classic insisted upon hosting a most elaborate celebration at the gloriously-appointed Coventry Garden, and despite an accidental double-booking with a local Nazi Party rally at the fault of the event host, it was a remarkable mixture of the upper echelons of both literature and anti-semitism.

All manner of celebrity were in attendance including the Poet Laureate of the British Empire's tennis coach and the devilishly-witty grandson of a man to whom William Blake owed twenty pound. It was a veritable whose-who and I took great pride and delight in being in attendance as a guest of honour of my incredible friend, dallying my way through a garden of cultured conversation, dazzled by rich chatter of literary magnificence and mildly concerned by slightly more tepid mutterings of the "capitulation of German Imperialism at the thieving talons of the modern Jew". But those were merely the opinions of Sir Penguin-Classic.

The highlight of the day's splendour was a reading of Joseph's work by the boy himself, atop a stage of marvellous construction that even red, swastika-emblazoned banners could not temper. My friend rose its steps to a wave of applause and cheering and the occasional impassioned female fan respectfully whipping her tits out in admiration. From his jacket pocket, Joseph produced a leaf of paper, from which he read.

"Thank you all for being here on this sun-blessed day. It fills my heart with an indescribable warmth to see each of your faces together before me, joined by a common love of poetry," Darkfire addressed the audience.

"My journey to this place has been one, perhaps more of luck than of talent and passion. Never have I thought to strive for a place on a stage such as this, at the behest of my success, and yet here I am. Fortune has shone upon me."

Several of the attending Nazis chose this moment to claim his success as an example of the supposed supremacy of the anglo-Saxon lineage. Joseph Darkfire, a man of impeccable moral direction, swallowed nervously, folded the paper back into his blazer and continued.

"I would say to some of those in this audience before me, who look at their misfortunes and call for someone to hold accountable, that I stand before you having dropped into a very different situation. My mind is not taken by who I must blame, but to whom I must owe thanks and favours. Rather than spend my thoughts fighting those who I believe draw me backward, I am allowed, by my circumstances, to bless those who have brought me up. Having not ever sought to hold others into account has allowed me the freeness of mind to afford the time and creativity and happiness to drift forward. I would say, to some, that it is firmly within your interest to perhaps cease your campaign to vilify, and to present yourself the opportunity to prove your believed supremacy in a more enlightened way; in a way that does not bring others down beneath you, but raises you above others. If you are better, prove it through living brilliantly, else you risk contradicting the greatness you claim to represent by yourself tarnishing that representation. We are, after all, one people in God's eyes and all that prevents our cause to love one another is the decision not to do so."

It was a beautifully-worded sentiment but the Nazis were having none of it and began pelting the stage with scrunched-up copies of the Treaty of Versailles until they were eventually escorted away by mounted police. After several minutes of confusion and the eventual re-admittance of Sir Leonard Penguin-Classic, Darkfire continued.

"Now that the Nazi threat has finally been dealt with once and for all, I would like to read to you two poems from my work, of which I am most proud. This first piece, in which I break down conventional gender stereotypes to develop a masculine mermaid figure, I have entitled 'Barnacle Sam'."

There once was a man,
named Barnacle Sam,
A highly-determined young Mer-man,
Such a worldly dear sort,
he was well-versed and taught,

To be fluent in Latin and German,
He was mainly renowned,
for the wonderful sound,
That came out of his mouth, pure and gallant,
And although half a fish,
our young Sammy did wish,
To perform for the king with his talent,
But he couldn't seek fame,
'cause the rules of the game,
Said singers could only be human,
Sam said 'I shall dance,
Though I don't fit in pants!'
They still told him 'No', now he's fuming,
His Dad said, 'My boy,
visit Great Sea King Roy,
'And beg of him legs for a figure,
'But beware of a curse,
'cause he might make things worse,
'Like that time that he made me an editor's note for the love of god
change this word immediately,
So Sammy went out,
half-human, half-trout,
And swam forth a-seeking a Sea King,
He found the old man,
eating fish from a can,
In a cave that was reeking and leaking,
'My Liege,' Sammy sung, with his lyrical tongue,
'Give me feet with the beat of a dancer,'
'Your wish is command,
on my word, you will stand,'
Said the King, 'By the way, you've got cancer',
So Sam as it seems,
should be near to his dreams,
His life should be fettered with humour,
But the terrible thing,

is the boy cannot sing,
Because there in his throat is a tumour,
Instead of the fame,
he is riddled and lame,
His mood grows increasingly emo,
No longer a trout,
all his hair's fallen out,
And he's not even taking the chemo,
It's a horrible state,
our dear Sammy's poor fate,
The throat tumour soon starts him choking,
But in spite of the pain,
he found terminal fame,
When he starred in an ad against smoking.

A round of applause erupted and persisted for several seconds until a booming, authoritative voice called out from the crowd and culled the clapping hands of the audience.

"BANAL," said the voice.

All eyes turned to its source, to see a man of not more than two years of age, reclined upon a beanbag toward the rear of the gathered crowd. He was attired in a pristinely-white nappy and a red t-shirt emblazoned with a charming cartoon of a cat. The man wore no shoes and his chubby, pink legs swung gaily above the grass. Upon his head was a top hat. With the assembled group's eyes upon him, he lifted a cigar to his infantile mouth, took a deep breath of it, and allowed the smoke to slowly escape. Upon the cloud's release, with his other hand, he drew a pacifier to his lips and then pissed himself.

The exclamation gave way to nervous mutters and whispers, and I harvested enough intelligence in short time to gather that this was none other than the famed children's literary reviewer, Michael-Steve Burrows. This was a man, despite his adolescence, who was revered throughout Europe as the ultimate authority on prepubescent literature and his presence at this small event was profoundly unexpected.

Atop his stage, Joseph responded to Burrows' obnoxiously-public critique by turning so ghostly a shade of white that a few Nazis returned to the area to attempt to vote him into office. But within seconds he regained his composure, humbly declined nomination, and continued to present his work.

"I hope you enjoyed 'Barnacle Sam'. In a way, I feel that it is somewhat autobiographical. Having not been raised under the blanket of a pair of loving parents, I often feel that I am not fully a man, and that half of me is missing. And so it is that to extend my naturally-bequeathed talents to the world is of tremendous difficulty."

The audience responded to such honest emotion with a collective sigh and warm applause.

"Next, I would like to read to you another poem from my compendium; one that I hope is a powerful and confronting insight into the abusive nature inherent in the unbalanced relationships that are toxified by vanity and capitalistic pursuit. It is called 'Cyril the Squirrel Goes to Court for Battery'. I wrote this whilst imprisoned at an orphanage, amid an atmosphere and a language ironically unfit for children, but I have censored the poem accordingly for younger minds."

Cyril the Squirrel was a regular guy,
With zero regrets and with hope in his eye,
A hero to family and people he knew,
With a penthouse apartment in a tree with a view.

One day he was sorting through his myriad mail,
Through ads for new ointments and oils for his tail,
When one coloured envelope captured his glance,
And within was an invite to Jack the Duck's dance.

Cyril did not think so highly of Jack,
After lending him money that he never got back,
And though the Duck's parties did generally suck,
There'd probably be girls there that Cyril could form healthy, respectful
relationships with.

He knew for the ball that he must look his best,
Shampoo all his fur and be wonderfully dressed,
He'd wear his best waistcoat, a hat newly made,
To make sure he'd definitely get himself a friend for a long time, not
simply a good time.

So he went to the Hatter and talked with Ol' Max,
A crabby dear Tabby, who could make lovely hats,
'Mate, I will wait, you'll create a great cap,
But none of that weird Lady-Churchill-type merchandise'.

With his hat on his head and with cash in his pants,
Dear Cyril the Squirrel made way for the dance,
He grinned from within as he entered the doors,
There were girls that he knew, and he knew they were socially
accommodating sole traders with all the applicable credentials.

The night started well, and all seemed so smooth,
'Til later, when Cyril was making a move,
To Mary the Wench he flirtatiously spoke,
During which, to his horror, his brand new hat broke.

Mary, dismayed, backed away from the scene,
For Cyril, un-hatted, was a mess to be seen,
'I'm sorry, Dear Cyril! You're all out of luck',
Without that fine wear, we can never go just hang out, maybe at
church or something.'

The very next day he returned to the Hatter,
Demanding refund for the horrible matter,

But Max held his ground and refused to comply,
And Cyril replied, giving Max a black-eye.

So the Hattery Cat made a Battery claim,
And it wasn't too long 'til the barrister came,
He read Cyril's rights and attempted arrest,
And he maced Cyril's face when he tried to protest.

Beaten and blind, they dragged Cyril to court,
The squirrel-ful jury would say what they thought,
Villainous Cyril the Squirrel, nonplussed,
As his crimes were read out to the people's disgust.

'This squirrel's a beast' claimed the man for the State,
'His mind is corrupt, full of loathing and hate',
The statements were met with agreeable tuts,
Over the sound of the munching of nuts.

'The squirrel was right to attack this here cat',
'A refund was due through the fault of the hat',
Cyril could realise his chances were moot,
As the curious jury shared glances and fruit.

The verdict eventually came loud and clear,
'Guilty' the word that poor Cyril did hear,
And off he was carted, to a terrible jail,
Where fruit was illegal, and acorns were stale.

Cyril spent months in a maze of steel bars,
And found himself frequently banged in the metaphorical emotional sense,
Ever regretting the pain that he'd earnt,
And never forgetting the lesson he'd learnt.

And since his release, and up 'til today,
Cyril the Squirrel backs firmly away,
Violence might seem very right to your gut,
'Til you're stuck in a jail with stale nuts and sore butt.

Once more, the air was saturated with rapturous applause. I had to agree with a man standing next to me, that the veritable assault of the audience's appreciation decisively penetrated the trenches of suppressed middle-class social resistance, overwhelming weaknesses in the line and manipulating the resulting breakthroughs by providing flanking opportunities via the rear of enemy positions.

But still, one among the gathered remained unamused.

"DERIVATIVE," Michael-Steve Burrows decried loudly from his beanbag.

The throbbing and electrified mass, having had their celebration so sharply ceased by the loud call of the infant cynic, bowed before a sudden uncertainty in their own tastes and fell shamefully to murmurs and contrarianism and the repeating of things they had read in the Daily Mail as if they were thine own considerations.

So effective was the might of Burrows' condemnation and his reputation, that several of the present white supremacists did tsk Darkfire and take shame in their race, and soon thereafter wholly reformed and started careers as socialist life coaches.

And yet the vicious critique was not complete.

"A piece of such clumsy prose and so odious a theme that I appear to have defecated and soiled my favourite cloth. But perhaps, as the towelling around my dirtied loins, could be a more worthwhile use for Darkfire's pages?"

The young reviewer had indeed shit himself in apparent protest, ruining a perfectly good beanbag. Nevertheless, Burrows' scything wit was of an unworldly class and the gathered crowd lit their eyes and expelled all air from their lungs in fits of laughter. My heart sank as I felt an onslaught approach my friend. He looked forlorn. Despite Joseph's dominion over words, he had not the malice to wield them as a weapon, and Burrows looked to exploit this unwavering decency in exchange for more of the people's favour.

"Darkfire, you do to the English language as I recently did to my mother's perineum!" He continued to howling laughter. "Let us hope it doesn't cause *another* divorce!"

It was a gut-aching sight to behold; this minuscule bully rendering my Joseph's heart to deflation in his proudest moment. I knew fully that something must be done, but I saw none willing to risk themselves to protect my dear friend. I then realised that his rescue must be completed by the only one who loved him enough to intervene; Me.

In response to Burrow's recent bowel movements, a lady emerged - his maid- to attend to him. As the crowd continued to heckle and thrum, the woman removed the infant's nappy and committed to the cleaning of his lower half. I saw my opportunity and assigned every of my faculties to the task of wit.

"Well," I loudly began, gaining the attention of the assembly. "Suddenly, all this insecurity and negativity and bitterness makes the most perfect sense."

As dramatically as I could, I raised my arm and aimed a pointed finger toward the wretched child, who looked back at me with slight confusion.

"For this man has…" I paused for effect, "a BABY PE-NIS."

For a short moment, silence took Coventry Garden as its captive. But in seconds, members of the gathered audience came to realise that Michael-Steve Burrows did in fact have a baby penis.

"Of course I have, you utter cretin-" the boy began, but it was too late. Others in the crowd offered their own take on the observation, firing off such cutting lines as "Yes, it is a very small penis" and "Good lord, my own penis is far longer and girthier than that man's penis".

Fortunately, the demographic was predominantly male, and if there is one reliable certainty in mankind's history, it is the compulsion of adult men to remain endlessly concerned about their masculinity and its physical manifestation that hangeth between their legs. And so, with merry abandon, did the hundreds of attendees gleefully point at Michael-Steve Burrows' yet-fully-formed pink-whistle and laugh and jibe and ridicule.

Burrows glared at me, attempting to joust my ensiform stare with his own. It was now of no use. I was yet to understand the enemy I had made, but in that moment, I was the honourable conqueror of a vicious tyrant.

"Mister Darkfire, put me down for two copies!" I declared above the din to my friend, who now wore a grin and eyes blessed with adoration. "Wouldn't want anyone to think *I* had a small, baby cock."

The effect was immediate among those in the crowd. Men flocked to the stage with handfuls of money, thrusting it toward Joseph in desperation, and when the on-site editions were sold out, they rampaged throughout the country's bookstores. Interestingly, the white supremacists all returned as one and bought a disproportionately-large quantity.

Following the chaos, 'Darkfire's Pocketbook of Poetic Erections' became an overnight sensation.

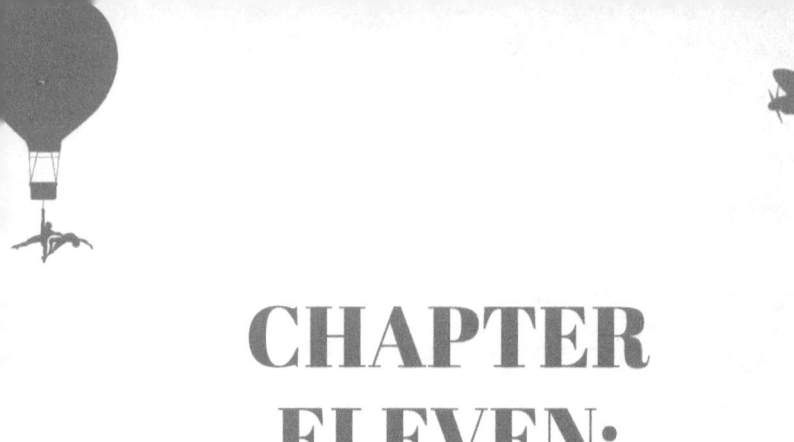

CHAPTER ELEVEN:

First Broadcast

I mmediately following my graduation from University, I was thrust onto the first stage of a new career. Belfast's strong Catholic roots offered a fantastic relationship with the Vatican, and having been so impressed by my commercial manipulation of the meek during my time in North Ireland, I received an invite to partake in a twelve-month residency with the newly launched Vatican Radio.

The year was fulfilling but mostly uneventful, although I was able to participate in one particularly historic moment as an interviewer on a talk-show programme called "*Chat*ican on the Vatican". The Catholic Church had recently discovered a not-before-published book of the Holy Bible and I was to interview their representative, a Cardinal Boylett, about its un-veiling.

My thanks to those at Vatican Radio who have graciously provided me with the verbatim transcript of that discussion, as below.

BS: Thank you for being with us today, Cardinal Boylett.

CB: It is my pleasure to be here, on this historic day.

BS: Now, may I ask you to tell us about this new holy text that you and your col-leagues have recently uncovered?

CB: Well, I should stop you there and clarify that this is not a newly uncovered piece of scripture.

BS: Oh, it isn't?

CB: Oh dear me, no. All texts as pre-scribed by our Almighty have been fully recovered by now and locked away in little wooden boxes to preserve their integrity.

No, this is simply one of the many unpublished holy books that we have within our Holy Archives that we haven't lost the key for.

BS: I'm sure this is news to the majority of our listeners. So how have these sacred texts avoided publication in the past?

CB: Well you see, the bible is a very lengthy thing, notorious for its lengthiness. It's a huge book, you know, very difficult to knock off in a single sitting and it's quite difficult to carry around with you. We did split it into two parts as I'm sure you know - due to the excessive lengthiness - with all the lessons about being a good sort of chap in one, and all the exciting bits with the smiting and the saucy women in the other. But despite splitting it into two parts, people still complain often of their lengthiness and send us letters with suggestions of things we should cut out. The removal of certain, weighty parts of Leviticus is the usual submission but conversely, we do receive frequent requests from politicians in Northern America asking us to *add in* bits that they've come up with. But yes, as a result of the lengthiness, there are some holy texts that simply didn't make it to the final publication. Nothing too important, mind you, nothing that would dilute the sanctity of The Almighty's message. There are things like a Gospel according to a lady called Beryl Jarvis, which is frankly a bit too exciting in parts to be taken seriously. We also cut out some of the more filthy psalms. So the reason that the Christian faithful have not been privy to the existence of this new work is because of the lengthiness of the current bible, which is something we'll take into consideration should we ever go forward with a sequel.

BS: I see. And could you tell us of the situation that has arisen, that has made the inclusion of this piece of scripture a decision of modern importance?

CB: Certainly, I can. You see, one of the problems that we're currently experiencing in the Vatican is that the popularity of Catholicism is on the wane. We have a waning popularity, you see. Historically, we've been incredibly popular. You could even argue that we were, at one stage, one of the most popular things on the planet, even moreso than cups of tea and those shiny gems that dangle between ladies' busts, much sought after nowadays. We were very popular, not so long ago, and we still are to a large extent, although it's begun to wane. Our popularity, that is. We have a weekly meeting on Thursdays - it used to be Sunday afternoon but a few of us are busy around then so we moved it to Thursdays because we're trying to get better at accepting change. And at these meetings, an unusually tall man hands His Eminence a piece of paper, and His Eminence shakes his head in a gesture of ever-dwindling confidence and tells us our popularity is on the wane.

BS: How much has it decreased, if I may ask?

CB: He's purchased a drum set and is taking lessons twice a week.

BS: Catholicism's popularity I mean, not His Eminence's confidence.

CB: Oh, I see. Well, he never has the exact figures, but he assures us, with convincing certainty, that things were definitely better in the past. And so, to remedy our diminishing popularity, we devised a cunning scheme to run a survey of two-hundred-and-fifty public school boys and asked them what we'd done to upset them. The answer was quite unanimous and surprising; they said that they found Jesus *unrelatable*. Now this was very surprising to us, because the *relatability* of Jesus Christ, the Only Begotten Son of Our Lord and Saviour, is very much what the whole Christian philosophy is supposed to be about. Jesus' entire job description is to be the relatable one; he's the sort of pretty receptionist figure at the hotel who gives you your room key and tells you where all the nice, local vegetarian restaurants are. There's a Trinity, you see. You've got God up there, he's very much in charge of the whole operation and he's making all the executive decisions. Then you've got the Holy Spirit who's doing all the admin work and the finances in the background, which is why you never hear too much from him. And then you've got Jesus, who's supposed to be the relatable one whose ethereal omnipresence doesn't give you the willies. That's why we put his face on all the merchandise, you see. If you tried to embroider the image of God, the infinite, eternal, and unchangeable being; a force of untold power, goodness, and truth onto a t-shirt or a throw cushion, nobody would know what it was supposed to be. That would be a very incomprehensible throw cushion. But put a picture of Jesus on it, giving you a cheeky wink, and people get the idea. So as you can understand, we were very surprised and alarmed to discover that people found him unrelatable.

BS: I see. And so the addition of this book addresses that issue of relatability?

CB: Yes, we believe that it does. You see, many people who completed the survey suggested that Jesus Christ comes across as a bit preachy. Of course, that was entirely the point when we put the first edition out, but times change and it's fair to say that, in this day and age, he does come across as a bit of a smug, know-it-all, do-gooder. I am not reluctant to admit that he even gets on my nerves at times. So me and the other lads down at the Vatican had a rifle through the archives and we found a book full of stories about Jesus being a bit of sod from time to time. We're releasing it as part of the New Testament under the title of The Holy Epistle of Relatable Cheekiness, popping it in after Revelations to try and bring the tone back up. That was something else that was mentioned in the feedback we received; lots of complaints of there being a bit-of-a-downer end to the bible that hasn't helped Christmas sales, which is a time of year when we should be expecting to overperform in our retail outlets. This wonderful new book tells of a delightful other side to the Son of God, in which he wields his holy magic to perform a few playful pranks on his less favourite disciples, and it goes into some detail as to how popular he was with the ladies, as of course he would have been at the time, what with his celebrity dad and all. There's a wonderful parable about weaning a fox onto white rum. I was particularly moved by that. And a bit where he dates a Filipino waitress for a couple of months before breaking up with her over her taste in music. The initial chapters start off a bit dark, I'll admit, but they get much lighter toward the end. As do his girl-friends, now that I think about it.

BS: And do we know which apostle penned this work?

CB: The book is believed to have been written as a didactic asset register by the manager of a local wine bar that Jesus co-owned with St Paul; a clever venture if you think about it, one that ties neat-ly in with other parables in the canon-ical gospels. We at the Vatican believe this unique, new insight into the infinite cheekiness of Jesus Christ of Nazareth of-fers the required sort of relatable good humour and wholesomeness that will allow our popularity to cease waning.

BS: Well, this truly is a profoundly his-toric moment in the history of Christian-ity. Is this available to our audience for purchase now?

CB: Yes, we at the Vatican are pleased to announce that the billions of bibles cur-rently in circulation are as of now he-retically out-of-date and will need to be immediately replaced with these new ones, which can be bought in all retail outlets of good repute for the small one-time fee of two shillings, followed of course by the traditional, on-going subscription of ten per cent of everything you ever earn.

BS: Cardinal Boyett, thank you for your time.

CB: Mister Smacker, thank you for yours.

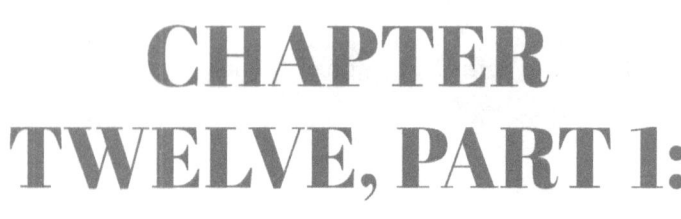

CHAPTER TWELVE, PART 1:

The Union of St. Cloud & Sloth

Through an act of spite, I found myself heralded as the Best Man at the second wedding of my one-time employer, Clara St. Cloud. Her entrepreneurial excellence had yielded her a tidy fortune, and so she was able to afford an entrance into high society by marrying a diminutive but nevertheless well-connected man named Remington Sloth. The Sloths had cleverly cashed out of the human-trafficking trade mere weeks before it had become unfashionable, and so they stood upon a mountainous wealth in its aftermath and now operated several ventures intended to cleanse their image, including an internationally-renowned charity that rehabilitated frightened bunnies, called 'Fix'a'matosis'.

The reason for my appointment to a position of ceremonial importance was due to St. Cloud's desire to offend her new husband's brother, who was alleged to have drunkenly offered to have a tight-fitting bracelet of hers resized at no expense; a comment she took to be an insult about her figure. Remington had little influence within the relationship and so offered only small resistance to the reassignment of his brother's role, and I was delighted to step in as, despite being placed in a certainly awkward situation, I was quite attracted to the offer of a new, cost-free suit as I had recently decided to temporarily become a gambling addict and required something formal to wear to race courses and, in related occasions, court.

St. Cloud and Sloth had spared little expense when preparing for their wedding day. They had managed to wrangle the short lease of a Royal Legion, located not more than a couple of hundred metres from Eltham Palace, after exploiting Sloth's Royal contacts and blackmailing Harold MacMillan with a claimed library of photographs of his penis. The affair was a lavish one and a dazzling dedication to a time of western history in which matrimonial over-expenditure was less about one's own tastes and more about causing others to feel meagre about theirs.

I felt nervous as the ceremony began because, as Best Man, I had been entrusted with the ferrying and handing over of the rings. But due to a particularly bold gambit that followed a morning of riotous dares and shots of "chicken-stock schnapps" in an alley in Durham, I had been rather cleverly tricked into bidding both rings as a tremendously-expensive bet on a two-year-old thoroughbred named But First Here's Moira. The colt itself was a magnificent racer, but sadly the competition in which I had been led to believe he would win was the Football League Second Division. Despite a respectable twenty-two goals and eleven assists in thirty-two games, he only managed third place and blew it in the playoffs.

In the pocket on my waistcoat, in which the rings were supposed to be, my fingers gently caressed a folded letter of humble apology that I intended to pass to the groom at the required time. It would be a slight embarrassment but I knew I could depend on fine British stoicism to relieve me of genuinely repressing consequences.

Still, there were flickers of anxiety as Clara St. Cloud commenced the reading of her vows.

"My Dear Remington," she began. "Ever since I had the joy of gazing upon you from afar all those months ago, so gloriously adorned and poised amidst the floral arrangements and the myriad stalls of the Annual Trentham Potato Festival, the flower of love has blossomed evergreen in my heart.

"It is often said that one does not attend The Great Trentham Spudfest with the goal of matrimony in mind. It is a place of industry, not of romantic fantasia. But yet we made it so. Together there, and since then, we have laid down passionate roots in the compost that is our lives. We have dug through adversity to claim the potatoes of our intertwined souls, and we have rinsed and washed them to serve alongside the gravy of our hopes and dreams.

"Remington. You are the banger to my mash. The brown to my hash. The roastie to my smash. The 'gou' to my 'lash'. You bring flavour to my life just as finely-sliced spring onion prevents bubble 'n' squeak from tasting like yesterday's roast dinner. With these starch-stained lips I beg of you that we should embrace each other as best friends and lovers, wrap ourselves tightly in tin foil and cook our love on 'high' for approximately seven minutes, to serve with lashings of butter and maybe some chives. I adore you."

There was a heartfelt patter of applause from the crowd and then a short break as two scantily-attired ladies handed out french fry samplers to the gathered. A single tear moved down Remington's face. Once it had been stitched up by a nearby surgeon and the audience had been dispensed morphine to deal with the trauma, the groom took to his own verse.

"My sweet Clara. My darling herbaceous perennial. As a child, my proudly-Irish father would always say to me; 'Only two things in this world are too serious to be jested on, potatoes and matrimony.' I never knew what he meant at the time because he said it *as a child* - and what I mean by that is that he did it in a high-pitched voice to ruthlessly mock my prepubescence - but it now makes the most perfect sense.

"It seems only yesterday that I liquidated zero-point-five per cent of my portfolio to invest in a humble potato farm, and even less time since I travelled to Trentham for our serendipitous introduction. I was stood proudly by my outlet for the eponymously-named Sloe as a Sloth Gin - a potato-based, juniper-infused alcohol beverage claiming gross profit of approximately sixty-nine-thousand pounds for the most recent financial year, with a projected gross of ninety-five-thousand in the coming year. And then my eyes met yours.

"Since that magical day, Sloe as a Sloth Gin has expanded its market share to an enviable thirty-nine-per cent in the UK, with aim to launch in the US in the fourth quarter, pending brand trademark and associated intellectual property protections. As has my love for you.

"Clara. Today our hearts merge as one, as do our vast finances and real estate holdings. Today our love, that has distilled from the humble potato, is fully fermented, and too powerful for continental European industry stands, and unfit for consumption by anyone under the age of eighteen without the consent of a parent or guardian whilst on private premises. I love you with the energy of an army of a million angels, and with a bank balance capable of paying for their presumably hefty per diems. Clara. I am satisfied to have you become my wife."

As Remington Sloth handed Clara St. Cloud a cheque for ten thousand pounds to dab her tears with, the congregation jeered and swooned. I did my best to contain my emotions, both wholesome joy and crippling guilt.

The celebrant was keen to move on immediately because he had better things to be doing.

"Who among you is the ring bearer?" he asked.

All eyes turned to me. I gulped in nervousness and withdrew the letter from my pocket. The room's collective gaze panned to the small piece of paper in my hand. What a damned situation I'd found myself in. *Curse you, But First Here's Moira! To hell with you for resting your first team against Yeovil Town to make an ill-fated cup run with promotion on the line!*

One can imagine my orgasmic relief when my crisis was instantly sidelined by the intrusion of a man, crashing loudly through the palace doors. This clatter of activity snapped the attention from me and I expelled a sigh of relief.

The man hobbled up the aisle. He was hideous. Monstrous. Women fainted at the sight of him and men tittered disapprovingly, before taking advantage of all the unconscious women. His face looked as though its right side had melted somewhat, causing the front-on silhouette of his head to appear in the shape of a kidney bean. Drool poured from the corner of his crooked mouth and dampened his ragged coat. As he stumbled between the pews, his catheter caught on a strip of decorative ribbon, pulling it from its holstering to spray dark orange urine onto the father of the bride. None had seen a more beastly sight.

A mouthful of spit exploded from his mouth as he bellowed, "Stop!"

Everybody had quite clearly already stopped, but we doubled our efforts and stopped even more.

"This union is unlawful!" the man declared. "This man and woman cannot become husband and wife in the eyes of the church!"

"Now, listen here," interrupted Remington Sloth. "The poor and the unattractive have no place in this Royal Legion, it is an environment suitable for those of us who have money and beauty. You must have at least one. Begone with you, back to the nightmare that whittled that which you claim to call your skull."

"Be silent, you fop of a man. This marriage cannot be registered, for the woman who stands next to you is already wed to another!"

"Who?"

"It is I, Captain Wesley St. Cloud."

The crowd gasped, mostly out of a sense of duty to the moment. There followed a short dialogue from Clara St. Cloud in which she explained her marital history; an important requirement as the audience consisted of only her more-distant relations who could afford the ten-pound entrance fee.

I had long since known of the fate of her late (or not) husband. Captain St. Cloud had not been a popular soldier, but by all accounts he was a brave one. Unheld by fear, he had advanced from the fire-torn trenches of Ypres like a sexually-frustrated Anglican leaving a marriage, until he met his presumed end on the field of battle. The men who'd fought beside him testified of his bravery, and had watched with their own eyes as the Captain was shot several times in the head, most likely by the enemy. Not even the fiercest imagination had humoured his survival.

Yet here he stood. As Clara St. Cloud drew her revision to a close, the man seemed to straighten his stance and push out his chest. The rags he wore were the mudden remains of the captain's uniform of the British Army. The woollen pom-pom beanie on his head had been knitted in the pattern of the Union Flag. This was a man who had returned from the land of the dead but had still found his life lost. He was here to reclaim it.

"They told me you were killed, my Wesley."

"I thought it myself at first. I lay in a foxhole for three weeks, amongst the rotting corpses of my fellow soldiers, living off filth-ridden rainwater and food delivered from a substandard local Chinese restaurant. Once I'd built enough strength, I pulled myself for miles through the mud to a small hamlet, and sought assistance from the locals. They helped me to walk again and gifted me employment. Though I could not speak or write the native language, I worked as the town's pharmacist and eventually successfully ran for public office. As mayor, I developed public transport infrastructure that connected the village to strategic government areas and propelled the local narcotic industry to never-seen-before profits. Our humble hamlet had grown to a full-sized ham. I was offered a young wife, the most beautiful belle in all the land, but know Dear Clara, that I remained loyal to you and we only did hand-stuff.

"Once we'd successfully connected the town to the capital via bullet train, I was able to return home. And now, here I am. I have fought through great adversity to be here. Death's talons tried to pull me down but I refused his way, ever-knowing that my one true love would remain in waiting for as long as she could. Be with me once more, my dearest Clara."

Poor Clara St. Cloud looked once at Remington Sloth, her well-to-do, established, gentleman groom. Then she looked at what remained of the face of her long, lost husband, Captain Wesley St. Cloud, the man to whom she was legally still married. Both St. Cloud and Sloth turned to the celebrant to seek wisdom or loophole that would allow them to continue to be wed.

The celebrant said "Probably not" and reiterated his earlier feelings about wishing to be elsewhere.

Clara St. Cloud collapsed in tears.

This whole spectacle, as dreadful as it had been for its immediate participants, offered a fantastic escape route for my ring-bearing atrocities, so I slinked back into the larger congregation. Together, for five or so minutes, we all watched as politely as we could while Clara St. Cloud wept at the monstrous sight of her reunited husband. Her sorrowful heaving escalated when a rather enterprising young lady in the audience put her hand up and offered to take her now vacant place at the altar. Remington Sloth shrugged and agreed, and together they were married after wrapping two halves of a torn-up apology note around their fingers; a moment that felt dramatically-less embarrassing for yours truly now that an exceptionally unattractive intruder had seen fit to squirt piss on his own father-in-law.

It was a relief to all that the only further drama of the day involved Jennifer Bambi choking to death on a canape. Other than that, it was a charming affair.

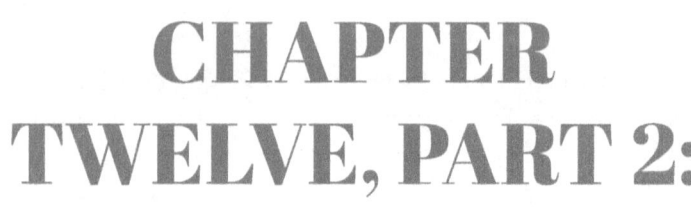

CHAPTER TWELVE, PART 2:

A Mourning in Paradise

I had only previously attended two funerals in my life; the one of Sir Derek Elrington, and a small ceremony for my dear mother. The latter was little but an exhibition of my father's contempt for the funeral industry, and took place on Upton Heath for the total expense of approximately ten pounds.

"There are very few ways one can spend a small fortune and have a rotten time, and funerals are one of those things," were Father's words, and strange ones indeed for the opening of a eulogy.

In contrast, James Ferdinand Bambi had insisted on only the finest farewell for his dearly departed wife and had organised a 'destination funeral' on a remote island off the coast of Mindoro in the Philippines.

"Jennifer would have adored it here," posited James. "A destination ceremony is what she always wanted, although I think she'd have preferred it at the wedding. Couldn't stand the thought of travelling with her when she was alive though. *Lovely* girl. *Ghastly* tourist. Always complaining about something. It was always 'James, what of all these wretched mosquitos?' or 'James, we've forgotten the quinine', or 'James, the malaria has rendered me immobile.' There was little pleasing her. But no, Jenny would have absolutely adored all this and she would be happy that people enjoyed themselves. She always said to me, 'James, all I want of my funeral is for people to smile!' She was quite adamant about that for some reason. People needed to be *happy* at her funeral. I suppose that explains why she was such an asshole to her friends."

The funeral had been a sparsely-attended affair. A mere two dozen of Bambi's invitees had the means to afford the travel and, of them, only eleven had successfully navigated their way to the *northern* Pandan Island. The others had spent the last few days a mile or so away, on the *southern* Pandan Island, waving frantically for help.

The funeral, wake and cremation had been included in a bespoke holiday package that included a five-night stay on the unpopulated isle where James and I now found ourselves. He was taking his beloved's death reasonably well and had suggested, on this particular day, that we should both drink an entire bottle of Tanduay Rum as quickly as we might manage and then see how high we could climb up a nearby palm tree. Gently we swayed, fifty feet in the air, trying to figure out a way down.

From his pocket, James retrieved a handful of coins and threw them to the sand below us.

"A local will sense those are there, and they shall attend to our rescue. The poor here can detect money like a shark to blood," he said, slightly racistly.

It occasionally occurred to me that Bambi was a dreadful man, but then I recalled how burdened he was by the cruel curse of tremendous wealth, and I instead took to sympathising. It was an imperative of decency that I should show understanding, and continue to be mentioned in his will.

Our conversation broke for a short while as we watched from our vantage as the misguided guests on the Southern Island, distant though they were, had apparently reached some civil agreement and started to build shelter. A ferry ran from the *north* island with bi-daily regularity, but the *south* was mostly desolate unless one agreed to pay a local to transport one and, from what we'd gathered by deciphering their smoke signals, such was the native poverty that nobody could break any of the affluent visitor's fifty-pound notes. Rather than give in and lose such a sum of money to a foreign economy, the guests had nobly decided to establish a colony in the King's name.

The tree to which we clung swayed slightly in the breeze, as did my vision, causing a harmonious inversion that made everything appear normal. Bambi was strangely nonplussed and smoked his pipe thoughtfully, occasionally knocking the ash into a coconut that he'd hollowed out to form an ashtray. His nonchalance was almost of concern, and I pressed upon it and asked him how he was feeling about Jennifer's passing.

"Hardly a time to ponder death," he replied, to which I offered my opinion that sitting fifty feet up in the air on the precarious cusp of both a deathly fall and alcohol poisoning might perhaps be one of the most ideal base camps from which to ascend the subject of an afterlife.

Smoke puffed from his mouth as he sighed.

"It does make you think, I suppose. What's the point of it all? No amount of earthly brilliance or success renders any value once you're dead. In the end, life is just a tiny tea break between two halves of eternity. All we have power over is our choice of dunking biscuit. I dearly hope there's something to be had in death but I've little expectation other than what I recall of prior to birth; not a sausage. Otherwise what are we all to do but pad our meaningless existences with enough comfort to make our blip tolerable?"

"A fine legacy lingers beyond our life," I replied.

"That thought is a thin slice of reassurance. Another layer of blanket to soften the thought of the ultimate end. At least Jennifer went in an instant, not toiling over a slow, dreadful decline. Mortality at least granted her the grace of surprise instead of the arduous reckoning most are destined for. It will soon be time for me to become old and watch the candle slowly burn down. What a horrible thought. What of me shall fail first, I wonder? My sight, my mind, my legs? Will I have lived happily enough to justify the wretchedness of that decay? Do I have a surplus of sweet memories to outbalance the coming bad? Will God send a dove to tell me when I've reached my peak so that I may end it with a knife to my wrist? Could I even muster the strength to sign out prematurely and save myself the humiliating descent? I ask you Baggy, with your youth and your future, what is the point?"

"Well, I suppose a scientist would come to say that we're here to reproduce and manifest our immortality in that manner. Perhaps you would find comfort in an heir?"

"Ah yes, intercourse. Jennifer and I tried that once on our honeymoon. We didn't think highly of it. All seemed a bit common for our tastes. And such a mess. The hotel carpet didn't dry out for almost a full week."

"My dear friend, I disagree with you. If, in your life you can cast a wake that never settles, others will ride upon your waves and something of you will live forever. That is not a hopeful fantasy, that is an undeniable truth that can be observed in every facet of our current lives."

Over on the southern island, the guests had completed construction of both a church, from which to establish an appropriately anglo-Saxon pantheon, and a school to educate their forthcoming children. The builders of the school had become so excited at the prospect of procreation that, the second they had downed tools, they located some female guests and commenced work on producing the children. Meanwhile, the builders of the recently-finished church were looking on in envy - disguised as righteous indignation - and furiously inscribed something onto a stone tablet.

"Tell me, Bambi," I persisted. "Who invented the log flume?"

"James W. Haines. A great man. His work has changed lives. He was the Da Vinci of his times."

"And tell me, Bambi. Would your great successes have ever emerged had this Haines not considered the feasibility of combining logs and water and gravity to spectacular effect? I think you know it's not true. You know his name by heart. When one day you have left the living, another will come forward to be hoisted skyward by *your* accomplishments. And *your* name will be spoken of in the same regard. Your greatness will not be forgotten. Your works will be referenced forever-more. The flumes of the thirtieth century will echo the name James Ferdinand Bambi. That is what your life is for. It is not a tea break. It is simply the preface to your immortality. And the better you write it, the more fantastic the story."

James didn't speak any agreement but I like to think I had tempered his doubts if only for the moment. Deep down though, I suspected that, among the population atop that fif-ty-foot-high tropical tower, it was not *his* concern that I was attempting to exile.

"Speaking of gravity and trees and the direction 'down', Baggy, it seems we're in luck," Bambi pointed.

Beneath us, a gathering of Filipinos were clustered at the foot of the tree, waving around a metal detector and shouting in Tagalog, "Coins! Wealth! Praise be to our savage, heathen Lord," or something to that effect; I couldn't understand a word, to be honest.

"Wonderful. Perhaps they have a nearby ladder."

"Bugger that, Baggy. Dinner's on in ten and I'm to unveil to the maitre'd The Alchemist's Breadstone. He reckons his cousin knows a guy in marketing who could give it the leg-up it needs. Come on, ol' boy. Aim for their shoulders," James re-plied. Placing his coconut ashtray onto his head as a makeshift helmet, he tucked his pipe back into his jacket and launched himself from the tree with all the free-spirited abandon of an extremely drunk, existentially-troubled man who'd just buried the love of his life.

I didn't monitor his descent, trusting not his results but his confidence in action. Instead, I took one last glance at the dis-tant southern island. By now, both the church and the school were on fire, and so were most of the women. Only four men and one lady looked to remain alive, and they appeared to have founded a two-party system of democracy. Elections were being held, and both candidates were promising voters that whoever elected them into office could have the remaining woman.

I silently wished them well, closed my eyes and, with one graceful leap from the palm's husk, crushed both clavicles of a man named Pedro.

CHAPTER THIRTEEN:

A Letter from
Michael-Steve Burrows

42 *Wimpole Street*
Marylebone, London

27th August
Dear Mister Baggy Smacker,

It has been almost two years since you ridiculed me in a reprehensible, juvenile manner. Do not think your actions have been forgotten. Do not think you can beg for my forgiveness or alleviate any of the suffering that I intend for you.

My reputation and my credibility inflate with each day, as does my "baby penis". As all three grow, I become better suited to bringing righteous justice down upon you and your little friend, Darkfire. With God as witness to my pledge, you will feel the wrath of my baby penis, which is actually pretty big these days, and you will rue the day you crossed Michael-Steve Burrows. Come judgement time, it shall be I who smacks your baggy, if you follow my meaning.

Please find attached three photographs of my penis and one impressionist watercolour of how it is predicted to look in five years' time, to be interpreted at your own decision. I've included a shilling in each shot as a means to define scale. Be it known that I'm not even fully erect in these photos, this is me basically flaccid. And to quote the wise and brilliant Pope Urban IV, "I'm a grower, and a shower." So have a good think about that, shithead.

Kind regards,

Michael-Steve Burrows

CHAPTER FOURTEEN:

The Gentleman Host

No sooner had my knuckles rapped upon the solid oak door of the finely-appointed Edwardian townhouse, did it swing open to reveal the most dramatically-attired gentleman I had ever bore vision upon. His upper body was adorned in a technicolour towelling robe, sequined to within an inch of tolerability. On his head perched something that at one time may have been a live peacock but now more resembled a tactical helmet. His trousers were made from stitched-together autographed programmes from various West End shows, and his knee-high boots appeared to be hollowed-out meerkats, to which little orthopaedic thought had been given.

"Oh my, oh my, oh my. Yes! Bless Aphrodite, yes! You will do most wonderfully. Come, my dear boy, seek comfort within my cosy antechamber, safe from the perishing, autumnal gusts," said the figure.

Though he gave no quarter through which to enter, the outside was fiercely chilling and I burrowed past his waist, into a fabulously-upholstered hallway. The furnishings were immediately lavish. The walls were papered with the most wondrous papyrus. The floors were carpeted with a triple layer of exposed goose feathers. Game hunting trophies were mounted upon all available surfaces with a sentiment of staggering extravagance, although it would have been much more appealing had some of them not still been partially alive.

"You are fond of hunting, I gather?" I asked, raising my voice above the various terminal bleating.

"Oh, yes, I am a very capable predator, my dear boy. So many of us in show business are. I shot all that you see myself. You see that boar there?" He pointed to a particularly bored-looking hogshead that hung above a fireplace.

"Majestic," I replied.

"I took her down with only a water pistol. Took a week from start to finish. I essentially had to wait for it to die of hunger. In retrospect, it perhaps would have taken *less* time had I not been continuously preserving its life with hydration. Nevertheless, the highlight of my trip to Siberia."

"What took you to that part of the world?" I inquired out of politeness.

"I was there working with the blind."

"That must have been challenging."

"Indeed it was. They were rarely on time and could barely keep the sled in a straight line. Walk with me to the parlour, won't you? I shall pour for us an exquisite drink, and we shall discuss your future."

I followed him down the hallway, into a room full of sculptures and erotic works of art, and erotic works of not-quite art. Marble erections, both architectural and phallic, dominated every crevice (both architectural and vaginal), and the goose-feathered flooring, which had terminated at the end of the corridor, gave way to a knee-high wading pool of Chartreuse. I removed my shoes and sloshed over to the impressively-stocked bar that ran along an entire wall.

"I would most love to take a gander through your artwork at a later point," I said.

"You're welcome to, though they have the most dreadful attention span and no anal sphincter, so be sure to mop up afterwards."

Just as I found an inflatable lounge to recline upon, a large grey cat entered the room and paddled toward the two of us.

"Ah, this is Mister Pepperbridge, coming to say hello. He is of immaculate pedigree."

"Russian Blue?" I attempted.

"Right-leaning libertarian, as with most felines I believe, though I find it best to avoid the discussion of politics whilst in Mister Pepperbridge's company as it provokes him to become feisty."

"I see. As it does with my father."

"Ah, but does your father claw at you whilst saturated in French liqueur?"

"Actually, yes, he spent time in prison for something quite similar."

As I watched the man assemble a cocktail through one eye, my other peered around at the room's curiosities, meaning I couldn't actually see anything clearly at all. I regrouped my vision and spied a particularly eye-catching artwork.

It was an intricately-detailed, painted wooden panel, upon which all manner of activities were taking place. The scene appeared to be of a shadowy underworld, peppered with naked figures engaging in various acts of non-church-approved hedonism, tucked away into darkened nooks. In the centre was a beam of light that descended from Hell's ceiling, and the men and women had been painted as if they were magnetised toward it. Floating high above the adultery, irradiated by the glowing shaft, was a devilish-looking half-mole, half-bat creature with a foul and bloodied grin on its face. In each winged hand it carried a decapitated human body, and though its intentions were clearly carnivorous, its feet were tethered by a rope that hung to the ground, from where dozens of male beings could be seen attempting to climb to apparent doom. In the right-hand corner of the work was a small white rectangle that read "£2 ONO".

I asked my gentleman host for the meaning of what I could see.

"Ah, yes. That painting is the legendary, lost lower panel of Hieronymus Bosch's 'Garden of Earthly Delights'. Once thought to be a triptych work, that most-glorious enigmatic piece travelled astray after its previous owner, Philip II, down-sized to a studio apartment in Valladolid and hired the aid of cheap removalists. I was fortunate to have picked it up at a car-boot sale in Bruges over ten years ago. As you can see, the oriental salesmen was flogging it for two pounds, but after some skilful haggling, I paid a nearby mercenary one pound to have him shot and I took it. It's an exquisite painting and I feel it stands on its own merit despite its separation from the more famous three panels, which I've always considered to be a bit on the shit side."

"It is ghastly," I could not help but say.

"Indeed. Ghastly, but enchanting. The world was not ready for Bosch."

"I see."

"Not culturally, I mean. 'Not ready' in the same way that it wasn't ready for the Spanish Flu."

My gentleman host handed me a wide-brimmed glass filled with an orange liquid that gradiented down into a darker shade. With a graceful flick of my pinky finger, I scooped out a small pill and took a long sip. It was indeed exquisite; a balance of sweet and sour, with a mellow texture that finished as a tickle of botanical tang.

"I call it Edgar Allen's Morning Stream, in honour of Poe's talent and alcoholism. It is based with mango juice and gussied up with gin, grenadine and a light spritzing of a special fluid produced by a convent of blind Macedonian monks. I can assure you of its exclusivity, as I've seen how long it takes them to learn how to aim into the bottle. I once became intimately friendly with one member of their rank. A charming boy, though they take a vow of silence upon joining the monastery; a habit I find irritating as I quite like to indulge in classical music when I find myself in the moment of being intimately friendly with a hairless European boy. But don't you worry. We eventually *came* to an *arrangement*, if you'll take the time for some friendly innuendo."

I vomited ever-so-slightly into my beverage, but fortunately just enough to change its taste to that of a Bloody Mary.

"Do you know," Lavender continued, "the Garden of Earthly Delights is considered by many interpreters to be an homage to the depravity of the seven deadly sins. Lust, Gluttony, Wrath, Envy, Greed, Pride and poor old Sloth. One for each day of the week, I've always thought. Mister Pepperbridge regularly commits four of them. Five, before I had him neutered… And surprisingly little Wrath after.

"But despite the analysis of the alleged experts, I've only managed to count to six in the original. I see all manner of sin upon those three famous panels, yet I see nothing that strikes me as Pride, and I believe I am fitter than most to identify her. I come from a long line of Pride, it runs through my blood. My father was proud. His father was proud. It may have skipped a generation with my young son, Tobias, as he has married into the Danish royal family, and not on the side of the aisle you'd think.

"But yes, I think Pride is what we're looking at in this fourth part of the work. That creature there is Pride. A beast that all aspire to without regard for those it discards, or those they impede or harm en route to her allure. Pride draws you in, sucks you dry and spits you back out onto the carpet when done. Something else I know all too well of, my boy.

"And yet, I've always actually considered Pride's sinful reputation to be of poor award. Pride has done so many wonderful things for our species. Pride pushes science forwards, it allows art to thrive, it pollinates cultural advance. Pride thrusts men to their limits, it makes women fight for equality and it allows children to form life-long ambition.

"*Vanity*, now *that* is something to avoid. I suspect, when the sins were originally translated, no ideal word for Vanity existed, and so Pride became the unfortunate avatar. Vanity is *truly* sinful. Vanity is Pride's hollow, vapid, evil cousin. Have you ever considered the difference between Pride and Vanity?"

I took a long sip at my glass of chemicals and made clear I did not.

"Well, it's quite simple, dear boy. Vanity is desperately wanting those around you to think you are spectacular. Pride is desperately wanting to convince *yourself* that you are. Vanity is a vulnerable wall, shielding no city; purely defensive, with nought to defend beyond its foolish architect. Whereas *Pride* is a mobile army, there to siege. Pride does not *need* to protect anything. It fights to the death because virtuous battle is its purpose. Remember those differences, my boy. Be sure to pursue the correct one.

"So," he continued, hoisting himself onto a lilo shaped as a small desert island, "The name is Smacker, is it?"

"Yes, Sir. Baggy Smacker."

"Well, young Mister Baggy Smacker, my name, as I'm sure you know, is Hillary Lavender and it is my pleasure to meet your acquaintance. News of your interview with the Vatican has reached all corners of England. You have become something of an acclaimed interviewer. Cinnamon-dusted fig roll?" He offered, as a small silver tray floated past me.

"Has anyone provided a bodily substance to their preparation?"

"Merely a sprig of mine own hair to bind the pastry."

Politely, I declined.

"Not to worry. Mister Pepperbridge finds them simply divine. Mister Pepperbridge!"

Immediately as called, Mister Pepperbridge emerged from beneath the surface of the emerald liqueur to splish and splash toward the proffered confection. Upon his destination, he revealed a small purse from within his furried coat and scooped the pastries into it and, once replenished, he dove back into the unseen depths.

"What a peculiar sight," I uttered.

"The vapours of the Chartreuse cause all sorts of wonder. Now, Smacker. Let us discuss why you are here. You come most highly recommended by the fool, Ernie Greenglass. He is quite mad, but nevertheless with a proven eye for spectacle. My contacts in Belfast have discussed with me your cunning and originality, and Ernie recalls something of an imprint being left by you. Is the world of television still your pursuit?"

"Never moreso, Hillary."

"Please, call me 'Hilary'. With a single 'L', as we are now friends."

"Yes, Hilary."

"You have chosen a fine path, Baggy, and you have found your timing well. We are at the dawn of a new era, the first light of mankind's latest glory. The age of art was born in the Renaissance, it was refined by Mannerism and Baroque chapters, it was beautified by the Romantics, complexified by the Impressionists, and it never strayed too far from being interesting when the Realists got hold of it. But now we stand at the foot of the mountain that is the new age, the highest and most modern echelon of human expression; what those of us in the television industry call... *Light Entertainment.*"

"Light Entertainment?"

"Yes, Baggy. Light Entertainment. Not too boring, not too exciting. Just enough entertainment to be considered decent. No scandal, no titillation, nothing that would encourage unwanted habits like dedication and dependency or expectation. Just enough to keep people entertained and educated.

"You must aim to create programming that would keep the youth off the street in the evenings, but not so compelled that they would pine for it should we need to relocate them in wartime. We want production that would be inoffensive so as not to cause the elderly to write in, but at the same time intriguing enough to deny them the time to write in about how there's nothing good on.

"That crucial balance is the key, Baggy. Light Entertainment is to be a coy lass whose flirtations must remain social and never coquettish. And it has been said to me by our mutual friend that you are a young man who lives very much upon the plateau that we seek to build upon. How did you and Greenglass come to meet?"

"I observed a stage lamp ignite and set him on fire. I suppose you could say that was my first taste of... *Light* Entertainment."

Lavender reached out and slapped me wickedly across the cheek.

"NO, BAGGY! Such black wit is far beyond the threshold of Light Entertainment, you naive fool! Do you wish to receive letters in the mail from the disgruntled masses?!"

"My apologies, dear Hilary. I... I lost touch with my sensitivities. I think it might be the vapours."

"Pray that it be, Smacker, for indiscretions such as that, even far milder, will attract the Great British public's most insatiable tendency; righteous indignation. It has brought down greater establishments than television in man's history, and it does not sleep through controversy unless it's to do with rugby league for some reason."

Lavender's striking of my face appeared to have inspired a feline dedication to mutual offence and called to action the claws of Mister Pepperbridge upon my inflatable lounge, and I found myself ever-so-slowly slipping beneath the green and gentle lapping.

"But despite your lack of experience, Baggy Smacker, I am willing to take a chance with you. There is some twinkle in your eye that tells me I am talking to a young man with the exact modicum of charm and a harness of basic English that would enable him to read pre-written jokes from an autocue and pretend they're off-the-cuff, and sustain the attention of the nation. I am putting together a variety show with all manner of acts, and I'm offering you the chance to be a part of its inaugural series. It *needs* someone cynical, scything and informative, and I think *you* would be perfect for my needs."

"I would be honoured, dear Hilary," I said, now submerged to my collar. My clarity had become blurred as my nostrils edged closer to the Chartreuse, and my eyes had begun to sting. I concentrated on sobriety as I was drawn powerfully to his offer and to unconsciousness.

"Then it is to be a deal, young Baggy. You are to be a star of television. Shall we drink to your future?"

I agreed that we should, and as he tilted his cocktail glass upward to quaff the remainder of his drink, I shared in the toast as I drifted underwater by submitting to a short drowning in expensive French liquor. As my lungs filled with fluid and I dropped to the room's depths, I observed a small submersible vehicle steering toward me, and as it drew closer, I saw the unmistakable whiskered face of Mister Pepperbridge operating its steering.

I awoke several days later in a Chelsea hotel, beside a non-disclosure agreement I didn't recall signing, and a note from Lavender requesting my attendance at BBC Centre in two months' time. I immediately took a letterhead and excitedly penned a message to my good friend, Joseph Darkfire, to tell him of how I was soon to join him as a modern man of esteemed celebrity.

I posted the letter with the vibrance of one who felt anything was possible. All evidence seemed to indicate that my path to worldly glory was now uncovered. But little did I know that Lavender's casual remark of wartime mobilisation was to become realised within years. For Great Britain was soon to be again ravaged by worldwide conflict, and the men of the planet once more decimated in their tens-of-thousands, and as before the widows and orphans of Earth multiplied in unprecedented numbers. And this fateful time, my own schedule was to be quite annoyingly interfered with.

CHAPTER FIFTEEN:

Light Entertainment

The much-awaited apple that I recently ate hit my tongue this morning, facing stiff competition from other things I recently ate, including a highly-regarded banana that I had around eight-thirty-ish. Unlike the banana that I recently ate, the apple that I recently ate was consumed as a palate cleanser to banish the aftertaste of the Earl Grey I recently drank, and not purely for the dose of pleasure and energy that bananas are more likely to provide.

"It's been a forgettable year for apples that I've eaten and heading into award season, there is still much opportunity for apples to stand out and take a shot at winning accolades. With that in mind, you would think orchard owners would be monitoring things carefully, and making sure any apples that I am to eat were of the best possible quality to see if they can't sneak in a late entry that will remain prominent in voters' minds. Unfortunately, it seems unlikely that anyone involved in the production of the apple that I recently ate will be marching up the red delicious carpet this year.

"The varietal of apple that I recently ate was a Pink Lady, the sort of fruit that consumers have come to expect to be crispy and sweet, like a sunburnt Clementine Churchill. It seems strange then, that the apple that I recently ate was in fact chalky and rather disappointing, like Stonehenge. There were certainly some lingering elements of sweetness, I will happily concede, but the desperate performance of that fructose, no matter how passionately it tried, could not transcend sufficient blemish to elevate the final product to notable heights.

"In the current, over-saturated world of apples that I recently ate, you need to get the basics right at the very least. It seems a waste that the apple that I recently ate, at its *core* got so many fundamentals wrong. In the end, the apple that I recently ate should have perhaps fallen closer to the tree. Back to you, Hilary."

The camera crew made various silent hand gestures to indicate that they had not, prior to going live on air, worked out a silent hand gesture to indicate that they had cut back to Hilary Lavender. So instead there was a moment's pause as somebody passed him a bit of paper with the words "We've cut back to you, Hillary Lavender" written upon it. After the host had sent back his own bit of paper to the set director that read, "Please, call me Hilary, with one 'L'", he smiled broadly into the camera.

Lavender sat with great majesty behind an opulently-designed desk that glowed with a spectrum of gorgeous colours sadly lost upon the monochrome broadcast. In his arms, slept Mister Pepperbridge, who purred loudly into Lavender's lapel microphone causing waves of irritated Britons to violently assault their television sets in the hope of correcting the buzzing audio. Embossed on the front of the desk, in striking art-deco typeface, read the words "Hillary Lavender's Spanking Good Time".

This was Lavender's second attempt at producing his own program, following an ill-fated series entitled 'Next Door's Pussy', in which two households would swap cats for a fortnight and have the resulting 'calamitous shift of dynamic' filmed in a documentary format. Sadly, the featured felines adapted to their new surroundings in mere minutes and appeared to surrender all prior memory of their previous owners, which made for a rather depressing watch. As such, it was abandoned after three episodes and a torrent of angry letters, mostly from disappointed elderly men whose expectations had been unfairly raised by the show's title. Lavender's reputation had taken a temporary hit, but he was expecting a more positive response from this new venture, though presumably the same sort of mail.

"Many thanks to Michael-Steve Burrows for that most excellent critique of his breakfast. Some well-articulated and high-value information there. I believe I will be staying away from that particular piece of fruit. Sounds like something of a *bad apple*."

The studio audience laughed and heartily applauded their own ability to detect a punchline and maintain a coherent memory for over fifteen seconds.

I had not known, as I'd signed my contract, that the vicious Michael-Steve Burrows would become my colleague. His great renown as a critic had no doubt attracted swathes of television offers and I considered it my damned poor luck that, of all opportunities, this was the one he'd availed himself to.

If the truth be told, I would still have gladly made the commitment even if aware of his pesky presence, but it did feel as if maintaining a relation with the devil was somehow untrue to my friend, Joseph Darkfire. Thankfully, Burrows' and my paths did not cross other than during the live broadcast.

"Well, viewers, next up we have another handsome young man who will be tantalising your desire for salacious affairs with his pioneering new 'Celebrity Gossip' segment! Here he is, ladies and gentlemen, our resident pop-culture expert; the oddly-intrigued, the concerningly-informed, the perversely-invested Baggy Smacker!"

I was intensely nervous. In seconds, the entire nation's eyes would be upon me. At that moment, I was lost for thought or word. 'How had this come to be?' I recall wondering. Why had I ever pined for this feeling of the most severe trepidation and self-doubt?

I was blessed with a pause in proceedings as the camera crew scribbled something into a notepad and passed it to me. The note reiterated that they had not had chance to properly communicate without speaking during a live broadcast, and that they had not established a system to indicate that I was now on camera to an audience of hundreds of thousands, and that they would shortly be sending a second piece of paper to let me know when I had been cut to. I folded the piece of paper into my pocket just as the succeeding note had been handed to me. I noted its contents and signed the attached form, confirming my recognition that the camera was indeed upon me, and mailed it back to the camera crew via first-class post.

I drew a deep breath, directed my gaze to the camera, and spoke.

"Good evening, England, Scotland, Wales, the British Islands, and various obedient sections of Ireland that the rest could learn from. My name is Baggy Smacker and this is Celebrity Gossip time."

For a segment theme tune, an off-screen organist played the opening bars of Rachmaninov's second piano concerto, which did an impressively-awful job of setting the tone. As it gave way to a more light-hearted xylophone melody, I looked to the teleprompter, where my own written words - heavily edited by Lavender - shone miraculously before the camera's lens.

"We start this week's land of slanderous scandal with a cheeky gander at Romania, where the incorrigible King Carol II has conjured yet another crazy controversy by suspending the national constitution and seizing emergency power of the country! More commonly renowned for his myriad, mischievous, marital misgivings such as his affairs with the sultry and sexy Magda Lupescu, it's no surprise that the prominent playboy has installed his authoritarian and corporatist agenda by centralising power to an absolutist monarchy! It seems that it isn't just the hearts of women everywhere that Carol II commands with a violent, anti-democratic stranglehold!"

I could feel nervousness drying my mouth and tightening my tongue, but thankfully to my left was a small wooden table with a quenching glass of water for such malady. I took a sip from it and rested it back down. There was a strangeness to it; a herbal, almost medicinal taste, however I resisted contemplation and pushed onward into my glowing script.

"Over to Germany, where naughty old General Werner von Fritsch has shocked his fans by resigning from the position of Commander-in-Chief of the German Army. Rumours run wild that the veracious veteran had been veering too far into No Man's Land or, to be more accurate, *Only* Man's Land, if you catch our drift. Several candidates have been earmarked by the Wehrmacht to replace the beleaguered General, favourite among them the not-so-popular General Walther von Brauchitsch, an appointment likely to go down with viewers about as well as the Hindenburg! Let's hope his menu options include less bratwurst and more strudel!"

The audience regaled in the whimsically-dressed homophobia but while comforted by my confident delivery, I was nevertheless ill at ease. My lips burnt ever-so slightly where wetted by the recent drink, and a just-so-familiar taste lingered upon my palate. I searched for something in my mind to replace the concerns but was shocked to instead find an inner-voice calling to blame immigrants for the tainted water. The first droplets of panic formed on my brow.

I quickly studied the next segment on the autocue; A series of very well-written, highbrow witticisms implying that Austrian President, Wilhelm Miklas, had taken a shit onto his father's chest. Suddenly, there was a mechanical popping sound and the words vanished. Seconds later, a carrier pigeon delivered me a scrawled note advising of calamitous technical problems with the autocue. On the flip side of the page, written in bold script, was the word "Improvise".

I took a deep breath, held my gaze to the camera and winked knowingly. Do not despair, I told myself. The famous diamond-tongue wit of the Smacker bloodline should suffer no holdback at a moment such as this. Effortless ad hoc charm was as much a part of my family spirit as alcoholism and juvenile atopic eczema. I invoked the lingual dalliance of my ancestors and allowed lyrical genius to flow forth from my lips.

"Our apologies, ladies and gentlemen. We appear to be experiencing some difficulties. If the autocue was any darker right now, we would insist it enter the building via a different entrance."

Piercing gasps rallied throughout the studio. Eyes widened. Without voluntary decision, my hand slapped against my mouth, aghast. What had I just said? It was certainly beyond the scope of Light Entertainment. My heartbeat rose to a gallop as my face strained of colour. I attempted to readjust.

"I, uh... I meant to say that... The collective power of the modern Jew-"

The lights in the studio were immediately dimmed. As I glanced for answers that would somehow piece together my behaviour, I saw Hillary Lavender's glass-like expression pierce into me. His look was a palette of emotions; Anger, disgust, confusion and betrayal. The tittering of the crew reverberated in my ears. Even the carrier pigeon committed to a heavy-handed metaphor of flying above me and defecating, with perfect aim, onto my lapel microphone.

I looked around more and spotted a face peeking from beyond the studio's set. It was none other than Michael-Steve Burrows. Unique to him in this room was the evil smile upon his face.

The water! I now remembered the peculiar taste, infused with nostalgia. It was the medicinal, herb-like flavour of the coltsfoot leaf. There was no doubt about it. The fiend Burrows had discovered my father's allergy to Coltsfoot Rock and employed it in a strategy to realise my downfall. He had trusted upon the condition's hereditary nature and his long-promised vengeance had been seized. Against my own free will, I had become a victim of chemically-induced racism.

A short hour forward and I found myself slumped in a chair, absorbing the beratement of a livid Hillary Lavender. At this turn in the relationship, the second 'L' was most definitely restored.

"You little fuck!" he roared. "What in God's name were you thinking? All that we have built is now ash! My career is ruined! I took a fool's chance upon you and this is how you invest your opportunity? Have you nothing to say for yourself, you ungrateful and bigoted young swine?"

I had no answer for the man. My father had found the brushing away of his racist tendencies of such ease, but I had not the comfort of a literary career to deflect with. To all who had observed the broadcast, I was nothing but a mere delinquent. My one great chance had been brutally hammered back into its hole by the devil himself; Michael-Steve Burrows. He had promised retaliation and, oh my, had he delivered upon his word.

I considered scrounging some sentence to present as a meagre apology to the man before me but, as I attempted so, the door of Lavender's office creaked open to reveal the diminutive stature of Michael-Steve Burrows. He was fully naked and, as was his habit, had recently shit himself. The unfiltered confidence of the auburn streams trickling down his infantile form only added to the smugness of the upturned demonic crescent that styled his wretched smile. He held a small jar of honey-sweetened pulped pumpkin in one hand and a spoon in his other.

"Gentlemen," he addressed, as he scooped mash from the glass vessel and smeared it across his dumb little face. "That was... something of a performance." He threw the food to the ground and laughed maniacally, and then cried for a bit, and then started laughing again. From his diaper, he procured a crayon and used it to draw an unconvincing picture of a duck upon the gilded wallpaper of Lavender's office.

"You cretinous beast!" I declared. "You foiled me all for your selfish pride. And not only myself, but dear Lavender too!"

"Don't blame the infant, Smacker," interrupted Hillary. "Have yourself some decency. You expect me to believe that a mere taste of an unpopular confection would drive men to such filth of mind? I am not blind to the agenda and motives of the common bigot!"

It was of no use to attempt to talk my way out of my insolence. No man in possession of functioning faculties would believe such a thing as my inherited troubles. I placed my head in my hands and begged tears to withdraw. I had been offered a once-in-a-lifetime climb for success and my footholds had fallen away so close to the apex. At this lowest point, even Michael-Steve Burrows appeared, for a merest, fleeting jiffy, regretful of his actions.

"It's too late for tears, Baggy," said Lavender. "Your time here at the BBC is at its end, for a man of such hate has no place in the realm of Light Entertainment. Perhaps one day in the future, the divisive dystopia for which you so seem so accredited might come to be, and fellows such as yourself might be given a platform to peddle your unsustainable, conservative rhetoric on automobile review programmes or pop music contests. But until then, the Great British public will not allow their taxes to be spent upon one man's xenophobia, especially when they all keep getting told off for doing it at football games. The doors to Television Centre are closed to your prejudices. You must now find your way through this industry via the rancid catacombs of independent broadcasting, where your horrific world views will be accordingly syndicated."

I pulled myself up and stumbled in a malaise of heartbreak out of the office. I stopped before Michael-Steve Burrows as I reached the door. His curt grimace was suppressed no longer. I pointed at his drawing.

"An unsurprisingly pathetic attempt. It hardly resembles a duck."

"It isn't a duck. It is a bunny."

"Why does it have a beak?"

"That is his carrot. Bunnies famously enjoy carrots."

"It has less artistic merit than the stains on your lower body."

"And yet so much more worth than your own portfolio."

"Perhaps one day you might view your own actions with the scathing critiques you are so infamous for. Maybe some good might come of your pitiful envy, and while you'll no doubt remain with your baby penis, perhaps some of your non-physical attributes might one day progress in age."

"Should my actions ever sway too far from my intentions, perhaps then I shall consider revision. But until then, I will decline such feedback from a person of such little achievement. Good day, Mister Smacker."

And so I left Television Centre and collapsed on its forecourt, and watched as the clouds above raced beyond me like the dreams of my youth, glowing with the sun's light before slinking away behind an unreachable horizon. My soul felt shattered. I suspect I had laid there for hours before security guards presented their concern and beat me viciously on the skull with batons until I agreed to stop being such a drama queen.

I found as miserable a public house as I could, and attempted to drown my sorrows but instead of sinking, they rode my misery as keenly as a group of tourists enjoying a spine-tingling log flume. Behind the bar, a radio crackled a news story. Britain had declared war on Germany. At that time it meant nothing to me.

Within weeks, nothing else would mean more.

CHAPTER SIXTEEN:

Headhunted

ollowing the nationwide broadcast of my supposedly hateful and radicalised tirade, I was immediately pestered by wave after wave of lucrative job offers to host talk-back programmes on independent radio. I turned down each role with a proud disgust, berating hopeful producers for attempting to lure me to their telegraphic lecterns to preach to their audiences of unwashed and vitriol-filled zealots. The more hurtful and cruel my rebukes, the more impressed they became and the larger the advertised salaries grew.

For an intolerable period, due to a dire need for funds, I was under the employ of a tremendously racist playwright named Cooper Ribbed-Blanket, among whose infamous works included such inflaming titles as 'Curry Your Anus'; a crude re-imagining of William Shakespeare's 'Coriolanus' in which the protagonist purged the ethnic poor of Calcutta and, rather than ultimately being killed for his misdeeds, ended up signing a record deal with Decca and marrying a ravishing sock-model named Butterfoot. Still, it remained somehow more tasteful than 'Quiet Down, Mousey Bitch', his modern translation of 'The Taming of the Shrew'.

For as long as I could, I maintained possession of my principles but despite noble refusal, Parliament eventually declared a state of emergency purely so that they might seize my principles via compulsory purchase. Before long, my principles were sold in an auction to the highest bidder, and I found myself summoned to a job interview against my will.

It had been several months since my capitulation at the infantile hands of the savage Michael-Steve Burrows, and much had happened upon the peripheries of my life.

Hillary Lavender - reluctantly now with two 'L's - had managed to delicately steady his ship and had quite expertly navigated the backlash of public horror that followed my incident. With strategic marvellousness, he and his team had placed the blame of my outburst on the rising tide of German fascism that had breached its dam and drawn Britain to conflict. This successful plan to quell racism using slightly-more-socially-acceptable racism was a revolution in the world of broadcasting, and would soon be employed to great effect in the forthcoming allied war effort.

Elsewhere, my father had been released from prison once again, fallen in with a rough crowd of deplorables and taken to the high seas as an ethical pirate, scuttling Japanese whaling boats for their cargo, selling it and donating the profits toward research into the creation of a range of dairy-free cheesecakes. I'd only had contact from him twice over the past year; once to call and declare his love for my youthful wisdom and exuberance, and pay comment to the smoothness of my legs and the tightness of my immaculate buttocks, and then a second time only moments later to advise I forget everything recently said as he suspected he'd gotten the wrong number.

Other companions seemed to have fallen off the face of the Earth around this time. Clara St. Cloud had finally found happiness after her estranged husband dropped dead one evening. The suspicious circumstances around his death were vastly outweighed by negative opinions about his personality, and once the coroner had been convinced to read a selection of testimonies reviewing the Captain's past behaviour, physical appearance and his refusal to adhere to public escalator etiquette, the agreed upon cause of death was listed as 'euthanasia'.

My most intimate friend, Joseph Darkfire, had been offered a six-month-long artistic residency in a children's treehouse in Castleford, following a successful bid from the Yorkshire Board of Tourism as part of their ongoing campaign "to not be quite as terrible as Derbyshire". He'd sent me some of his work, seeking feedback and citing a creative blockage that he could not dislodge.

As I sat down in Askham Bog,
Atop a most inviting log,
I saw a Yorkshire terrier dog,
And it stole my sandwiches.

I sat in silence on 'til noon,
And watched the sun switch phase with moon,
I hear we'll get a Sainsbury's soon,
I'll buy new sandwiches.

Never one to extinguish the flame of Joseph's craft, I responded to his letter with one of absolute praise, suggesting only that perhaps the choice of breed of dog might seem too obvious and that possibly 'Waitrose' could provide better scansion.

And so it was that, despite the rumblings of violence from across the channel, the world felt oddly silent. No more alone did I feel than dragging myself through the gauntlet of recruitment without a friend's ear to lean upon, but I nevertheless found myself mysteriously summoned to a brick townhouse in Buckinghamshire. With nothing better to do with my time, curiosity claimed me. I soon caught a train from London and jumped off at Wolverton.

After brushing myself off and stemming most of the bleeding, I made my way to a building garnished with a black metal sign reading the name "The Stables". Following a stern knock, the broad door creaked open to reveal a minute woman. "Oh no," she said. "We've just had them done, thank you."

"I think you are mistaken, madam. I have an appointment for an interview, as per this letter here."

"No, no, no. The man from the Legion did them last Tuesday. We've no need for another coat."

"I'm not here to offer my services as a painter, madam."

"Painter? Who said anything about painting? He knitted charming frock coats for the cats. He does a wonderful job of it, and at a very reasonable price. The last man charged double and made the cats look like whores. We'll not be changing back. Not unless we adopt Protestant cats."

"Madam, I have come as requested in this communication. I plead with you to read this."

"Oh, I can't read that."

"Might you fetch your spectacles?"

"Wouldn't help. I never learnt to read English, you see. Portuguese and Latin, I went with and I'd say I never made a sillier mistake in my life. Tried to take up classes a few years back but, as you might imagine, couldn't fill in the forms properly because of the language barrier. Ended up enrolled on a three-year course studying amphibious naval strategy. Didn't even realise my mistake until halfway through. Just thought traversing the oceans, armed to the teeth and ready to invade was all part of the English-language experience. Shoot first, write a letter of apology later - That's what we were taught. As a matter of fact, I don't even speak English."

"What do you mean?"

"Desculpa, não falo inglês."

"I asked what you mean."

"Me desculpe senhor. Eu não falo inglês."

I stopped and took breath. Absurdity of such a degree could only mean one thing; This was surely a test to overcome. Someone had requested my attendance, yet before me was an obstacle that I needed to be thwarted in order to fulfil my intrigue and determine who exactly had summoned me.

In my era at Queen's University, I had taken Latin classes. I thought carefully and recalled a time when Professor Wainwright had once seduced me to a night of whispered mystique, in which he dispensed to me a great number of what he called "The Nonpareil Scriptures". These, he said, were the ethereal summonings through which man could conjure the will of almost any human soul. I recalled only one of them to heart, but it was all the Latin I knew to muster. I caught the crone's gaze and spoke with all the timbre I held.

"Cūrātrīcem tuum alloquar."

The effect was immediate. The animation of the crone's face stalled and a whiteness overcame her eyes. The door creaked wide open at her side. I had told her, in the language of ancient Rome, that *I wanted to speak to her manager,* and a deeply-imbedded Anglo-Saxon dread had compelled her.

"Please. Come in. We've been expecting you."

I stepped through the doorway and found a modern, deceptively-large room beyond the disguise of the Edwardian facade. I held the door, so that the women might enter behind me but as I looked back I saw her climb onto a bicycle and mumble something about it being her turn to organise the week's meat raffle.

The room I had entered was not dissimilar to the foyer of a medium-to-large-sized branch of a reputable building society, complete with a medium-to-large-sized security guard who appeared to be sleeping in one corner. Were he any bigger, he might have managed to do so in two. Before me was a reception desk, unattended but for a provocative bust of Clementine Churchill upon its ledge, with a sign hanging from her neck that read "Closed until Octember 32nd". I noted - with keen instinct - that this was all very silly.

Right and to the rear of Dear Clemmy were two doors, each with its own guard. Assuming that the mystery of my beckoning might lie behind one of these two portals, I approached the two men who addressed me with contrasting expressions.

"Hello, young sir. My name is Eric, and this here is my colleague Ernest."

"Good day to you both. My name is Baggy Smacker, and I have been requested here for an interview. Might you know to whom I should be received?"

Eric reached into his jacket pocket and revealed a sheath of paper from it. He handed it to me to read.

The answer to your questions rest upon the other side of one of these two doors.
Should you choose correctly, your divine purpose will become closer to revelation.
Should you choose incorrectly, you shall be sent lacking, back to inconsequence.
There are two guards whose wills you are to manoeuvre.
One guard will always tell the truth.
One guard will always tell a lie.
Good luck.
Oh, and don't bother that other security guard. He's not part of it. We found him dead when we came in this morning and the coroner has had a bit on, so he hasn't been able to schedule him in yet. Nasty business, but what can you do? These things do happen and, let's be honest, you can probably tell that the man was in poor health. It's quite sad really. Not even a wife or next of kin to notify. Always was an odd chap though, so understandable. Always rambling on about Japanese cartoons and antique weaponry. Don't get me wrong, I'd never condemn a man for maintaining a healthy hobby, but it was relentless at times. Even insisted on bringing a pistol from the Great War every day as part of his uniform. We did tell him it wasn't a real bank, but he just sort of sighed and looked into the distance and said "You try telling that to the Tax Man". Really odd chap.
Anyway, sorry to rant.

I breathed deeply and eyed both men. There was nothing about their attire to suggest difference or a clue that might distinguish honesty from dishonesty. Similarly, the doors themselves were identically marked, offering no guidance.

"Ernie," I began, "might you tell me through which door I should enter? The left or the right?"

"I can assure you, Mister Smacker, that the left door is through which you should step."

"But Ernie, are you the guard that tells the truth? Or are you the guard that tells a lie?"

"I am the truthful one, of course."

"Ah! But is that not precisely what the dishonest guard would suggest, were I to ask him the same thing?"

"I do not know, Mister Smacker. You would have to deploy such an inquisition in his direction."

"Eric," I commanded, "Which of these two doors is the correct option?"

"Mister Smacker, as a man of sublime honour, I can tell you that it is in fact the right door that you must enter."

"And should I trust your colleague, Ernest?"

"On no condition, young sir. Ernest is considered a king among liars."

Eric intervened, "Actually, I fear that it is you, dear Eric, who is known for his deceit."

"On the contrary, Ernest. Your untruths are known throughout the land. The schemers and the charlatans of all England proclaim your duplicity as the highest of its form."

"Such lies, my dear Eric, for we all know whose name is inscribed atop the throne of fallacy and down the columns of the temples of shameless perjury!"

"We do indeed, Ernie. I saw that name myself reaped into the fields of fools and thieves and phantoms of fakery and fabrication and falsehood for all the world to see. 'ERNEST:', it read, 'A GODLESS MERCHANT OF ENDLESS CANARD!'"

"Well that's funny, Eric, because I'm pretty sure you're such a fucking liar that your wife cheated on you and left you for your brother."

"Wha-? Christ, man, you know that isn't true."

"Oh, so you're lying to *yourself* as well these days?"

"Veronica was lost at sea - that's what it says on the death certificate. There's no need to conjure rumours just because this guy's here."

"Lost at sea?! That's an odd way of saying she's being spit-roasted to senselessness by a shipload of sailors." Ernest pointed at Eric and turned to me, "Can you believe this guy?"

"Well, that's what I'm trying-" I started, only to be interrupted.

"You know what, Ernest? At least I had a fucking wife?"

"Yeah but did you though? Maybe legally, but is it really 'your wife' if they're fucking half of Buckinghamshire?"

"Oh, you are a real piece of shit, aren't you?"

"I dunno, maybe this guy should decide?"

As the two continued, I crept forth and back between their erupting diatribe and the lifeless corpse of the other security guard in his corner-tomb. From the dead man's holster, I daintily ejected the slightly-rusted, antique Webley Bulldog .450 revolver. As I returned to the warring guards, I dangled it enticingly with my index finger looped around the trigger pull. Their quarrelling was still in session.

"Which half of Buckinghamshire, dear Ernest?" I inquired.

Their bickering ceased, and both men looked around with hesitance.

"I- I beg your pardon?" asked Ernie.

"With which of the halves of Buckinghamshire did Eric's wife enter into copulation? A simple question, to which you must furnish an answer; true or false?"

"Well- Uh. When you specify 'half', are you asking geographically or… Socioeconomically perhaps?"

"Ah yes. Let me narrow down the choices for you, so that you might provide your answer. Or shall we rephrase the question as… Was the half of Buckinghamshire, with whom Eric's possibly-deceased wife intimately laid, the half that excluded yourself or the half that included yourself?"

The two men exchanged glances of distilled uncertainty. I prompted them for an answer.

"Yes or no? Ernest. Did you sleep with Eric's wife?"

"I- Uh…"

"You must answer. Rules are rules."

Ernest closed his eyes and breathed deeply.

"I mean, maybe a bit-" he began, but immediately Eric snatched the revolver out of my hand and pointed it at his companion.

"You truth-telling fiend! I knew it! I saw the way she looked at you during trivia nights, as you so smugly were able to get all the answers correct whilst I scored zero every time!" he cried out, and pulled the trigger.

It was made evident by the chaotic explosion that the gun's former owner had paid as much attention to the condition of the antique as he had his own resting heart rate, and it was with a deafening bang that both men's skulls were ripped apart in a puff of claret.

Once the men's bodies had thudded to the floor, I knelt carefully at the keyhole of each door and looked through. Through the door on the left, I could see a man wielding a cricket bat in a menacing way, before a large mural that read "WRONG!". Through the door on the right, I saw a large mahogany-filled room complete with an opulent wooden desk at which sat a man in possession of a most familiar face.

I stood up straight, brushed fragments of bone from my coat, and opened the right door.

"Baggy! Glad you could make it," said the face.

"Wouldn't miss it for the world, James," I replied.

"Take a chair, old friend and let me pour you a drink? No whisky, I'm afraid but I do have some questionable gin to which I've added black tea in an attempt to make it appear more sophisticated."

"Has it worked?"

"Almost."

I sat at the desk and faced James Ferdinand Bambi. Together we raised snifters and toasted each others' health, both of which immediately took a significant hit as soon as we swallowed.

"I am as delighted to see you as I am unsurprised that you managed to outwit our little gauntlet of conundrum, Baggy."

"Took barely a minor twitch of a mind such as ours, James."

"That business with the two guards was my idea, you'll be unsurprised to hear. I first heard such a riddle in a tavern in Basseterre a distant time ago."

"Ah! The parabolic enigma of a salt-weathered band of merry sailors, no doubt?"

"No, I read it on the back of a coaster. There *were* sailors present at the time, though they were far more interested in a slightly-easier riddle on the other side that read 'Drink Basse-terre Dry!'. They were doing an excellent job of it."

"I see. Well, it was a marvellously deployed quandary and, I've no doubt, an excellent filter that only the sharpest of thought could pass through."

"Indeed, it is. Simple, yet elegant. One simply asks either guard which door *his counterpart* would say is the incorrect one. You weaponise dishonesty against truth. The truthful guard, when asked, will tell you that the dishonest guard will lie, and point to the incorrect door. The dishonest guard, when asked, will mislead you of his colleague's honesty, and again direct you to the incorrect door. Then one simply chooses the door that is not suggested."

I elected not to tell James Ferdinand Bambi of my circum-vention of his test, including the two lifeless corpses that lay at his door, and instead chose to acknowledge that my later-al intuition would render me perfectly qualified for whatever task lay ahead.

I could see that my old friend had something to tell me. There was a twinkle in his eye that suggested much more than a fanciful job interview, and as much as I wish to embrace the reverie and nostalgia of a long-awaited reunion, my soul had been itching for purpose ever since the on-stage debacle that had thwarted my ascent.

"James, tell me, what is all this about?"

"Yes, you're right. Let's get down to business. Baggy, Great Britain again finds itself at war. The people on the streets might not yet know for certain as of this moment as the first bullet has yet to be fired, but it is soon to come and prepara-tions are underway."

"I feared such a thing, James. Might you reveal the belligerents?"

Bambi reached to a drawer at his desk and pulled from it a sheet of paper with a reassuringly-small list of European nations.

"This is a list of all the countries that Germany *is not* going to declare war upon," he said, un-reassuringly.

"My god. Were they not convinced by the previous result?"

"We did ask them about that. They told us they want a second opinion."

"Well. Let us furnish them with one. Do the Americans know?"

"Yes, we sent them a coded request asking for alliance."

"And how did they respond?"

"We're not sure yet, we haven't been able to decode the one they sent back. We've got a division in Milton Keynes working on it around the clock. It looks hopeful. The front of it bears a photograph of FDR urinating the word 'Victory' into a sandy knoll. Could just be overcompensation for the wheelchair rumours, but we're optimistic."

James prepared another drink and took on an air of uncharacteristic seriousness. His tone became sobering and his broad shoulders tightened, only partly due to the taste.

"Baggy, Britain is not as strong as it once was. It is far from the might it wielded before the last great war. Wounds are still being licked, but the enemy we face is stronger than ever."

"What part am I to play, James? Tell me what needs to be done."

"We can't beat them with brute force. We can't rely on alliances. We won't outlast their supplies. We certainly cannot depend on attrition to bend the tide in our favour."

"Then what must we do?"

"We need to be creative, economic, savvy and intelligent."

"That sounds achievable."

"By 'We', I mean the Government."

"Oh my."

"There is some dim hope though, Baggy. His Majesty has at least seen wise to employ the services of those such as myself; those of us proven in a craft that necessitates more than sheer thuggery and violence to succeed."

James continued, "Not more than a month ago, I was beckoned to the King's court to pitch what I thought would be no more than royal amusement. I'd had a wonderful idea for a log-flume-inspired Sushi Train franchise, in which the food would remain pleasantly moistened after a culminating plunge each circumnavigation. That way you could use the sushi left over from the day before and people would assume it was fresh, thus saving precious pennies. However, upon ending my recital, I was taken aside and told two very important things. One, what I have told you here today and how I could help. And two, that His Majesty would not be investing because he'd been to a Sushi Train the previous week and they had refused to let him drive the train.

"The British Empire will not win this war, Baggy. But the British *People* can. We've run out of guns, bullets, soldiers and generals. We've even had to ask the French to have a bit of a look around for all those horses we left there last time. But what we do have is a new generation of Briton, for whom intellect and cunning and the dream of glory rank highest among aspiration. These are the people who will win this war. People like yourself. This will be your moment, Baggy Smacker."

It seemed James had more to say, but I had heard enough. I rose from my chair and held out my hand for him to take.

I had felt the first stirrings of heroism tug at my heart when I spoke to the recruiting officer at the Crystal Palace all those years ago, but since then waters had muddied and my path had become tangled and overgrown. I did not feel that I had entirely lost my way, but it was certainly not as clean a route as I'd hoped. But all this now changed. From the encroaching thicket, I had emerged into a clearing, central to which was this new, radiant sense of belonging and I was intent to beam toward it, like a moth to the flame.

James Ferdinand Bambi, my oldest friend, reached forwards and took my hand in his.

"I'll do it, James. I'll carry out whatever task needs to be done. I will fight for England, for Britain, for the World. For His Majesty and for my own honour, I will give every ounce of will ever breathed into me by the gods. Everything I am will be spent upon one focus, and that is to usher in a new era of glory and greatness."

"Good chap, sign here," James said, thrusting an application form into my hand.

Within the hour, I was Sapper Baggy Smacker of the 701st Sanitation Company of His Majesty's Corps of Royal Engineers, on a train to Chatham to master the fine arts of subterfuge, espionage and intrigue under the guise of a conscripted underling. Prior to boarding, I took time to submit one final telegram to my dear friend, Joseph Darkfire.

DEAR JOSEPH STOP
I AM ONWARD TO GREATNESS STOP
MEET YOU THERE SHORTLY STOP STOP
NO JUST THE ONE STOP STOP
REMOVE THE LAST STOP STOP
NO LISTEN TO ME STOP
STOP WRITING STOP STOP
PLEASE LISTEN TO ME STOP

REMOVE ALL THE DUPLICATE INSTANCES
OF STOP STOP
THIS IS RIDICULOUS STOP
I HAVE A TRAIN TO CATCH STOP
JUST SEND THE FUCKING THING AS IT IS
STOP

And with that final communique on its way, I climbed aboard without looking behind me and began the biggest chapter of my life so far.

CHAPTER SEVENTEEN:

The Reignition of Europe

In the world of military intelligence, deception reigned. And so it was that I sat, just over one year later, heading toward the European continent on a Royal Navy transport boat that we had quite cleverly disguised as the No. 157 to Canford Heath.

Our instructions were clear; should any Germans attempt to board, we would simply decline by telling them that we didn't have any small change, and unless they happened to have the exact amount, they'd need to go to the bank. And if they did happen to have it and then ask what we were doing in the North Sea, we were to explain we'd taken an incorrect turn at Lower Hamworthy and were waiting until we encountered a roundabout so that we might turn back.

My comrades and I were clothed and accessorised in every way so as to resemble a flock of grumbling, regional pensioners and, despite no apparent attention from enemy forces, it was agreed that every so often one of us would roll down a window and shout out a politically conservative opinion about immigration policy to amplify the cunning facade. To provide further cover to our imitation of an innocent piece of British public transport, we had made sure to depart the dock thirty minutes after we'd told people we would.

The past year of my life had been uncoiled at Brompton Barracks where I, along with esteemed comrades in arms, trained for destiny. In a few ways, life at Brompton was not dissimilar to my experiences in Beeston Orphanage, although without the dire sense of apathy. Our dormitories were as cramped, our schedules were as rigid, and our meals were apparently as prepared by creatures without conventionally-human taste. But for now, I was at least driven by purpose, excitement and a patriotic justification to shoot alpine folk musicians.

The 701st Sanitation Company was (and remains so in historical documentation), by all appearances, an unassuming division of the Royal Engineers, responsible for the construction of frontline latrines, hygiene facilities and plumbing, among other important tasks such as separating multi-ply toilet paper into more economic quantities and verifying the authenticity of phone numbers scribbled beside offered services above the urinals. But this was nothing more than a ruse for our true armament - deception. We were one of the Special Operations Executive's most devilish and secretive espionage units.

As the alleged architects and constructors of frontline infrastructure that very few wished to observe in progress, we were afforded a perfect veil for our more devious goings on, far forward of the regular infantry and sapper divisions. No one would blink an eye, friend or foe, as we slipped behind enemy lines with undeniable innocence, yet intent on wreaking a range of havoc that would decimate the inner-workings of the German military machine through ingenious subterfuge, whimsical double-bluffing, and the merciless 'top-decking' of their cisterns.

The first weeks at Brompton were gruelling, and not purely due to the physical exertion required for the initial phase of standard infantry training. I had decided in my wisdom that, to convey the confidence and bravado that might render me a tempting candidate for future leadership positions, I would spend substantial effort establishing myself as the company prankster and, due to the nature of our objective, I was offered almost limitless chances.

During the first month, while others were foolishly wasting their time fortifying camaraderie and ordering their attention to studies, I laid the grounds for a hilarious scheme in which I introduced tarnished shellfish to the Barrack's water supply. Over the following weeks, two-thirds of the company became infected with cholera, culminating in a death toll of approximately one hundred sappers.

Thankfully, the good-hearted nature of this wonderful jape was as well-handled as the epidemic, and the top brass rejoiced in what they acknowledged to be a decent, British, team-building ribbing that had also performed as a marvellous exercise in purging the immunocompromised chaff from the ranks. Furthermore, the staggering onset of symptomatic diarrhoea across the compound provided a steady tide of learning opportunities for our face-value endeavours of sanitation management, so little surprise surrounded my immediate promotion to the rank of Lance Corporal.

In the name of goodwill, I used my entire subsequent pay cheque to commission artistically-interpreted family portraits for each widowed spouse, so that they could hypothesise what might have been, along with handwritten letters offering personalised dating tips for the near future. These gestures would result in a veritable onslaught of wartime correspondence between myself and several dozen of the more grateful women, which gradually began to consume so much of my time that I was required to outsource responding to a wing of eager-to-please German prisoners of war. Regrettably, this ostensibly helpful team of POWs included some high-ranking members of the Abwehr, many of whom escaped confinement after convincing a jaded widow into matrimony and inheriting their British citizenship. By all accounts, this was a poor situation, but I still considered it to be quite a feeble over-correction when I was demoted back to Sapper and blamed personally for allowing key members of German military intelligence the opportunity to work-from-home with their new families therefore extending the overall length of the war by two-to-four years.

Similarly to Beeston, my year at Brompton was made memorable by the introduction of colleagues who would play significant roles in the years to come. The 701st was not a small company but, due to the secretive modus operandi, intimate exposure to our peers was not encouraged or developed. Despite my demotion, I was still considered to be an extremely gifted asset, and as such found myself registered to a section of six men who would lead the most deadly and dazzling espionage missions of the war to come. It was these men, months later, who sat alongside me, dressed in moleskin jackets and tweed sports coats and theatrical bigotry, as we sailed from England.

Occupying the back row were twin brothers, Sappers Terrance & Harold Wellington. Born two months apart to different fathers, they had been separated at birth and did not meet again until turning eight years old when they happened to bump into each other in the mosh-pit of a Vera Lynn concert. At the 701st Sanitation Company, the Wellingtons took particular expertise in explosives, both incendiary and dietary. The combination of their studious wits and clinical finesse would strike at the core of the German war effort, rendering its foundations unstable through methods such as brutish firepower and leaving chicken to thaw overnight at room temperature.

Two seats to my rear sat Lance Corporal Alex Silverchair, a master of foreign language, duplicity and haggling. He was a man of unusually slender appearance, with long blonde hair and impressive breasts. Alex spoke over a dozen languages in a light, dulcet voice, through a captivating shade of maroon lipstick. All agreed that Silverchair had something mysterious and magnetic about him, from his boyish prettiness to the coy way in which he insisted on urinating and bathing behind a nearby bush. None in the company were as perfect for engaging the clueless enemy in face-to-face confrontation, and leading them astray through an undeniable charm offensive.

To my forward-left was the hunched pose of Sapper Heinrich Glühwein, an odd chap with an unplaceable accent and a tendency toward introversion. He claimed that his unusual dialect originated from western Wales and, whenever inquiry ventured further, would shriek "Meine identität wurde kom-promittiert!" into a fanciful cufflink on his sleeve, which he assured observers was the Welsh translation of "Your interest in my hometown flatters me but I now must retire for the evening for I have become quite sleepy".

Lastly, presented in the minutely-detailed regalia of the Wilts & Dorset Bus Company at the wheel of the bus, was our leader, Lieutenant Stephen Edgington. I had first met him early on in my days at Brompton, prior to his commissioning, and we had become immediate friends despite a considerable age difference. Edgington was arguably the most intelligent and quick-witted man I had ever met, and his confidence and optimism seemed capable of absorbing any bullet, shrapnel or ordinance that the enemy could fire his way. He might have been an Officer in rank, but he remained a friend to all and would often be found playing cabaret numbers on the company piano late into drunken evenings, with a band of merry soldiers at his side. I'd been so enthralled by one particular Coward-esque ditty he'd performed for us at the birthday celebration of a far-less-liked Lieutenant, that I'd asked him for a copy of the lyrics so that I might share with Joseph Darkfire next time our paths crossed.

Sailing past at noon most days,
I view a sign and read it says,
For merest sixpence I might graze,
On suspiciously inexpensive steak & chips.

I judge the post both once and twice,
In awe and wonder at the price,
And wonder if the taste is nice,
Of suspiciously inexpensive steak & chips.

Surely must there be a catch,
For such a tiny price attached,

Perhaps the beef's a faulty batch,
In suspiciously inexpensive steak & chips.

I can't believe a treat so cheap,
For steak and fries served in a heap,
This greatest value I must reap,
For suspiciously inexpensive steak & chips.

At just a cost of shillings, five,
Their profits surely take a dive,
Perhaps the cow is served alive,
With suspiciously inexpensive steak & chips.

I knew this claim could not be real,
Nobody tenders such a deal,
One could survive on just this meal,
Called suspiciously inexpensive steak & chips.

But dare I risk to break the spell,
And buy the meal and find too well,
The haunted reason that they sell,
Those suspiciously inexpensive steak & chips.

I'd rather wish that all's not lost,
And dream of steak at such small cost,
Rather than finding someone's tossed,
Marinaded cow genitals onto a barbecue and attempted to pass it
off as meat so they can sell it at a really cheap price, and then just
sit back laughing in the kitchen saying, 'I can't believe he's eating
bovine penis! What an absolute twat!.'

Happy birthday, Second Lieutenant White! Hope you enjoyed your
meal! The men of the 701 send their regards!

Edgington and I bonded over our love of poetry, sport and playful sarcasm, and he even taught me two of the more important chords on the cor anglais so that I might accompany him in a merry waltz when leisure time permitted. He suggested I could learn the others in my own time although, in his experience, "very few people would ever want to hear them".

For the company's biannual revue, we co-wrote and starred in a critically-observed production entitled 'The Pockets of Yesterday's Pants'; a thrilling mystery of a nobleman who is unable to pop out to the shops because he can't seem to find his house keys. The divisional newsletter documented its universal praise with such sentiments as 'a sensible length' and 'possessing the wit of a post-incarceration Oscar Wilde'. Edgington's committed acting performance received particular note, sparking rumours of a promising career in infomercials. But despite the best efforts of a titanic food-processor industry and the tantalising offer of moderate-quality steak knives, he was devoted to his King and country, and pledged his energy to the war effort.

We both shared a past in television, although his was lass-scandalised than my own. Following graduation from Southampton Solent, Edgington had created and directed a ground-breaking series for the BBC called 'Undercover Earl', in which members of the House of Lords would secretly disguise themselves as members of their own staff, to the witness of a television crew who would document the ensuing social awakening. Sadly, only six episodes were ever filmed prior to the outbreak of war, and its production was terminated following the unfortunate death of guest star Baron Rhayader who sadly suffocated during an ill-fated attempt to manipulate a fitted bedsheet.

The authority yielded by Stephen's eventual promotion afforded him the capacity to register me alongside him for the most daring assignments that the 701st had to offer. It was by his hand that I was picked for this first major operation of the war, citing my cunning and confidence as invaluable attributes for the task. Personally, I suspect my inclusion was as much to do with his desire for my companionship as it was my competence as a soldier, for though he was a man of incalculable assurance and calm, my friend Edgington was still as human as all were.

It was not without some trepidation that we sailed across the North Sea, uninterrupted other than for a small raft of Scottish tourists who hailed us to ask if we were going any-where near Corfe Mullen. We were immaculately trained, briefed and supplied, but there was always to be danger in heading behind the steel curtain into enemy territory.

This had been a year of excitement, of challenge and of immeasurable growth, and the culmination was this deadly ad-venture that would change who I was at my innermost core. I had counted on deliberation and drive to guide me to my calling, yet I found with increasing regularity that the world around me had far greater influence than I could ever have anticipated.

CHAPTER EIGHTEEN:
Operation Front Wipe

Our objective was simple; make contact with Polish resistance fighters of the Armia Krajowa, before locating and freeing the six prisoners of war that had been classified as indispensable to the allied effort. Our methodology, conversely, was intricate, masterful and feasible to only the most brilliant minds of the British S.O.E.

Thanks to some fine work of the Wellington twins, the team had discreetly scuttled our transport two miles off the coast of Gdynia, much to the annoyance of the Royal Navy who had been too frugal to purchase travel insurance. There was no other choice, however, for secrecy was paramount.

Upon our arrival, we were to lay low and remain undetected by the mighty German occupation; an easier feat than we'd initially anticipated as we'd written the date of departure on the wrong page of our calendar and had arrived two weeks before the invasion of Poland. Instead we spent a delightful fortnight hiking through the nearby hillscape, drinking Żubrówka and fraudulently ordering complicated, time-consuming flatpack furniture to the houses of opposing military leaders in an attempt to distract them and slow down their advance.

When the enemy forces finally arrived, we sought protection in the dining room of a vegetarian cafe owned and operated by teetotallers; a location in which we knew Germans would never care to enter. Nevertheless, we were not too out of reach of the sounds of conflict in the streets of Gdynia, and our concealment was almost compromised when we made the mistake of adopting a company mascot in the form of an exotic blue parrot that refused to stop screeching verses of Hayim Nahman Bialik poems at passing troops. Once the bird was dishonourably discharged and ridiculed by panels of comedians on the world service, we each did what we could in the ensuing weeks to bide our time and stem the gushing arteries of war.

The Wellington brothers, whose creativity for menace and destruction at no point ever lapsed, concocted a most brilliant plan to redirect the hastily erected plumbing of German latrines back into their own kitchens and water tanks. After the brothers had tunnelled far beneath Poland's crust, Sapper Terrance meticulously coordinated explosive contraptions to detonate in perfect concert, just as Harold had lured the enemy troops out of earshot with a series of dramatic monologues on the topic of possible improvements to FIFA's interpretation of the Offside Rule. Regrettably, it happened that the outcome of the sabotage merely resulted in diverting a urinal pipe to a water tank utilised primarily in the production of Bavarian-style pilsener, and thus had no noticeable impact.

Not to be deterred, Lance-Corporal Silverchair committed to a scheme of such mystery that none of us ever fully uncovered it. All we perceived was that, on quiet nights, an unassuming German officer would be lured back to the cafe and taken by Alex into a room out the back. Following soundscapes of giggling and pleasantry that could last well over an hour, the two would emerge; the officer holding a mixed expression of confusion and embarrassment, Alex holding a camera. The officer would then sign a piece of paper and verbally agree to not be involved in the war anymore because it was silly, to which the Lance-Corporal would pat them tenderly on the buttocks and order them a taxi cab to Belgium. I felt it not worth impeding my comrade with worrying questions but do to this day wonder what Machiavellian exploitation took place.

Sapper Glühwein was somewhat more reserved. We put it down to understandable culture shock, geographic vertigo, and other such disorders that often plague the Welsh, but supported him as much we could. It seemed to bring Heinrich much comfort to write to his parents - named Wichtige & Geheimnisse, as penned on the envelopes - and regale them with stories of who we were, why we were in Poland, what our exact coordinates were, and how, due to a clerical error, we'd forgotten to bring any bullets for our guns.

Alas, it fills me with guilt to acknowledge that these presumably heartfelt journals of a young man at war were never delivered, for it was I who was responsible for outgoing letters each morning. In the name of physical regiment, I would attend a daily swim in the port, almost always forgetting to remove my clothes, shoes and the fanciful satchel that I'd purchased from a local child to ferry provisions and mail. I blamed my mistake on the years of uniformed attire in the academic wading pools of St Adjutors and, in the name of morale, I thought it best not to mention my miscoordination to my squadmates until the war was safely won.

While the others combatted idle hands, Edgington and I devised plans to make contact with the Polish underground. Several guileful schemes were hatched, including hypnotising the entire populace of Gydnia using an advanced radio wave emitter that would send enchanting pulses throughout the city that, when processed by the human mind, would politely ask if any guerilla fighters cared for a spot of tea on Wednesday, around lunchtime. Eventually that plan was abandoned, as the radio wave emitter in question had not yet been invented, and so we settled on putting an ad in the paper. In the name of deception, it was cleverly coded.

6 backpackers seek accom.
On holiday from the exotic west.
Looking for locals to show us the sights.
Must be willing to party so ferociously that peaceful democracy is
restored to continental Europe.
Will supply our own Żubrówka.

The advertisement ran in the personal section for two days before we received correspondence, however the initial responses were not, in fact, from the expected Polish resistance but from marketing companies looking to profit from what limited wartime tourism was available. It wasn't until a week later, while nursing severe hangovers from a four-day-long wine tour across the Subcarpathian Voivodeship, that a brick was hurled through the cafe window with a note tied to it. It read "Meet at midnight, Church of Saint Michael".

Excitedly, we commenced preparing provisions, readying equipment and hurriedly learning Polish, until a second brick flew through another window with a note saying "Ignore last brick". A day later, the meeting time and place were rescheduled in a similar manner, and we left for our true mission under cover of darkness, careful to avoid the broken glass and invoices the landlord had left us for the cost of window repair.

The Church of Saint Michael was the sort of religious building that made you feel slightly sorry for God, as one would a relative receiving a pair of second-hand shoes at Christmas. According to the locals, it had been rebuilt several times over the past few centuries, ostensibly by four different people, each with declining enthusiasm, architectural prowess and budget. It was, however, a comfortable base of operation for the Armia due to its proximity to a local naval base and a twenty-four-hour gelato stand.

Our six-man team approached carefully, noting a flicker of candlelight through the barred windows. Edgington turned to whisper to us.

"Righto, chaps. This is the spot, but let's not be foolish; this could easily be a trap. So we're playing it safe. Smacker and I will approach the door to the vestry. Silverchair and Glühwein are to cover us."

"But we don't have bullets, sir," voiced Alex.

"Not with that attitude," Stephen replied, with a piercing confidence that halted further logistical concern.

"Wellingtons, I want you to rig our exit path with whatever you've got. If Gerry is in there, we retreat at our fastest speed and light them up when they pursue. If things go awry, split up, and meet back at the cafe for debriefing and a nightcap. Understood?"

We all nodded in silent acknowledgement, except for Heinrich who cleared his throat very loudly and shouted, "Okay, British colleagues. We shall now make our move."

Edgington and I crept quietly toward a small door at the side of the church. We'd earlier decided not to go through the main door for fear of causing a commotion, and also because there would certainly be a collection plate nearby and we hadn't anything on us less than a banknote. I expressed to Stephen that I could feel us being watched, to which he comfortingly assured me that it was probably just God. His explanation made a tremendous amount of sense if one believed in that sort of thing, and so I thought nothing further of it until we reached the vestry.

But there, as we reached for the iron door handle, we heard the distinctive click of a pistol hammer being pulled back. Both of us froze in place as we felt the cool press of metal gun barrels against the back of our necks.

"There's no need for hastiness. Who goes there?" I asked.

Edgington suggested that it could still quite possibly just be God, though that seemed increasingly unlikely.

Tensions rose when a voice from behind us spoke in stern, clear German.

"Wir haben nicht damit gerechnet, dich so bald zu sehen," said a female voice.

"We mean you no harm. We're simply Danish sex tourists who have come to visit the wonderful Orwolo Pier, and be with beautiful Polish women. My name is Malthe and this is my virulent friend Alfred," Edgington brilliantly ad-libbed.

"If you are sex tourists, then why are you entering a church at midnight?"

"Uh, for forgiveness. We must attend the confessional post-haste. We've had a tremendous amount of sex and feel like we owe someone an apology. We haven't even found time to visit the pier, because our minds are filthy and must be spiritually cleansed."

"But this is a protestant church. There is no confession to be had."

"Right, yes, that's what I said to Alfred here, but he felt we stood a pretty good chance of converting them back to Catholicism and working our way to purity from there. But you're right. A protestant priest would most likely *endorse* our behaviour, if anything. We demand to experience guilt that only the Holy Catholic Empire can inflict."

Edgington continued to improvise with stunning grace, but my attention was lured to the floral waft that had come to hang in the air since the Germans had ambushed. There was something very familiar about it. It was fruity, yet tart and it took me back to a time in my youth. Yes... Rhubarb. And then, I realised that the German voice itself was one I had heard before.

"The weather's not as bad as forecasted," I dared to blurt.

The German voice went silent for a moment. I held my breath while I waited to see if my gamble had paid off.

"Well, well, well. Young Mister Smacker."

I turned to my captor and saw the face of Katrina and another armed female.

"Katrina. It has been some time. You look well." I noted, with relief, that she was not dressed in the uniform of the occupying German force. "And what are you undercover as this time I find you?"

"I am not undercover. I am with the Polish resistance. We do not all support this war in Germany. How is your father?"

"Still on parole."

"Ah yes. An unfortunate circumstance that was."

I moved to respond but had forgotten to resume the breathing I'd stopped several paragraphs ago, and instead passed out for a short while. When I regained consciousness, I found myself inside the church vestry lying on a makeshift mattress fashioned from torn-up copies of The Holy Epistle of Relatable Cheekiness - which, due to a kerning error within a parable about the ex-communication of a heretic named Clint, had been hastily recalled by the church in recent years due to an increase in the public call for legalising non-heterosexual marriage.

"Smacker, nice of you to join us," said the voice of Lieutenant Edgington, who was leaning against a stone wall, eating from a small pot of gelato.

"Not a problem. Is the war still on?"

"I'm afraid so. I understand you're already acquainted with Katrina. And this here is Maria, head of the Gydnia AK division."

I had not initially paid much attention to Katrina's comrade-in-arms, but in the candlelight of the cathedral's interior, her beauty was inescapable. She had an appearance that was all at once feminine, fierce and thoughtful, as that of a post-coital black widow spider weighing up whether to consume a sexual partner who owed her a small amount of money.

"A pleasure to meet you, Sapper Smacker," she spoke through a serious Polish accent.

I attempted to respond but was so taken aback by Maria's elegance that I stumbled over my words and accidentally asked for her hand in marriage. The grace and swiftness with which she declined was utterly captivating.

"So, what brings you to Gydnia in this time of such chaos? Where is the rest of the once-mighty British Expeditionary Force?"

"They will come eventually. But there's preparation to be made before that can happen. And some of that preparation requires resources that are currently stuck in German war prisons. They are why we are here."

"And who are *they*?"

"Two SOE agents. Their names are confidential."

"Then how will you identify them?"

"They have been instructed to whistle the Warsaw Concerto over and over again until we find them."

"Will that be loud enough?"

"It shouldn't matter. It's an impressively annoying tune, so we're to look out for prisoners with black eyes and other severe bruising."

"Do you know where they're being held? There are dozens of German POW camps across Poland."

"We know. This is why we've conjured a most brilliant plan, sculpted by the finest minds in British intelligence. Firstly, my team and I will compose a hit jazz number of undeniable catchiness. I'll be on piano and vocals, Baggy here will be on the cor anglais and our squadmates will form the backline, with the exception of Silverchair who doesn't believe in catchy music. Once we've got the piece just right, we'll head to the studio for production and mastering. Following that, we've been given an absolutely tremendous marketing budget, to really get our names out there. The Crown has seen fit to provision us with two million pounds to promote our sound and sell out the Teatr Wielki, and from there we'll make the jump to venues like The Old Vic and Carnegie Hall and the Box Hill RSL. Once we're world-famous, the invites from chat programs will start pouring in, and soon enough our faces will be shared around the planet for everyone to see. Once we have the attention of Earth's entire population, we pop the question live on air, and ask if anyone's seen two badly-beaten men who won't stop whistling the Warsaw Concerto. We leave a mailing address with the studio, and wait for someone to let us know where the agents are being held. When we know the name of the camp, we start digging. We tunnel right underneath the Germans and set explosives which we'll trigger precisely when something good comes on the television, so response will be at a minimum. Once we've blown through the surface of the prison, we free our men and make our apologies to everyone who isn't being rescued. Then we close the hole, get our men safely back to Paris, and go undercover, posing as orthopaedic surgeons while we await further orders."

"That is certainly a plan," Katrina agreed.

"Yes, a veritable tapestry of cunning and intellect."

"And what role will the Armia Krajowa play in all of this?"

"We need someone to carry our instruments to and from the tour bus."

"I see. Maria, come. We shall discuss privately and see if this is in our interests."

Katrina and Maria exited the vestry.

Within the room was a statue of Jesus Christ performing a handstand while entirely nude; another recalled sentiment from the Vatican's fumbled foray into expanding its brand.

"What do you make of all this?" I asked Stephen.

"Christianity?"

"Yes. Do you believe in the omnipotence of a higher being? Was there ever a Jesus of Nazareth?"

"I suppose I tend not to think about it, Baggy. But as you have asked, I suspect I'm divided."

"How so?"

"Divided in that, I lean toward the idea that there might not be a God. Certainly not an attentive one. And by all written accounts, not a loving one or merciful one. But I firmly believe that there was once a man named Jesus who suggested we all try being a bit nicer to each other."

"Yes, that seems true."

"And, with some tragedy, I would say that the part of the bible I believe to be the most true is the bit where he kept suggesting that, and so a group of people decided to kill him."

"Yes. People can be…"

"A bit shit."

"Precisely. And don't even get me started on what heaven must be like, if indeed it exists. Over ninety-nine per cent of its population would be from the distant past. The chances of bumping into someone who isn't racist would be mathematically zero."

While we spoke, Edgington had been rummaging around cupboards and drawers, and finally found a stash of communion wine. We raised our bottles to Poland and awaited the return of our new comrades, however, their short conversation drew out far longer than either of us had anticipated.

After several bottles of claret, we fell asleep and remained so until the next day, when we were awakened by the loud creaking of the church's main doors. To our surprise, in marched two black-and-blue, rough-looking middle-aged men, struggling to whistle the Warsaw Concerto through clearly-chipped teeth and split lips, followed by Katrina and Maria.

Shock and marvel left our chins limp.

"How on earth did you manage such a thing?" Stephen asked Katrina, after clipping the men severely around the ear until they stopped whistling.

"Maria went to the cafe and *borrowed* your two million pounds, and used it to bribe the guards into releasing the prisoners. It was very little trouble. As I have said, we Germans do not all support this regime."

"Right, of course. Well, jolly good thinking."

With the rescued agents in tow, we returned to the cafe and considered our next steps. It was decided, as a group, that we wouldn't complicate our debriefing by notifying headquarters of the Armia's contribution to our mission, and would instead tell them everything had gone perfectly to plan in the exact fashion we had devised. Besides, we had already put a non-refundable deposit down on the music studio hire, and now had time to kill as a result of achieving our objective several months prior to initial estimations.

With the time available, we released an album of jazz covers of traditional Christmas songs, but unfortunately, without the two million pounds for marketing to lubricate our way through the cynicism of the music press, the record was a commercial failure and we were thoroughly lambasted due to what critics considered to be "uninspired, lifeless reimaginings of much-loved tunes, with a wildly misplaced release date of late January". Admittedly, the timing issue was completely our fault as we'd gotten Jesus' birthday and that of Clark Gable mixed up. So, with our mood ever so slightly dampened, we sent a postcard to the Royal Navy asking if they wouldn't mind coming to pick us up.

For our voyage to the safety of Paris, we forwent the same discretion of our arrival as James Ferdinand Bambi had co-ordinated with what remained of the Polish Navy to allow a heavily armed, nuclear-powered log flume into the port of Gdynia. We climbed aboard to set sail for France, and only missed it by a mere few kilometres. After a short detour through Belgium and several heated arguments with locals over whether or not Flemish was a real language, we arrived in the French capital. There we linked up with members of the Deuxième Bureau who smoked at us rather aggressively, listened to our exploits and then lectured us as to how they would have done it better.

My first taste of war had been an unmitigated success and I believe, at the time we arrived in Paris, the experience of that first mission set an unsustainable precedent for what was to come. For there was heartbreak and death and anguish just around the corner. Foolishly, I thought the enemy might be thwarted without my having to fire a gun at a human being and I clung on to the optimism for as long as I could. A change to that viewpoint was imminent. But for now, there was Paris.

CHAPTER NINETEEN:

My Parisian Distraction

ollowing our debriefing, we were permitted a term of leave for two weeks, in which we might relax, recover and rehabilitate our fatigued souls. However, my fortnight of reprieve blew out somewhat, following a night of drinking absinth so heavily that I managed to wipe out all memory of having ever joined the army.

In lieu of my own recollections, I deemed it necessary to invent a temporary past and so went by the name Norbert Charolais for a period of time, and managed to maintain the ruse of nativity despite having almost no grasp of the local language. I found that I could deflect detection of my true heritage by responding to any question asked of me by sighing loudly, leaning back in a chair when possible and simply saying in French, with as much feigned disgust as I could muster, "So. It's come to this, has it?"

I took employment as a credit analyst for one of the capital's smaller banks and, for a short while, led an idyllic life in Paris, spending my days staring out of an office window that was blessed with a magnificent view of a gift shop that sold posters of the Sacré-Cœur, and spending my evenings drinking Pinot Grigio in an alleyway with a dishevelled, foul-smelling man who also suffered amnesia and complained about being continually voted in as the Mayor.

As the summer days fluttered by, it felt as if the war had drifted away from the continent, and I felt so at ease that the greatest shock I was made to deal with was unexpectedly falling in love.

She was called Clotilda Antoine, named after the infamous American slave ship due to her parent's long-held family tradition of being appalling. She was one half of a pair of conjoined twins who, against all odds, had survived to their late thirties whilst sharing a single body. Her sister, Seraphique, controlled the left arm and leg and oversaw most internal systems, whilst Clotty dominated the right side, respiratory workings, lower bowel functions and, eventually, my heart.

With dark, flowing hair and pointed-but-handsome features, there was something reminiscent of the Mona Lisa about Clotilda, especially as, due to the sisters' condition, tourists were always queuing to take photographs.

The circumstances of our meeting was peculiar, to say the least and, were it not for Hermes' aim to inspire our love, we could have easily travelled a much different road. One warm morning, her sister and she walked into my unassuming office with the determination and cool indifference of a Danish sex tourist entering an orphanage.

I offered them a drink. Seraphique requested a pint of gin. Clotilda asked merely for some sparkling water, as she was driving. Once settled, we approached the topic of business.

"I wish for your establishment to tender me a loan of fifty-thousand francs so that I might finance a technological enterprise," Clotilda spoke in immaculate English. "This is for my own agenda and not anything to do with my sister, Seraphique."

To be successful in the world of credit analysis, there is no more highly desirable quality than cynicism, of which I have always been eternally blessed and, as such, Clotty's last comment stirred my attention.

I bided myself some time by dividing the ingredients of a mimosa between the two stunning ladies and asked them if, whilst I committed to the paperwork, they would enjoy watching an erotic film I happened to have early access to, entitled *Académie des Soldats : Opération à Moscou*.

With them distracted, I hastily searched the bank's records for anything related to Seraphique Antoine and was not shocked to discover evidence of default. Not even a full year beforehand, she had taken a loan of equal value for the reported intention of producing a working prototype of an 'elevator cancel button' that would allow a user to undo an incorrect press made when they were running late for work (a foolhardy attempt at innovation that even today baffles science). Initially, payments had been met within contractual agreement, but eventually had petered out and ultimately ceased altogether.

As the credits of the film scrolled, I resumed our business and explained that the bank, at this time, could not offer further credit to the Antoines' partnership.

"Possibly you misheard me, Monsieur Charolais. I am not in any variety of partnership with my sister."

"With respect, Mademoiselle Antoine, I suspect you are attempting to fool me. Both the amount and the intention are identical to that submitted by your sister."

"My sister's credit history is of no relevance in this matter."

"I do not see how that can be the case."

"We are two different people, Monsieur Charolais. You would not have cared to examine my sister's records were she not physically present, and she only is so due to our conjoinment. For you to deny this loan would be a clear case of ableist discrimination and should you pursue a rejection, we will have no choice but to sue you for the princely sum of one hundred thousand francs."

I marvelled at the sisters' cunning and pardoned myself to talk to the bank's manager, who immediately approved the funding request and fired me on the spot at the request of his new customer. Yet I held no qualms about my termination and instead found myself so instantly infatuated with Clotilda that I asked her out to dinner that same night. To my utmost surprise, and despite her sister's objections, she agreed on condition that she had final say on the restaurant.

We dined alfresco at one of Montmartre's most charming restaurants, *Le Jambon d'une Semaine,* to which Clotilda threw platitudes and a coupon. She introduced me to the head chef; a charming lunatic named Gerard Montreal who presented me with a friendly wink and a rendition of his oft-repeated catchphrase.

"I always say, *you are what you eat,* Monsieur Charolais!" he remarked, twirling his apron gaily while juggling garlic cloves, among other similarly French activities.

Most assumed this idiom was nothing more than marketable whimsy, but later in life, Gerard would reveal a more serious interpretation when he attempted to wriggle out of a charge of grand larceny by cannibalising a man who was not physically present at the scene of the crime. The jury were unfooled but the consumed victim was once quite rude to a dog, so Gerard avoided prison and instead spent three weeks spell-checking graffiti on behalf of his local community. Though he had circumnavigated the harsh isolation of a high-security penitentiary, the trauma of his heinous act would eventually drive him so criminally insane that he was no longer fit for work within any respectable institution, and ended his career in shame as a person who designed and administered pay-per-hour hospital car parks.

Despite his troubled future, the man could most certainly cook and in a gesture of unrestrained opulence, I ordered everything on his menu in an earnest effort to impress. It wasn't until the sommelier uncorked the sixth bottle of Chateau Lafite that I realised I'd been holding the wine menu as I'd done so, and was now in tremendous debt. But I had no room in my heart for regret; the following morning, I would declare both bankruptcy and my love for my darling mademoiselle.

I was, at first, in fear that my feelings for Clotilda might be unrequited, but it soon became clear that the attraction was a mutual one. I appreciated her careful hesitance in the earlier days, empathising with the instinctual self-preservation of a person in such a unique relationship with her close twin. But brick by brick, the walls of Jericho that surrounded her softer, more vulnerable inner sanctum fell away to the triumphant horn-song of my adoration.

Soon enough, we were as in love as two could people be, and about two-thirds as in love as three could. I would perform serenades upon her lavish apartment balcony with sweet rhapsody from my cor anglais, until her neighbours delivered several volumes worth of signed petition requesting to have me stop. Instead of music, I settled for poetry and, though Clotilda was not receptive to flattery, she absolutely adored insult to her various social rivals. One in particular - an obnoxious duchess named Meredith D'Arc - caused her the most vexation and so I wrote the following.

I don't expect a girl that cooks,
Or reads the smartest, artists' books,
Or wows the world with wondrous looks,
So long as she's not Meredith D'Arc.

Her nose would be so slightly bent,
Her wage would barely cover rent,
She'd be not-quite-from-heaven sent,
But more importantly, not be Meredith D'Arc.

Her poise and habits might be strange,
Her mind would rank in middle range,
Her flaws should seldom ever change,
Unless they include 'being Meredith D'Arc.

Beauty wouldn't mean a thing,
Nor shape, nor wealth, nor clothes, nor ring,
She wouldn't need to dance or sing,
Especially not as poorly as Meredith D'Arc

She'd never be the very best,
With hair unmessed, or heirs impressed,

Nor blessed with excess breast on chest,
But at least she wouldn't be Meredith D'Arc.

My ideal girl might seem a bore,
But why insist on so much more?
She's not that short, annoying whore,
Called Meredith D'Arc.

Clotty was so thrilled with my prose that she commissioned a mural to be painted on the residence opposite the D'Arc's, featuring the poem alongside a quite merciless caricature of Meredith. To add flourish to her prank, she went on to pay an arsonist to burn down her rival's manse with everyone trapped inside, proving once more her playful yet committed competitiveness.

Our love seemed eternal, however we were faced with one insurmountable obstacle; Seraphique. Whilst Clotilda's affection and loyalty were never thereafter in doubt, her conjoined twin sister looked upon our relationship with contempt and envy, and she would sabotage all activity when she could, as she tried to dampen the flame of our passion.

When we would dine out in any of the glorious Parisian restaurants that Clotty had three-for-two coupons for, Seraphique would purposefully order meals that had ingredients that the twins' shared body held an allergy to. So many beautiful evenings found their end in a bush or drain cover by the side of the road, as my crimson and bloated darling ejected cuisine onto the Parisian curbside.

When I would plan a night at the cinema, Seraphique would court her own date the night before, to the same film, forcing her sister to see it twice. Even when Clotilda would attempt to preserve the mystery by blindfolding herself and employing the use of earplugs, Seraphique would merely bide her time and whisper spoilers at us and other patrons, or insist on buying multiple extra large frozen colas from the lobby so that the persisting need for urination would interrupt our attention. It was times like these that I was so thankful that my Clotty was in control of the Antoines' lower bowel.

As one might imagine, the worst of all this animosity came during the act of love-making. What should have been moments of the finest intimacy were foiled by Seraphique's constant commentary and criticisms. She would deploy all manner of distraction during our passion such as loudly rating my performance on a one-to-ten scale, or reciting anecdotes involving the prowess of former lovers. She would schedule coital arrangements of her own, immediately subsequent to ours, so that I was forced to hurriedly dress and make leave without so much as a farewell kiss from my dear Clotilda, and then await her in the next room whilst attempting to ignore the sounds of some other man making love to approximately four-fifths of my darling.

An inevitable and unsurmountable breaking point came at Seraphique's most devious moment. In a gesture of surprising magnanimity, upon arrival at the sisters' apartment, I was met with a gift from the adversarial Antoine. I opened a delicately-designed case to find a pair of intriguing spectacles held within.

"I saw these in a boutique in a quaint district of Eindhoven, and immediately considered you, Norbert. According to the seller, they are perhaps the most desired item in all of Europe, second only to peacetime! And even then, I would imagine it depends upon how many sons you have!"

"Clotty, you never told me you had travelled recently!"

"I was distracted. We have business interests there. Livestock, primarily. The war has quite decimated the dairy industry."

"The ravages of fascism?"

"The opposite, actually. The nation's cattle have unionised and have seized the means of production. 'The Mooist Insurgency' they're calling it. And it occupied my entire attention while I was there. So imagine my surprise at Seraphique's expedition and generosity," Clotilda replied with a shared elation fuelled by what appeared to be a respectful moment of reconciliation.

"What a flattering present! Thank you ever so much, Seraphique. What on earth are they?"

"The Dutch call them Neuken-Ogens. They are said to have lenses that harness the long-journeyed light of Venus to help one penetrate the very soul of a romantic partner during the caterings of lust. With these, you can see a love more deep than you had ever thought imaginable."

"Oh my! What a perfect gift for a sibling's lover! We simply must try them at our earliest opportunity, Clotty."

With hindsight now an ally, I should have expected deviance. In my life, I have found that people rarely convert from a serpentine manner to an enchanting one in so little time, especially when they have just visited the Netherlands. But the inebriation of love had swindled me to want a better version of my lover's twin sister, and I fell head-first into her deception.

As soon as allowed, Clotty and I made love, and I immediately noticed the difference in our fornication from behind the Neuken-Ogens' glass. It did not feel like a brilliance of chemistry spurred by the eminence of Aphrodite, but I decided it polite to continue on in the name of appreciation.

When the love-making concluded, Seraphique revealed her cruel fraud. The spectacles were not at all graced by the magic of mythical spirituality, but simply goggles in which mirrored frames had been horizontally inverted. And upon learning this, I realised that the twin I had just been gazing toward and thrusting upon with lustful embrace was not at all my beloved Clotilda, but her witch-queen sister. Through treachery, I had cheated on the love of my life.

At first, Clotty felt we might persist. She implored that, in time, she could forgive me for my adultery. But as she wept into one shoulder, feebly attempting to conjure a way out of our predicament, Seraphique snarled into the other, reminding me that at no point had she ever offered her consent, and that if we did not abandon our union, the courts would hear the cries of rape.

It was approximately at this time that I remembered I had enrolled in the British Expeditionary Force, and that my services were required to restore peace and good fortune to Western Europe. I begged Seraphique to allow us one last night of romance in which to properly recite a farewell to Clotilda, but she denied us, declaring that she had decided to become a lesbian and would not permit any further penetration by a male.

And so I left the greatest love and returned to my post in Paris. I attempted to shield myself from the trauma of heartbreak, but I was thenceforth irreparably changed. Under the shadow of war, nihilism faced off against hope within me, and an altered Baggy Smacker emerged from the fire-torn husk of Norbert Charolais.

I could not decide if I had more or less to live for. As damaged as I felt by the shockwave of an exploded soul, I harboured a faint hope that someday, in a future less-filled with bullets and bloodshed and ambiguous credit histories, perhaps it would be possible to heal and replenish whatever reserve of energy a young man maintains for the colossal effort of being in love.

One thing, though, was for certain as I resumed my position within the barracks of the 701st Sanitation Company; the fresh callous upon my formerly-tender heart was about to make me a considerably more effective soldier.

CHAPTER TWENTY:

A Glorious Retreat

As my relationship with Clotilda Antoine passed, so did the phantom known as Monsieur Norbert Charolais. In his place, I re-emerged as Sapper Baggy Smacker of the 701st Sanitation Company, conveniently in time to avoid defaulting on a debt owed to a Parisian restaurateur of approximately twenty thousand francs.

Upon return, I was immediately marched to the office of a Major who demanded to know where I'd been for the past several months. Thinking on my feet, I told him I'd been sent undercover to infiltrate the Oberkommando and assassinate the enemy head of state, and had been close to doing so up until my holiday visa expired. The Major pondered this thoughtfully and checked with his superiors, who agreed that it sounded likely as German frugality among visa extensions was apparently the thing holding up the long-awaited American declaration of war.

I returned to my quarters to find a considerable heap of unopened mail from all manner of friends, family and others, and I poured myself a glass of the wine that I'd smuggled back from my interim existence as I sat down to read. It was a welcome relief to see written updates and well-wishes; especially so for the ones that were addressed to me.

According to correspondence from my father, he had been allowed to cut short the life-long lettre de marque he had signed on condition that he conscripted for war; an offer he accepted and manipulated when he discovered that the ethical Pirate Captain he was contracted to had not specified *which* war. Instead of enrolment in the greater conflict in Europe, Father opted to join the three-day-long Legionnaires' Rebellion in Bucharest as a Catering Advisor, initially on the side of the Iron Guard but eventually defecting to the winning side fifteen minutes prior to ceasefire.

Although he avoided fighting the more dangerous battles of the western front and was even able to remain based out of

London whilst sending his Typex-encrypted recipes to allies abroad, he did still somehow manage to lose the lower half of his left leg and suffer a troubling bout of chloracne following a fierce firefight sparked by broken promises regarding the cleaning schedule of a shared kitchenette.

After dispensing of an envelope containing a dimly-lit photograph of Preston the Cocker-poodle's genitals along with a note asking if I was currently awake, I opened another piece of communique from which I learned that Joseph Darkfire had answered the King's call and was currently part of the British Expeditionary Force attempting to thwart the German advances in north-eastern France. A wave of distress assaulted me at the thought of sweet, artful Joseph holding a rifle, but I was soon calmed to read that his officers had, as all do, identified his delicate nature and reassigned him to the position of the company's bard. I was furthermore unsurprised to learn that he had single-handedly held off a German recon unit with a song about two elderly same-sex field mice falling in love and opening a bed & breakfast in Aberdeen together, and that it was of such melodic beauty and such lyrical ambrosia, forty-five enemy soldiers completely reassessed their prior months of merciless blitzkrieg and elected to shoot each other in the head, giving Darkfire, for a brief period, the highest single kill-count of any individual serving in the allied forces.

I scavenged an ink and quill, with which to respond "Ha!" in a letter of my own, and paid the quartermaster for a first-class stamp to ensure its quickest delivery to my dear friend.

Among the last of the letters I perused was one from Clara St. Cloud, who had apparently leaned away from conventional entrepreneurship and had instead committed her retirement to a philanthropic infatuation with aviation.

Dear Young Smacker,

I will forgo floral salutation as I have no doubt you are successful, satisfied and secure in all manner.

I am writing to let you know that, in recent years, I have invested a great amount of my attention and wealth to the advancement of British aeronautical endeavours. I consider it to be the most interesting and modern revolution, and I intend to go down in history as its most vocal proponent. But on this front, I have fierce competition, and I require the assistance of your tight, youthful, throbbing wisdom.

I have sent a letter, in synchronicity to this one, to your Commanding Officer, compelling him to temporarily release you from your commitments to His Majesty's service so that you might immediately be summoned to Calais. I have little doubt he will acquiesce, as he and I have history, and I once permitted him to gently molest me at his mother's wake as a gesture of pity.

Kind regards,

Clara St. Cloud

My intrigue had been piqued. No sooner had I finished reading, did my Commanding Officer crash spectacularly through the dormitory door amidst a flurry of concerned lawyers, and I was hoisted to a train carriage destined for the seaside town of Calais. Once there, I was given cryptic directions from a mysterious gypsy, who spoke in riddled tongue and had me march "thirty miles as the sparrow flies east" at which point "I would meet my destiny". I reached approximately halfway until it occurred to me that I might have just taken advice from a homeless person, and made the wise decision to instead telephone Clara via the number she had cleverly included on the rear side of her letter. Once she confirmed she was waiting at a sandwich stand a mere dozen metres from Calais Central Station, I eagerly returned.

"Baggy, you've not aged, even for a second," Clara bellowed as we approached.

"And you yourself continue to blur the lines between middle age and suspicions of some kind of vampiric conspiracy of devil-worshippers that have, through the most perverted means, mastered eternal not-quite-youth!"

In each other's embrace, we reminisced over our wonderful shared memories, making sure to do so several times over so it seemed like there were more of them. I regaled Clara with tales of my life-changing military endeavours so far, and in return she talked of a delicious-but-carb-heavy muffin she had consumed in Prague.

As fond as our small–talk was, there was allegedly no time to waste. Clara St. Cloud hailed an ornate carriage hauled by homeless men who'd been promised respectable employment and, to their surprise, she yielded a whip with which to strike them to inertia, and we headed south at an impressive thirty-five miles per hour.

We eventually arrived in a muddied field that had been hastily converted into a makeshift airport. This was evident by the presence of several long runways, two large hangars built for the accommodation of aircraft, and a line of roughly a dozen holidaymakers who were queueing up to shout violently at a nineteen-year-old clerk for their inability to control the weather.

At Clara's behest, we made our way to the smaller of the two hangars and entered via a side-door. As she fumbled for a light, I could see that the warehouse was empty beyond a single structure at its centre, concealed beneath a draped white cloth.

I did not require explanation, but did not wish to deprive my friend of her great unveil, and so allowed her theatrics as she swept the sheet from the vehicle beneath.

"Behold, Baggy. My magnum opus!"

With a sharp hoist of her arm, Clara St. Cloud ripped away the fabric concealment to reveal a two-seater fighter aircraft, adorned in almost the exact livery of the Royal Air Force, but with "Sample only - Not for individual sale" written in several important areas.

"It is glorious, my friend, Clara. This is for the war effort?"

"Yes, Baggy. This is the culmination of my tiresome actions and investments from the past several years. I have little doubt that this craft will long be considered the saviour of Britain. This will decide the battle of the skies. Here, in this shed, you are one of the first to witness the saviour of Europe!"

As flourish, Clara performed an erotic, excited dance that endured in reality for minutes, but in my mind for years.

"What is it called?" I inquired, as a means for her to stop.

"This, Baggy, is the St. Cloud Clatterfart Mk1. As you can see, it is a two-person interceptor, destined for fame in the conquest of air superiority between Britain and France. At great expense, I have directed the production of this prototype. And at further expense, I will ensure that its deployment against the Germans will turn the tide of violence toward the favour of good."

I was quite absolutely in marvel.

"Whatever took you to this ambition?" I asked.

"Rivalry. And also spite. And also envy. You see, a friend of mine, from far back in life, had pursued similar intent and, having recalled how thoroughly irritating I considered her to be, I simply had to contend with her for the status of Great Britain's revolutionary in military aviation."

"Ah, I understand. Few things power the world more fiercely than contempt. I once publicly condemned a small baby for the size of his penis. Few moments since then have filled me with a similar pride. Tell me, how does the Clatterfart differ from the offerings of your rival?"

"I'm glad you asked, Baggy. Aircraft, as you might know, are quite famously limited by capacity of weight. This is one of the many reasons why we disallow heavily-pregnant women and semi-professional golfers from the role of pilot in the RAF. It is also why, on our more manoeuvrable craft, we limit operators to one."

"Of course."

"Interceptors, or fighters, are required to be as light as can be. Yet to lose a dedicated gunner on an offensive aircraft is to lose so much of its threat. To fire straight from the nose means one cannot concentrate on flying. And so I thought, would it not be worth more to continue the focus and accuracy of a two-man team, and instead concentrate on the reduction of weight elsewhere?"

"That makes perfect sense, Clara."

"And so I found elsewhere to reduce weight; Ammunition. Perhaps the most heavy and cumbersome component of the lone wolf aircraft. And I found a solution to it that will benefit both aerodynamics, physics and the overall cleanliness of the standard British household."

"Tell me."

"Cat hair."

"Cat hair?"

"Yes, indeed. Cat hair. Were you the owner of a cat, you might know the condition. Car hair is simply everywhere in a good home. We have a device, an electric vacuum cleaner, and I suspect we harvest around a kilogram of car hair per day. Well, at least we would if it did not clog the mechanics of all it encounters. So often did I find myself condemning modern technology for its inability to overcome the simple confrontation of domestic cat hair, that I saw no reason as to why it could not offer the same interruption to the intricate components of a sophisticated piece of enemy aircraft or armour or, given sufficient allergy within their ranks, personnel.

"And so, I have worked in coordination with some of the finest minds in British manufacturing, and several mid-tier ones, to equip the Clatterfart with cannons that fire cartridges of compacted cat hair that, when aimed toward the propellers and engines of another fighter or bomber, really get in there and fuck everything up."

"And it's enough to bring down an aerial opponent?"

"Much of the time, yes. And even if it does not, it absolutely decimates the warranty."

"My friend, this is absolutely astonishing technology. How close is it to a state of production?"

"Close, Baggy. And in asking, you have touched upon the reason for your hasty summoning. I need a pilot to become intimate with the tendencies and controls of this prototype so that I can start turning the heads of the Royal Air Force."

"I am flattered, of course. But why me? I have no experience operating an aircraft."

"Oh, you're not to be the pilot, dear boy. You're to operate the canons and perform ancillary tasks, such as diarising the pilots' thoughts and preparing their sandwiches for mid-flight indulgence. It is I, Baggy, who will fly the plane. And when the day comes, and the top brass of His Majesty's government behold the undeniable might of the St. Cloud Clatterfart Mk1, and they beg for me to sign the contract that will authorise them to commence construction of thousands of units, the only caveat in my eager response will be that I be bestowed the privilege of heading the first wing that enters battle over the skies of Europe, and also the rank of Air Chief Marshall along with total tactical authority over British Fighter Command."

"Reasonable demands, considering your offering," I replied. "So you have had pilot training?"

"Yes, I took several over-the-phone lessons with Amelia Earhart's mother and I'm confident I've got a pretty good handle on things. She taught her daughter, did you know?"

"Did her daughter not allegedly crash?"

"Yes, although the mother did mention that she'd forgotten to coach her daughter to crash less often, so it is understandable. With the aid of retrospect however, she came across as incredibly wise and affordable."

"I see," I responded thoughtfully. "So, I suppose the next question is, when do we start testing the Clatterfart?"

"Now, Baggy."

"Now?"

"Unless you have a more important war to get to?"

I confessed I did not and, minutes later, I found myself assisting Clara St. Cloud with climbing up a small cabin-side ladder and into the pilot's seat. As I climbed into the rear gunner's position, a small runway truck drove into the hangar, pulled up alongside the Clatterfart and began loading luggage and refreshments into its cargo hull.

"There's a latch at your feet, Baggy," St. Cloud advised. "Open it, and you'll be able to access the hull. How about pouring a gin and tonic, for good luck?"

Though cramped, I clumsily put together two drinks and my friend and I clinked them together on beat with her commencing take-off protocols.

Initially, the control tower advised of a twenty-minute delay due to runway and airspace congestion, but once

Clara St. Cloud explained that she was incredibly affluent, we were permitted to ferry out of the hangar and go for it. I finished my gin and tonic, and surveyed the apparatus within my own semi-detached cockpit. Before me was a small television screen, inanimate to begin with but, once I'd flicked the correct switch, it burst to life to show a black-and-white image with a crosshair at its centre. To my right side was a flight stick, and when I moved it tentatively, the screen moved in harmony.

Minutes later, we were directed to a length of flattened mud that someone had optimistically signed as being a runway. I admit to being slightly nervous, not least because Clara's first attempt at taking off resulted in her getting lost and having to stop to ask someone for directions.

"You'll want to keep heading the way you're heading, and when you see a sign that reads 'Runway End', you'll want to be turning upward, alright?" We were advised by an elderly farmer.

We thanked the helpful local and, once Clara had emptied her change pocket and tipped him forty-thousand shillings in coins, we returned to the starting point.

Our second attempt was slightly more fruitful, with at least one of us taking momentarily to the air. However, this was less due to the magic of aviation and more a result of St. Cloud accidentally pressing the button that triggered her ejector seat. Once a team of engineers were sent out to retrieve her from a nearby glen, we reset preparations and tried again.

This time, we took flight and it was spectacular. All inhibitions of mine vanished immediately as I fought against gravitational force to gaze out of the side of the cockpit, and observed the earth fall away from us. Everything below shrank from full-scale, to model village, to miniature train-set, to ant colony. As we ascended, the aircraft banked to the east and I could, for a moment, see the tan ribbon of Calais' coastline belting France's emerald pastures from the glittering vastness of the English channel. Beyond that, the distinct white peaks of either Dorset or Dover broke through the ocean's royal blue, and proffered a glimpse of distant green that struck me to sobriety. There was home, a place I had not given much thought to in a very long time.

My coma of awe was broken by an obnoxious buzzing noise, and a message flashed from the console announcing that the pilot had requested a ham, cheese and pickle sandwich. I reached into the cargo hold and pulled forth the ingredients, but struggled to take my eye away from the majestic visions outside. Once I had handed Clara St. Cloud's food to her, I couldn't help but pour a finger of gin and toast silently.

"It's quite amazing, isn't it?" Clara chimed.

"Yes, it's breathtaking."

"It's the pickles, you see. It's all about the pickles. There's only so much one can expect from English cheddar and ham. But the pickle spread, from Derby I think, is absolutely divine. Do help yourself. I have crates of the stuff at home. The gentleman who owns the company that makes it once struck me in a dream, and after I sued him for the emotional trauma, he paid out in pickle spread."

I opted against distracting myself with hunger and instead continued to stare in wonder. As the aircraft weaved left and right through the air, I basked between the comfort and longing for England on one side, and the confronting closeness of the Western front on the other. Yet from above, it all seemed suddenly so pointless.

I would have preferred to enjoy the serenity for longer, but a crackle through the radio snapped both of us to rigid attention.

"Hallo, hallo. My name is - good lord, let's see if I can get this right the first time for once - Field Marshal John

Standish Surtees Prendergast Vereker of the British Expeditionary Force. There you go, nailed it I think. James, did I get all my names right? JAMES. Pay attention, boy. Did I get all my names right? Yes? Excellent. Sorry, this is Field Marshal Vereker and this message is intended for the audience of all private aircraft and seacraft currently within the vicinity of the English Channel, North Sea and Strait of Dover.

"So, look, I can't be sure how much of the news you've all been reading, but the war isn't going terribly well right now and we're in a bit of a spot. Specifically, that spot is a small patch of beach in France and, well, it's not looking terribly good at the moment. The Germans have us fairly well cornered, hats off to them, and - there's not really an easy way to say this - well, we're a bit fucked if they come any closer.

"So this correspondence is something of a mayday call. We've got quite a few men stuck down here - James, how many? Well, count again."

There was a short pause in the transmission.

"Right, sorry about that. So there's about three hundred thousand of us down here, essentially the entire British army and we're a bit out-done.. Don't ask me how, there'll be plenty of time to go into that later. But for now, well, we could all really do with a lift home and a spot of tea and maybe a nap. Then after that, we promise we'll nip back over and defeat the Germans at a later date. So, James will read out some coordinates, and if any of you who are in the area could just sort of pop by and pick up your share, we should hopefully have all of us back in Dorset before the pubs close. James, you do your bit."

As James began to read out the location of the remainder of the British Expeditionary Force, Clara St. Cloud craned around to look at me with a smile on her face.

"Well, Baggy. Seems as if we've an opportunity to test the combat readiness of the Clatterfart. Are you ready?" I took one more glance toward Britain. Prior to that moment, I'd not ever considered myself patriotic or nationalistic. But although to observe the continents and islands and waters from on high was to minimise their scale, it did so in a way that made them feel vulnerable and pocketable. From the ground, as a youth, England felt vast and expansive; a vicious, existential labyrinth with no end to struggle and anxiety on any side. From above, it appeared innocently verdant, with an elderly fragility in need of conservation.

"Quite possibly the most ready I have ever been," I replied quietly.

As soon as confirmed, Clara wrenched at the flight stick and steered us toward our new destination, only having to land for directions once. In little over fifteen minutes, we were flying low over the French coastline, and could clearly observe the chaos down on the beaches under us.

As St. Cloud took the Clatterfart to lower altitudes, the thousands-strong swarm of soldiers sharpened from a brown blur to identifiable figures. Many were crouched in foxholes that had been either hastily dug or carved out of the sand by enemy artillery. Others had built a giant sand castle from which to defend against the eventual German onslaught, although the tide was coming in so they had instead declared war on the ocean and could be seen hurling grenades into the waves in an attempt to thwart them.

On the southern end of the beach, some of the more sporting Germans had downed their firearms and offered to sort out the conflict via a series of volleyball tournaments. While the bloodshed was minimised, British sports funding had been at its lowest in decades and the unarmed enemy advance seemed somehow more brutal than it had before.

"Eyes front, Smacker," Clara St. Cloud commanded, with all humour lost from her voice.

In the near distance, a formation of small dots could be seen approaching from the West. It took only seconds to fly closer and identify them as I'd feared; a four-strong wing of German bombers, heading toward the coastline where, no doubt, their objective was to strafe the beachhead and riddle the BEF with bullets and bombs.

"No fighters, as far as I can see, Baggy. But those are Heinkels. I can't make out what series from here, but I'll wager there's more than enough weapons on those to protect themselves," Clara confirmed.

I took a deep breath and another look toward the beach. The only British success story to be seen was a platoon of soldiers who had successfully out-fought the owners of a kayak hire stand, and even *their* closeness to escape was brought to an end as their top-loaded luggage of souvenirs capsized the vessels the moment they breached the waves.

"Our boys down there look like sitting ducks," I said.

"They look comfortable?"

"No, they... Not ducks sitting on a couch so much as... I... Look, I've not given that expression enough thought I'm afraid. What I mean is, we don't have a choice, Clara."

"I'm glad you agree. Man those guns with all your focus and grit, Baggy. We're about to test much more than this *aircraft's* resolve."

As we turned to engage the enemy head-on, I gave the control stick of our craft's armament a wiggle, before lining up the reticule with the lead bomber. Gently, I held my finger over the trigger and reminded myself to breathe.

I watched the digitised image of the enemy as they came closer and closer. From a pixelated cloud of grey, distinction invaded every area of the monitor's screen, and it wasn't long before I could clearly make out the detail of the pilot's swastika face tattoo, the fanciful Nazi trinkets atop his cockpit console, and the words "Go Milwall!" threaded into his t-shirt.

"Fire on my count, Baggy," Clara St. Cloud commanded.

I steadied myself.

"Three."

I took a deep breath. A burst of enemy bullets spat at us, although none seemed to make contact.

"Two."

I applied the lightest touch to the trigger, ignoring the clicking and associated flashing of the "Gin & Tonic Requested" alarm that Clara had chosen at that time to utilise.

"One!"

With the enemy aircraft firmly in my sights, I pulled the trigger. An almighty "WOMPF!" rang out, followed by a shockwave from both sides of the cockpit and a screech of a very startled cat who had apparently been mistaken for a large reel of ammunition. As soon as I'd fired, I felt a vicious tug of G-force as Clara immediately yielded upwards, out of the way of the oncoming Heinkel. I hoisted myself in my seat, to a position at which I was able to crane back and see behind us.

Initially, it appeared that the wing of enemy aircraft were totally unharmed. All that looked beyond normal was the small white circular outline of what I presumed to be the cat's parachute. I flinched as another spatter of gunfire emitted, and this time I heard two sharp cracks as bullets found their target.

After one or two seconds, I saw the effects of the cat hair, as the lead Heinkel began to produce white smoke from its left wing. Moments later, the white had turned to grey, then to black. As St. Cloud levelled out and banked to her left, the first flickers of flame could be seen.

"Clara, you genius. It has worked!"

St. Cloud responded with more passive-aggressive pounding of her service request, and I quickly scrambled to pour her another celebratory cocktail as she lined up the next bomber for us to strafe. By the time I'd added the slice of lemon, our first target had sputtered to a stall with a left engine engulfed by flame.

When I passed through the gin and tonic, Clara downed it in a single gulp.

"Ready for another?" she asked.

"Don't you perhaps think we should attend to our immediate threat before indulging in more drink?"

"Another German craft, I meant, you silly boy. But actually, now that you mention it, yes, I would also like another drink please. Something special to mark the occasion. And quickly."

I fumbled with a bottle of cinnamon whisky and limoncello, and thrust it into St. Cloud's waiting hand, just in time to return to my primary duty and wrench the targeting stick so that it centred upon our next opponent.

By this point, the Germans had become aware of the harm that the Clatterfart was demonstrably capable of, and the sporadic bursts of gunfire had become sustained pattering, with shots continuously snapping through the wings and fuselage.

As before, I waited for Clara's countdown and pulled back the trigger confidently as another Heinkel fell into my aim. Once again, we banked away, although this time I felt no need to confirm destruction. Even had I wished to, when we turned, we did so to immediately face an oncoming enemy fighter that had appeared from someplace close to nowhere, and I felt as though my blood had dropped several degrees in temperature.

For the next minute, in silent terror, we attempted to manoeuvre away from the enemy's sights. Clara St. Cloud pushed the Clatterfart's flight stick to its limits, tilting, rolling, banking and diving, trying with all her might to turn the tables and have the interceptor within the range of our weapons. But to no avail.

By now, the bombers had departed our small piece of airspace, but the impact of German bullets could still be felt and heard. St. Cloud was a naturally talented operator, but the pilot of the enemy fighter was evidently an ace, and it seemed as though, for not a single second, were we out of his aim.

It appeared inevitable that, eventually, my dear friend Clara St. Cloud rolled left when she perhaps should have leaned right. Instead of evasion, we turned directly into the path of the German fighter and a terrific crack of gunfire tore through the whistling wind. A smash of glass and a whimper of pain followed, and I knew immediately that we were in trouble. From my position rear to my friend's, I could see marks of blood against the aircraft's instruments.

"Clara! Are you okay?"

Meekly, Clara tapped with diminished strength against the cocktail button. I grappled for nearby bottles once again and poured us both shots. When she downed hers she did so, not with the usual zest and theatre of an affluent alcoholic declaring a satirical feud against her liver, but in a manner that felt more akin to a solemn toast to something larger than the moment.

"Clara, concentrate. We simply need to land, and we can have you attended to. Perhaps a cream cheese and cucumber sandwich might perk you up?"

She coughed first but then croaked, "My dear Baggy, I think that the time for cream cheese and cucumber sandwiches might have passed."

"Nonsense! They will return to fashion soon enough."

"I speak not of fashion, Baggy. All sandwiches sit somewhere upon life's timeline, and very few I suspect linger afterward. Possibly the ones with corned beef in them. But cream cheese and cucumber sandwiches do not. Although I suppose they're quite popular at funerals, so they're admittedly very much near the end."

"Come, Clara, this is not the end. This is not how you bow out of this world. We simply need to land and we shall be fine."

"Baggy, I am not attempting to be coy or heroic. I am hurt. Considerably so. And my ejector seat has already been deployed. I feel life seeping from me with great swiftness. It is a strange feeling, I'll grant you, but no more stranger than the fact that I am at peace right now. This aircraft... My legacy... Was she not beautiful?"

I stifled tears. "She was beautiful, Clara."

"Imagine how jealous that fucking bitch rival of mine would have been, had she seen our flight, Baggy. Will you write to her for me? Something along the lines of 'Our inaugural voyage was as fruitful as your diet is not, you girthy tart' or something to that effect."

"Of course, yes, I will write to her. With all the juvenile contempt and sarcasm that I might possibly muster. Did you know I once called out a baby for the size of -"

"Yes, you've mentioned that previously. Look, Baggy, you must eject before it's too late. You might think it a shame to leave me, but you know more than many that my life has been a very full one. I have zero regrets and I have zero ambitions unfulfilled. You see, Baggy -"

St. Cloud was interrupted by the pneumatic pop of my ejector seat exploding upward through the cockpit into the sky-blue vastness. I attempted to wave goodbye as I evacuated and explain that we were getting concerningly proximate to the earth so she'd need to forward me any further advice via mail, but it was not clear that she'd registered my departure.

The ejection fired me upward enough to offer a decent overview of all below me. My dear friend, Clara St. Cloud, careened into the English Channel with an emphatic splash that her cousin, James Ferdinand Bambi, would have been so very impressed with. She did so, within a tomb of her own over-achievement and, though I wiped tears from my eyes, I felt confident that she could not have seen a more fitting death.

The German fighter, having downed his opponent, lost interest in the Clatterfart and saw no reason to pursue me. Instead, he turned back to the west to resume the escort of the remaining bombers.

On the beach below, things were going as poorly as before, with wave after wave of Germans attacking allied positions, as well as wave after wave of actual waves bringing the British-built sand fortress to such ruin that the National Trust were already gating it off and charging one pound per entry. Germans were occupying all podium positions of the volleyball tournament, and were handing out hastily-crafted participation trophies to French and English soldiers in a display of sportsmanship so patronising that, years later, an international tribunal would declare it a war crime.

At the apex of my trajectory, a parachute deployed and I drifted calmly downward, observing the world in a way similar to a disinterested God who'd forgotten how to fly. A small hatch flipped open at the arm of my chair to offer two possible options for landing; 'Sensible' or 'One to tell the grandchildren of'. I elected the former, as it had been something of a day and, after hearing a small whirr of mechanics, I found myself sailing toward the beachhead.

When I crashed to the ground in a cloud of sand, I resisted the urge to stand up immediately and instead lay in the tender sun, staring up at the endless blue above, of which I had so recently been a resident. I could hear the bustle of soldiers around me, and a distant thud of artillery and mechanical violence. I felt a sense of urgency, but not a strong one. My recent sentimental shroud of wonder and confused patriotism had been neutered by the loss of someone who I had great love and respect for.

For a very long while, I lay in the sand and wracked my brain for a reason to rise up. When I could summon not a single one, I decided that I might enjoy ending my life there and then, and simply sink into the coastline of France and fulfil my desires for legacy with knowing I had contributed to this war with at least two downed German bombers. I could be done with any further stress of grandeur, once and for all. Tens of thousands had died with less merit. There was no shame in calling it a day.

Sadly though, a small cat, dragging a parachute from his collar, stamped toward me and deployed the most viciously odorous defecation directly adjacent to my head, and I was left with no option but to hoist myself out of the Clatterfart's ejected gunner chair and resume life.

I assisted the feline in detaching the tangled rigging of the chute and he meowed gratefully.

"Good lord, sand as far as the eye can see. Have I landed in the world's greatest litter tray?" he asked.

"No, you're in France," I replied.

"Ah. Not far off then," he said.

We chortled heartily, exchanged further needlessly-critical witticisms at the expense of the French, and then bid farewell.

I watched him saunter inland as I considered that I might possibly have been concussed from the trauma of landing.

I looked to the ocean, at the approximate point I had seen Clara and the Clatterfart crash through its surface. It was a significant distance from shore, and I had no means of overcoming such a swim, let alone submerging to any useful depth. I considered a prayer or some form of eulogy but suspected St. Cloud might resent the prospect of some god interfering with her tomb of gin and pickle spread.

Instead, I turned to the land and realised I would have to rejoin the theatre of war if I wished to somehow be relieved of my predicament. Of all the engagements along the beach, the sand fortress was the closest, so I set toward it. Given my experience in treading water in the deep end of Saint Adjutor's Comprehensive College of Excellence, I surmised that I was most-equipped to battle against a slowly-rising tide.

By the time I reached it, the east-facing wall was being rebuilt behind the safety of a well-dug moat. I approached the building unarmed and not in uniform, but was permitted entry after the guards at the main door confirmed my nationality by feeding me a spoonful of instant custard and observing whether or not I complained.

Within the walls of the fortress, all manner of activity was to be observed. On one side, a group of soldiers were sitting at a table, comparing pleasant shells that they'd found on the beach and formulating a business plan to create jewellery to sell so that they might bribe German soldiers to allow their escape. In another corner, Officers of a middle-class background were calculating how many non-commissioned soldiers would need to be sacrificed in order to form a human landbridge from their current position to a well-reviewed seafood restaurant in Southampton.

But there was one small area of the sand castle's inner sanctum that instantly caught my eye, for against a small space of wall there was a seated figure, with knees up against their chest and arms clamped around their legs. As soon as I saw him, I ran to my dear friend Joseph Darkfire and, once he registered my approach and stood, embraced him with perhaps the strongest hug I had ever managed in my life so far.

"Baggy! Is this a dream?"

"Before I walked through those doors, I wished it had been. But now, to see you, I hope I am wide awake."

"How did you get to be here? I received your letter this morning. I was so utterly touched to see you had written the word 'Ha' in response to my comparatively-extensive communique that I had put a substantial amount of time and thought toward."

I explained to my friend how I had come to have been deposited on the beaches of France and, upon hearing of the recent loss of someone dear to me, he broke down into tears of empathy and began to commence compiling an extensive anthology of poems about loss and death and entrepreneurial women with above-average-sized breasts. Before he could become carried away, I slapped him across the face to restore his focus, to which he cried more and attempted another publication about the trauma of violence.

"Joseph, we need to get off this beach," I said to him.

For a second, his eyes still welled with tears, but they were then dried by a resolve I had not seen in him before. He breathed deeply, wrote a single, forty-eight-line sonnet about stoicism, and stood up.

"You're right, Baggy. Neither of us end here."

"Agreed. What's the plan? The tide looms and this fortification will soon fall. We need to get out of France."

"We know. We've tried everything. We made boats out of sand, and they fell apart. We attempted to form a sub-aquatic tunnel from sand, but it sank to the bottom of the channel. All we have is sand. We're running low on ammunition, and the company commander has poor credit so we can't afford to purchase any more."

"What forms of communication do we have? Is there a radio?"

"I'm afraid not. We had one, but the quartermaster reassigned its batteries to a microphone for last night's karaoke competition and they have since depleted their reserve."

"I see."

The moment I responded, an almighty explosion knocked us both from our feet. Joseph and I were blasted to the floor, and when I opened my eyes from the shock, the glaring blue sky and fine light sand were replaced by a gothic grayscale. I could identify my friend, looking back at me, but all else was clouded in smoke.

Neither of us was hurt, but it was clear that men around us were, as several voices could be heard saying such things as "Oh, that should be fine once I've run it under the tap" and "There's no need to call the doctor on a Sunday when we can just wait until the week when it's a bit cheaper."

I had felt dazed enough from the fiasco of the Clatterfart's maiden voyage, so it was Joseph Darkfire this time who rose to his feet and pulled me from the sand.

"The German artillery is firing upon us, Baggy. We need to get out."

I considered playing Devil's advocate out of a sheer sense of masculine obligation but felt a change of heart when a second enemy bombardment landed on the shell-sorting table and destroyed approximately two shillings' worth of terrible jewellery, along with a dozen men.

Joseph and I rushed through the doors of the castle, battling against our panicking comrades, until we broke free of the smoke and debris, and fell gasping onto the sand. I took a glance behind, past the crumbling structure, to see a platoon of bib-wearing German volleyball players looking for a more serious challenge. To the north, I could see the regrouping of the stolen-kayak-hire division attempting to re-enter the waters of the channel, having finally decided upon an appropriate weight allowance for fanciful trinkets.

"That's us, Joseph," I said, pulling my friend out of the sand with me. "Can you swim?"

"No, Baggy. No orphan has ever been able to swim. Buoyancy requires the love of at least one parent."

I was fairly certain what he had said was incorrect however we were without time to engage in debate. Instead, I took his hand in mine and pulled him northward until we were in line with the kayakers. By this time the soldiers were about a hundred metres from the beach. I attempted to yell and attract their attention but my exclamations were drowned out by crashing waves and distant artillery.

"Joseph, we need to swim out to them. Hold onto me and kick your legs. Can you do that?"

"I don't know that I can, Baggy. You see, orphans cannot kick their legs-" he began, before I interrupted.

"Joseph, I have lost one dear friend today. I shall not be parting ways with another. I promise you, you can do this. I have helped fellow students to survive through entire lectures at school with minimal effort on their behalf. Please believe in yourself with as much awe as I believe in you. You will hold tightly onto me, you will kick your legs, and you will live another day. And when all this is over, we can have a nice cup of tea and address some of the fucking ridiculous theories you have about your being an orphan."

Joseph Darkfire took a long look at the aquatic expanse beyond and breathed out deeply. Then he returned his gaze to mine and spoke.

"I'm ready."

Together, we waded through the breaking waves until we found ourselves submerged to our chests. From that point, Joseph placed his arms around my neck and we began our attempt to swim as one. Initially, I was pulled under by the weight of my friend and I resisted my own panic as I sensed his. When I bobbed back above the surface, I gasped and told him to kick. Joseph kicked and, after several seconds, we surged upwards and forwards.

The kayaks had made minimal progress and were still at a reachable distance, and after only a few minutes of coordinated floatation, we were close enough to call out for their attention. At first, we were sensibly ignored but our cries became strained enough that one soldier paddled around to face us.

"Hello, chaps. Right bit of bother back there on the beach," he said.

"It certainly was. Look, we require assistance. Have you space for us to board?" I responded.

"I'm afraid not, old boy. I've already jettisoned enough souvenir lunchboxes today and I shall not be losing any more profit."

"Please! We need to get back to England. If you will not allow us aboard, might we cling to your hull and be dragged across the channel?"

The soldier eyed us thoughtfully and finally relented.

"Of course, chaps. Grab a hold and resume your kicking. I expect you to sell at least one carton of lunch boxes each, but we can discuss the terms of your debt when we reach land."

Once the soldier had completed his one-eighty turn and was once again facing England, I held onto the kayak's aft, and both Joseph and I returned to thrashing our legs. Within little time, our craft was back in formation with the others and, at first, a tide of relief could be felt. It seemed that we were going to make it.

I craned my neck for a final glimpse of the French beach-head and saw chaos. The partially-ruined sand fortress was under heavy bombardment by German artillery. The remaining English defenders were attempting to repair its walls, only to be thwarted by refusal from the National Trust which had managed to have it heritage-listed in record time and wouldn't allow alteration without the correct permit fees paid. Thousands of English soldiers were still trapped on the beach without a prayer.

At the height of futility, we saw traces of hope. Ahead of us, the distant silhouettes of all manner of ship could be seen and I realised that the broadcast that had tempted Clara St. Cloud to diversion had been heard back home. Civilian sea-craft of every variety were making their way from the southern coast of England to northern France, presumably not simply for shopping. The kayaking soldiers even cheered as a jet-ski sped by, hauling an inflatable banana boat behind it.

With Joseph still clinging onto my shoulders, I allowed myself to momentarily relax. I stopped kicking my legs, closed my eyes and allowed myself a moment of peace.

An explosion rang out immediately. Though Joseph and I were mostly submerged, the shockwave pushed through the water and launched us away from our kayak. Somehow, we managed to stay together but the same could not be said of our paddling comrades. I was not sure if we'd been targeted by torpedo, missile or artillery round but something German had clearly managed a direct hit on one vessel that had obliterated its occupant and shredded his surrounding squadmates.

Our own pilot was now slunked over, most assuredly dead, with his boat in two pieces. Somehow we had been spared a similar fate having been so close to the waterline but every kayak around us was now in bits and slowly sinking.

"Kick, Joseph, kick!" I cried out, feeling the deadweight around my neck. While he managed a modest thrust and maintained his hold, I suspected my friend to be injured as he did not speak back. Desperately, I climbed through the debris and bloodied waters, looking for any form of floatation to rely upon. All of assistance I could find was a carton of lunch-boxes emblazoned with the slogan "I've Done-Kirk", which provided temporary respite and a sensible chuckle but were clearly not water-tight.

I could not see any sign or evidence of whomever had launched the attack. There were no longer planes in the sky and no German boat craft about. If a submersible had been responsible, then it clearly saw no urgency in plucking us from the channel to accommodate as prisoners of war.

At this point, we were desperately far from both coasts. I kicked and pushed against the ocean as much as I could, and although Joseph had at first managed to maintain collabora-tion, he was weakened to the point that all his energy could muster was just enough to keep his clasp around my neck.

Valiantly, I expelled every calorie of energy within me and I could feel myself becoming exhausted. I clung to another passing carton of souvenirs - this time plastic water bottles that read "Visit Tolerable Calais!" - but they too sank quickly once under the weight of two people. As the kayaks and bod-ies around me submerged, I faced the reality that I would need to either part ways with Joseph Darkfire or die.

But what would life be without that immaculate friendship? As I gave all I had left to keep us above the surface, I consid-ered survival alone. In my life, there had been no greater inspi-ration than Joseph. Yes, I had friends who had achieved great things but few had done so from the hopelessness that he had. Clara St. Cloud had lived a life of affluence and industry, as had James Ferdinand Bambi, but they had been blessed from the start. I had always gauged my own worth by comparing myself to Joseph. Not out of jealousy, or cynicism, but out of genuine admiration. I realised that I felt, truly, that he was a better man than I was, and nothing could illuminate that more than abandoning him to die without meaning in the chilling waters of the English channel.

I continued to kick. I continued to flail. I continued to gasp for air. I continued to do all I could to keep Joseph Dark-fire alive for as long as I could. Yet all I had to give was not enough.

My muscles grew sore and my lungs burned from desperate panting. Slowly, with each stroke of my arms growing weaker and weaker, I sank downward. With all I had left, I pushed my face out of the ocean one last time and drew the greatest breath I could, before submitting to the inevitable.

Together Joseph Darkfire and I were to drown.

But then life reached out, as it so often does, and decided otherwise at the very last. As I closed my eyes and resigned myself to those final moments, I felt something wrap around me, followed by the rough pull of ensnarement and a viciously mechanical tug upwards. Seconds later, Joseph and I burst through the ocean's surface and continued to be hoisted as I attempted to make sense of what saving grace had denied Death of our company.

A fishing net surrounded the two of us and to our side the blinding white hull of a small trawler had appeared. As we ascended, we passed the name of the boat, inscribed in cursive text upon its starboard; "*Randy Scandy Alexandy*".

When we were dumped onto the deck of the vessel and untangled from netting, I found myself being whipped repeatedly with a fishing rod by none other than my father, who had assumed that Joseph and I were engaged in a lovers' suicide. I tamed his homophobia by filling him in on what I'd been up to over the past few years, and after fifteen or so minutes he agreed to stop beating me and would instead just throw an occasional haddock at my head when I wasn't looking.

Finally, I had a chance to inspect Joseph and could see that he was indeed injured. A deep gash ran from his left ear to his forehead and blood was flowing steadily. I did what I could to bandage him and relayed the urgency of his need for a hospital to my father, who agreed to set a course for England as soon as he'd fished all the souvenir lunch boxes out of the water to sell to locals in Guernsey, who he claimed "would be made speechless by the technology".

Once I had assisted him in doing so, we made way for home, and I slumped against the deck of the boat in complete exhaustion. The last few hours had undoubtedly been the most intensive of all my life. And though I knew heartbreak would soon resume at having lost Clara St. Cloud, I felt proud that I had at least saved Joseph Darkfire from a similar fate.

Before that moment, I don't recall any such feeling of existential contentment. But to be able to determine objectively that I had been instrumental in prolonging a friend's mortal coil was an awakening moment. If only, I am now able to dread in retrospect, it was the last time I would need to do so.

CHAPTER TWENTY-ONE:

A Temporary Ceasefire

The world moves to a different rhythm in war. Time seems to accelerate and decelerate at its own accord, priorities shift by the hour, and constant urgencies create situations that normally would seem unfathomable. It was this unbridled erraticism that meant I found myself, months later, exhuming a corpse from a cemetery in Bristol Cathedral at midnight alongside my nemesis, Michael-Steve Burrows.

Though to say he was assisting would be an overstatement, as he stood by idly whilst I manned the shovel, citing his still undeveloped limbs as an excuse to avoid labour. Burrows was mysteriously physically unchanged since our initial introduction, although he now wore an obviously-prosthetic, oversized penis atop his natural one that dragged along the ground as he walked. Despite the clear fakery and its filthy condition, Michael-Steve would still boast about it at every opportunity.

"I tell you, Baggy, sometimes it's a curse," he sighed. "To be so endowed is to be subject to such responsibility. I attended a wedding not more than a month ago, at which the father of the bride accidentally tripped over my impressively-long member as he walked his daughter down the aisle. And if only that were the worst moment! The marriage itself was abandoned midway through the groom's vows, as his wife-to-be declared that, having seen the length of *my* penis, she could never be married to anything less. Oh, it was quite the embarrassment. Be thankful you're not so awfully jinxed as I. I tell you, Baggy, there are very often times when I in fact miss my - what did you call it? My *baby penis?*"

It was easier to ignore Michael-Steve's embellishments as, if one were to point out how clearly artificial his attachment was, he would attempt to prove the naysayer wrong by urinating through it, out of a small hole he'd cut at the end. Having seen him do so twice to an audience of horrified officers in the dining cart of our train to Bristol, and out of respect for the nearby departed, I elected to avoid the spritzing of another performance.

We had come to be working together at the need of His Majesty, whose Special Operations Executive had determined that Michael-Steve Burrows, just as myself, would play a key role in Britain's fight for superiority in military intelligence. After I had escorted Joseph Darkfire off Father's boat, to the safety of medical aid, I reported back to my unit, expecting to return to the 701st Sanitation Company, to link back up with my friend Stephen Edgington. Instead, I was rushed to a tactical picnic in Hyde Park, which the now-Captain James Ferdinand Bambi was chairing as well as contributing a plate of flapjacks to the spread.

Also in attendance were Lieutenant Michael-Steve Burrows, naked as always, as well as a government representative from the Ministry of Secondhand Gossip, and an elderly, non-uniformed woman whom no one could recall inviting but had provided such a thoughtful array of pastries that it felt rude to eject her.

The moment I arrived, anger surged through me as I laid eyes upon the wretched fool who had destroyed my TV career, though I did my best to hold my tongue. Rather than mirror my maturity, Burrows attempted to discreetly operate a small hand pump which inflated his mud-ridden mock-cock to what was presumably supposed to resemble an erection.

"I know I can't speak on behalf of everyone else, but there's something about a fine English morning such as this that *really* gives me the horn," he commented as I sat down.

"What in God's name is *he* doing here?" I asked Bambi.

"I'm aware of your shared past, but there is no time for such pettiness in war, gentleman," James replied. "Lieutenant Burrows has shown impressive intuition and leadership in previous operations. You both have. And now fate has seen fit to unite the two of you. There will be forever after the conflict to refresh your disdain for each other, but you must realise that while hatred might seem an overwhelming emotion from inside, from outside, there are very few things smaller than it. Do you both understand?"

"With respect, Captain, I do not think you know the full breach of his man's treachery," I responded.

"With respect, Baggy, I do. I know that he destroyed your career. But I also know that I provided you with a new one. And I might also point out that you have irreversibly damaged his own sense of self," Bambi opined, indicating Michael-Steve Burrows' unconvincing appendage. "And you might well find that you've more in common than you initially thought."

I conceded that my old friend had made his point.

"But now, to business. First of all, I'd like to extend my thanks to you all for making the journey here on such short notice," said Bambi. "I would like to offer further gratitude to the people of the Ministry of Secondhand Gossip for taking the time to provide gluten-free items among their offering of freshly-baked savoury muffins for this most-vital tactical picnic. Whilst we have no celiacs present in the armed forces, due to how irksome they are, the incredible density of these goods will undoubtedly serve as a powerful and much-greener alternative for conventional ammunition as our current stocks gradually dwindle.

"I have summoned you here today to prepare for what might possibly be the most important operation of the entire war. It is said, the only way to truly defeat a serpent is to sever it at its head-"

"You could drown it," interrupted the elderly lady.

"What?"

"You could drown it, if you needed to."

"Right. Yes, I suppose you could-"

"Fire, also. You could put it in the oven. I highly doubt a snake would survive for too long in a hot oven," added the representative of the Ministry of Secondhand Gossip.

"Have you tried just humanely relocating the serpent? I mean, I'm sorry to be *that* person, but we don't have a great number of snakes. It's very unlikely that it would be venomous. There's a man in the phone book who'll do that for a small fee," suggested the woman.

"It... I... There's not an actual serpent."

"Well, it wouldn't be the first time someone has mistaken *this* for one," Michael-Steve Burrows chimed in, hoping again to draw attention to his penis. "And let me tell you, it most certainly shoots venom, if you'll indulge a little euphemism."

"Be quiet, all of you," Bambi ordered. "We are going to attempt to eliminate the head of the serpent *figuratively*, by removing the German Chancellor from power. It is the opinion of the S.O.E. that the German military is driven primarily by adoration of their Fuhrer, and that his retirement would irreparably compromise the structure and morale of the entire Wehrmacht."

"You specify 'retirement'," I interjected. "Why not simply have him assassinated?"

"He'll be martyred, should he die, which could well incite them further. They're a strangely-angry bunch over there and that is why we suspect this is a better option. If he were to die in office, someone would take his place. If he makes the decision to leave the position wilfully, people will assume the hours are bad or it's all a bit too stressful and not worth the salary, and hopefully they will call the whole thing off."

"That makes sense. So, what's the plan?"

"Operation Saltbeef," Bambi replied, pulling a package of dossiers from his tactical picnic hamper to disperse to each of us. For the next while, we sat on the tactical picnic blanket, reading through the briefing, with only the sound of the elderly woman's disapproving tutting breaking the silence.

To my mind, the plan was a masterpiece. Allied intelligence had confidently confirmed that the root cause of the German Chancellor's thirst for aggression was due to the insecurities that manifested following his rejection from a prominent art school. To cunningly exploit this, we were to find a dead body, dress it as a member of an admissions board for a popular university, and attach a briefcase to its wrist containing letters explaining that the only reason the Fuhrer's submission failed was because of his potential for genocide. Furthermore, we would hint heavily in the documentation that, should he actually provide evidence that he was a pretty decent chap at heart, he would be eligible for a scholarship at the Birmingham Guild of Handicraft.

Once we had disguised the corpse convincingly, we were to airdrop it from a hot-air balloon into a strategically-selected German hamlet and await its discovery. From there, it was expected that the documentation would quickly make its way up through the chain of command, and it would be only a matter of time until the Chancellor was made aware that all he had to do to get into art school would be to apologise and politely tell his armies to stop attacking the whole world.

And so it was that, only a couple of weeks later, I found myself in Bristol, digging up the body of a recently-deceased woman who had died with an outstanding library fine and was therefore owned by the British Government. Upon hearing that a corpse was required, I suggested dragging the English Channel for the remains of Clara St. Cloud, who would have been only too happy to have once again been contributing to the allied effort, however the team sent to find her brought the incorrect shoes and so the search was called off at the last moment.

With a final grunt, I heard the sound of the shovel hitting wood, and I climbed out of the grave. With the assistance of Michael-Steve and two lengths of rope, we hoisted the coffin out onto the grass and removed its lid. Fortunately, the corpse was in good condition as the woman's death happened shortly after she'd mistaken a bottle of epoxy resin for sunscreen prior to leaving the house for a day trip to Sandbanks. She was declared dead after she was found attached to a bus-seat hours later, perfectly embalmed and with a notably pleasing tan. The Minister of Defence had personally approved her appropriation after hearing that, in her so-recent living state, she had a reputation of being needlessly outspoken about the correct way to cook steak, and as such had no friends or family who might care to visit her grave and notice her absence.

We loaded the corpse onto our shoulders, carried her to a waiting motor car, and drove her to a nearby salon where British Intelligence's finest hair stylists were waiting to permit her one last makeover. Sadly, it was unlikely to be her most glamorous.

"We're going to do a poor job of dying her hair and give her the worst possible haircut we can manage," explained the technician.

"Why?" I asked.

"Because she needs to look like an artist."

"Is that common among artists?"

"Very."

"Why?"

"No one knows for sure."

"Right, what else?"

"For clothes, we found these scraps of mouldy denim that we're going to staple together to make trousers. For her torso, we've created a t-shirt with a reductive cartoon satirising a complex issue sequined onto it. As well as the decoy documentation, we're going to include a letter that implies she is in debt to a payday loan company and has been attempting to make repayments with vastly overvalued watercolours of her cat. And finally, we're going to give her two tattoos, the first being a reference to a piece of popular culture, and then a second follow-up tattoo on top of that suggesting that the piece of popular culture might not actually be something she ever enjoyed and that she was simply being ironic when getting the first one. Oh, and she'll also be wearing a beret."

By dawn, the corpse was reborn as Doctor Artemis Longhorn, Professor of Sculpture, Architecture and Advanced Glitter at the Yeovil Town Academy of Acceptable Art. The transformation was as convincing as it was morbid but we all agreed that, among the many reasons for one's lifeless body to be exhumed from its final resting place, an operation such as this was among the least perverted.

Mine and Michael-Steve's work was far from over. Our next objective involved travelling to Blackpool to hire a hot-air balloon, and although we managed the train trip with less embarrassment than our previous journey, it was quite difficult to explain to our fellow commuters as to why we had a freshly-painted corpse in our company. Eventually, Michael-Steve came up with the brilliant idea of responding to any inquiries of her presence with a compelling lie.

"Pay her no attention and save your concern. She has been recently exposed to jazz music and is in a fugue state." To this, onlookers would nod compassionately and cease all probing as to her inexplicably-terrible haircut.

We arrived at Blackpool Pleasure Beach and met with our contact; a dark-skinned, grey-haired, almost-mysterious man who asked that we refer to him as Switchblade. We declined, explaining that we did not find him quite mysterious enough for such a moniker due to his employee name badge that revealed his actual name to be Dwayne Lipton.

As per standard British military protocol, we had been provided with precisely half the amount of money required to achieve our goal and were expected to use our cunning and guile to fulfil the remaining amount required to hire the hot-air balloon from Dwayne. This time, it was I who concocted an ingenious scheme that involved drying out already-used tea bags that we found in bins and then reselling them to Australians who, well into the modern day, could seemingly not notice the difference. After two weeks of substantial profit, we exchanged our fledgling tea company for a four-day hire of Dwayne's hot-air balloon and prepared for the final stage of the mission.

The flight from Blackpool to the German town of Offenberg was approximately six hours' travel in desirable conditions, so we filled the basket with books, musical instruments, and bottles of wine so that we might be well-occupied. Worrying that we might still become bored to a state of inattentiveness, we invited three members of a travelling theatre troupe aboard to perform a condensed version of Macbeth. Michael-Steve Burrows warned further that, should the flight stretch for longer than anticipated, we ran the risk of becoming distractingly peckish, and thus ordered a week's worth of highland hams, cheeses and breads. In a rare moment of mutual respect, I acknowledged his foresight and complemented his efforts with the hire of a sommelier, pastry chef and a man who owned six differently-shaped cheese knives and would only let us borrow them if we dropped him off in Bordeaux.

As a result of our immaculate preparedness, when we finally took off, the hot-air balloon was only ever able to elevate twelve-foot off the ground. And so our flight from Black-

pool was more a tour of Western Europe, in which we floated through the high streets of England, fanned defensively
by concerned Britons away from their houses and toward
the general direction of Germany. When we bobbed over
the cliffs of Dover, we splashed lightly into the channel and
maintained just enough buoyancy to remain above the water,
though only after we'd ejected the sommelier and pastry chef
once lunch had been served.

By the time we had reached the French coast, we had eaten
and drank enough to have doubled our ascent and would have
quickly approached our destination had we not agreed that
three is simply not enough thespians to adequately perform
Macbeth, and so lowered a rope with a one-pound note attached at its end and fished for out-of-work actors. Four mime
artists later, we dragged once more along the cobblestones of
European boulevards, steering past obstacles by orchestrating
simultaneous cheese-belches as bursts of propulsion.

Finally, we approached the German border, to the annoyance of the man from Bordeaux who, once he realised we'd not
bothered to include his destination as a stop on our itinerary,
demanded to be lowered to the ground, which was currently
three metres away. But as we weighed his request against the
idea of simply murdering him, throwing him overboard and
using his cheese knives as payment for the actors who we had
learned, too late, were registered for equity, a most fascinating
thing happened.

As we entered enemy territory, a very sudden thermal
thrust pushed us upward, no doubt generated by German
smugness or some such phenomenon. Though it did not pro-
pel us to our mission's required height, it suddenly made the
effort of lowering our guest much more difficult, for we were
now floating at a considerably-more dangerous twenty-or-so
metres above the ground.

The gentleman had, by this point, overheard our discussions around the convenience of homicide, and had since then generously offered us the cheese knives as a gift, to which Michael-Steve and I were so deeply humbled that we acknowledged we could not bring ourselves to kill him, certainly not with all these opportunistic witnesses around.

So it was decided that the actors - desperate to prove their excellent physical condition - would climb out of the basket and form a human chain from our position in the sky to the surface of the earth, down which our guest could descend and hop safely off into the lush green countryside. Immediately, the actors stripped to their waists at the request of no one, and began assembling themselves into a ladder of clasped hands, wrists, ankles and feet.

As our guests straddled the side of the balloon's basket, I looked ahead of our trajectory and saw something of concern. Penetrating the crisp and verdant pastures below and before us was the brutal, grey-steel angles of electricity pylons and, while we were safely away from the erections themselves, between our altitude and the earth, powerlines hung at a height that would cut apart the living daisy-chain that precariously dangled from our vessel.

I attempted to capture my colleague's attention, but Burrows had become preoccupied by his ongoing insecurities about the dimensions of his masculinity.

"I say, Baggy, seeing us drifting up here with such a flesh-link that lags beneath us, it reminds *me* of a simple walk to the local market!"

"I suspect it does, since our protrusion is portrayed by actors," I wittily responded in my head, several hours later while having a bath.

My anxiety continued to rise as we reached closer to potential tragedy. The gentleman from Bordeaux had navigated down past four of the seven actors and was nearing a height that would allow him to safely disembark with only minimal injury. I called out to him to explain the urgency.

"Good sir! You must jump the last of the way! Look before us! Danger looms and we must preserve these other souls!"

By this time, Michael-Steve too had observed the impending disaster and joined my beckoning. In response, the gentleman looked up, presented us with an explicit gesture of his hand and then revealed, with his other, that he had dishonestly repossessed the cheese knives and had them hidden within his coat.

Now with no way to pay the actors and no concern for the life of the treacherous man from Bordeaux, Burrows and I agreed to desist compassion and see how things played out.

Firstly, we floated above the powerline and became caught against it approximately two actors down. As we came to a halt in the air, the gentleman continued his disembarkation and reached the last rung of the ladder. With a hand of his own still within one of the final thespians, he touched down onto the emerald pleasantry of rural Germany and ended his life there. The human tether formed a perfectly conducive arc between the power lines and the earth, and for the next agonising minute or so, every member of our organic landing gear sizzled into extinction.

At the moment of contact, I had been leaning over the basket, observing below, with my hand atop that of the first actor that clung to the rim, and it was only Michael-Steve Burrows' initiative to roughly grab me and pull toward the other side of the basket that permitted me to survive the moment. With the stench of cooking flesh dominating our attention, neither of us acknowledged until several months later that he had saved my life.

As death passed through it, the human ladder fell apart and dropped limply, piece by piece to the earth. With the sudden loss of encumbrance, Michael-Steve and I were whisked upward into the air, and immediately clambered to find the hot-air balloon's manual, which advised us on how to reduce our altitude before we rose too far for our lungs to manage.

Rendered sober by the trauma of the electrocution of eight men, we committed to comfort-eating the remaining food and agreed that it was only in the best interest of our mental integrity that we imbibe the remaining wine. Once replenished, we focussed on the operation at hand and left no more room for catastrophe.

Without further incident, we completed our mission and deposited the deception-laden Artemis Longhorn in the town of Offenberg, before returning hastily to England. We would learn later, that despite achieving our objective, the desired reaction from the German Chancellor would not end the war. Due to a turnover of administrative staff at the Birmingham Guild of Handicraft, when the Fuhrer eventually called to inquire about the promised scholarship, he was informed that they had no record of such an agreement and that he would be required to pay the standard ten-pound entry fee as per all other entrants. Inflamed by such indignity, the response from Berlin was to prematurely trigger an ill-advised winter offensive against Russia.

Nevertheless, Michael-Steve Burrows and I were hailed as heroes upon our return. Operation Saltbeef might not have been the catalyst for peace talks as had been hoped, but the unfortunate fatalities of those that comprised the human ladder had a silver lining. The strain that the grounding of the powerline had put upon the German electricity grid had caused significant downstream dramatics that had been intercepted by British Intelligence.

We both were presented with the coveted Medal of Squirrelly Deviousness in a ceremony that could only be described as 'having happened'. Immediately afterward, we were corralled into a room with top military brass, and also a man named Gavin, where we were exhaustively debriefed and asked as to how we'd managed to bring down such devastation upon the enemy's infrastructure. Hesitantly, we explained that we'd sacrificed the lives of approximately seven creatives and one foreigner, and while we initially worried that we might be court-martialed for such moral expenditure, we were soon reminded that we were dealing with predominantly conservative minds when they announced our initiative a resounding economic success.

Following Saltbeef, the S.O.E. immediately commenced acquisition of all available balloons in the home nations and began sending them floating from positions in France, across the border into Germany, to wreak complete chaos upon the electrical grid, as well as a multitude of hens nights back home who would now need to establish other means of festively portraying a penis. This new operation became so immediately successful at such minimal cost to the British government, that the human ladders of out-of-work actors were gradually replaced with simple tethers of copper, which were slightly more expensive to employ but weighed less.

CHAPTER TWENTY-TWO:

The Beginning of the
End of My Beginning

ollowing Operation Saltbeef, I felt grateful to be re-united with my old unit of the 701st and temporari-ly relieved of the tiresome company of Michael-Steve Burrows and his delusional protrusion. It would not be long before we would see more of each other, but several months passed without having to bear his sarcasm and insecurity, and in its place I was treated with the resumption of my friendship with Stephen Edgington.

During the unplanned intermission of my service, the squad of troops with whom I had travelled to Poland had not been resting on their laurels. While I had been whisked into the air by Clara St. Cloud and the machinations of James Ferdinand Bambi, the 701st had been pivotal to allied success, both in the field of war and upon its periphery.

At the time that I returned to the team, the company had been piloting an incredibly ambitious experiment - code-named The Glamorgan Project - to weaponise 'the pain of embarrassment', specifically in an effort to distil the exact feeling one experiences upon taking the stage to sing karaoke, to realise that they had only ever previously sung the chorus of the song they had chosen and were completely unfamiliar with everything in between. It was hoped that, should it be found possible to somehow physically metabolise that sense of total pathetic hopelessness, it could be deployed as a war-head against large groups of German soldiers who would shrug awkwardly and attempt to make light of their idiocy for about three and a half minutes, before ordering a taxi home, drinking two bottles of lower-shelf chardonnay, and crying themselves to sleep.

Unfortunately, just as a breakthrough had been made, the laboratory held its annual "Bring Your Child to Work Day" and a particularly inquisitive son of one of the lead scientists mistook an unattended vial of pure shame for sarsaparilla, thus swallowing six months of scientific discovery. The child survived and appeared to be unaffected at first but tragically, in what would years later be confirmed a direct result of the ingestion of music-related regret, grew up to become Tom Jones.

To our credit, much of the 701st's objectives involved ending the war in the most peaceful manner possible. Bloodshed and violence were always considered a barbaric last resort, to a point where the company adopted the motto "Let's settle this like we've got dinner reservations tomorrow" and employed the depiction of a Buddhist guide-dog play-bowing through a concentration camp in its insignia. As such, our strategies heavily involved psychological manipulation techniques intended to soften the enemy's mental resolve, rather than blast a hole through it.

This included a brilliantly-conceived plan of mine to pay celebrated actor Greta Garbo twenty pounds per week to attend German late-night chat shows and suggest that she was only sexually attracted to quitters. Following her inaugural appearance on a programme titled "Hallo Hallo, es ist Samstag", British Intelligence immediately intercepted reports of hundreds of enemy soldiers abandoning their posts, as well as evidence of a significant impact to the predominantly female-powered war industry due to women who had recently had enough time off from their husbands to determine that they were lesbians.

I suspected I might be in line for promotion, such was the operation's success, however the seemingly-inevitable collapse came when a tabloid newspaper photographed Garbo shoelessly playing footsies with Field Marshal Fedor von Bock in the garden of a bed-and-breakfast in Hamburg. The German general was declared dead a week later in suspicious circumstances, along with the effort to compel German attrition, my promotion, and his family. A month later, Greta Garbo re-emerged to the spotlight alongside a bearded, reportedly-mute lover named Todd Grunt and didn't mention another thing about the war on German TV.

Our attempts to prematurely end the conflict seemed to continuously come up short so, for a while, we shifted our focus to rescuing allied prisoners of war through ingenious means. Our methods were varied and mostly unfruitful, though we did get excruciatingly near to success by working with the scientists of American Intelligence, with whom we committed to discovering the complex system of pheromonal communication utilised by the common black ant hive.

We considered that, should we empower selected humans with the ability to communicate silently over vast distances, we could then coordinate prison escapes with minimal risk and baffle the enemy with our apparently magical intuition, similarly to how the Royal Air Force had managed the invention of radar. Sadly, little came from this as key personnel resigned from their positions, fled the country and used the technology to sell small tubes of questionable perfume in airport bathroom vending machines. Edgington and I both agreed to apply what remained of the pheromones to ourselves, to see if we could communicate in a manner similar to ants, but after several days of exposure we felt completely unchanged beyond an increasing desire to walk in single file to the capital city of the nearest matrilineal monarchy and attempt to fuck their Queen.

Despite the less-than-excellent results of our endeavours, the S.O.E. acknowledged the intellectual ingenuity of the 701st Sanitation Company and saw fit to reassign us to the thriving boffin hub of Bletchley Park. We were permitted to set up a workspace in Hut 21, provided we vacated it on Friday evenings so the weekly regimental drag bingo night could go ahead as per normal, but we made cunning use of our quarters' ulterior designation following a chance meeting with a curious young lady named Mavis Davis.

Edgington and I quickly accepted that decrypting German communication wasn't our greatest strength, and instead spent much of our time designing a conversational card game aimed at couples living within failing marriages. However, we soon realised something was amiss about Hut 21 and began to notice strange goings-on that suggested we weren't the only ones calling the building home. In the mornings, we would find papers had moved in the night, crumbs were found on tables, and a floral scent lingered in the air upon our arrival each day. In addition to these small clues, it also appeared that someone was gradually assembling a two-tonne, special-purpose supercomputer that eventually took up approximately two-thirds of the floor space.

Initially, we assumed it to be the work of mice, and so set up several traps about the place, baited with an expertly-curated selection of midlands cheese. After two days without result, we considered that perhaps our lure was too sophisticated for the rodents of Buckinghamshire and replaced the dairy product with a single Chesterfield cigarette upon each device. The effect was immediate.

The next morning we arrived to find a shy, young blonde girl writhing in discomfort and a cloud of cheap tobacco smoke. Once we had unhooked her from the contraption and apologised, she introduced herself. Mavis, we discovered, was currently working out of Hut 7, but had dreams of something greater, and so she had been sneaking into our workspace at night to build a computer, called "Brilliant Tim", capable of deciphering the most complex of German encryption.

Edgington and I, fully aware that we were spectacularly failing to earn our keep at Bletchley, immediately asked if there was any way we might help and get some sort of credit for doing so.

Davis then educated us on the basics of codebreaking and computer processing, of digital analysis, of pattern recognition, and complex cypher decryption, and then showed us how feeding a punch card into her supercomputer made a satisfying 'ding' sound. It was this last part that Edgington and I found we excelled at. Mavis Davis went on to explain that each punchcard represented an intricate alphabetical sequence, and depending on the arrangement of holes in accordance to a relevant letter in the alphabet, and the time of day, and the current temperature, and the mood of the cypher operator, and several other factors, Brilliant Tim would either emit the aforementioned satisfying ding when the output was invalid, or a truly orgasmic gong sound when a code had been successfully broken.

In pursuit of this mysterious and desirable audio, my colleague and I enthusiastically hatched yet another ingenious example of our seemingly-endless resourcefulness. The very next Friday, we attended the company drag bingo event and convinced its participants to use a hole punch rather than their usual felt-tip marker to record their results onto playing cards that we had fashioned into the precisely-required format necessary to allow them to be fed into Brilliant Tim. By the evening's end, we had several hundred completely randomised punchcards that could be interpreted alongside a piece of German encryption. Stephen and I were both elated at our success, and only slightly dampened upon Davis' revealing that, statistically, we would need millions more to get a result using purely random input.

Despite Mavis' less-than-hopeful response, Edgington and I were not men to be easily disheartened, especially when the Bletchley Park quartermaster had started poking his head around to ask nosy questions such as "What exactly are you doing in here?" and "Who the hell is ordering two hundred pounds worth of midlands cheese every week?"

And so we conferred with the host of drag bingo, a sultry, well-breasted and long-legged Scotsman who went by the stage name Roberta the Bruce, and allowed for us to pilot a marketing campaign for the weekly event. After learning that Greta Garbo was still on His Royal Majesty's payroll, we arranged the upping of the celebrity's fee to thirty-pound per week in exchange for her agreeing to be tattooed upon her lower back with the most scientifically seductive phrase British Intelligence could develop. Following the permanent application of the words "Bingo participants loosen my taps, thus moistening my most treasured succulent" onto the starlet's spine, attendance exploded so vastly that a relocation to a larger venue was necessary and, after three months, Roberta the Bruce and his end-of-week bingo act were comfortably filling Kenilworth Road stadium in Luton with an average audience of just over ten-thousand. Such were the ticket sales that Luton Town Football Club's sponsors insisted the team played their games at the same time so that their advertisements might finally be viewed by someone.

A priceless expression of astonishment conquered the face of Mavis Davis when we first arrived on a Monday morning with a sack of over one hundred thousand punch cards, which we dutifully entered into Brilliant Tim over the course of the next days, eagerly anticipating the forthcoming, elusive gong of revelation. Davis was however correct in her estimation, and we continued to collect and process well over five million punch cards over the next weeks with only the moderately-satisfying sound effect as our reward.

Our prize was eventually delivered on a dreary, rainful Wednesday evening, at a point when morale had reached something of a low. Mavis Davis was absent during most of the day while she attended to her normal duties in Hut 7, and so it was only myself and Stephen present at the pivotal moment. It was my turn to process punch cards and manage the supercomputer, while Edgington enjoyed his cheese break and examined a magnifying glass through another, larger magnifying glass in an attempt to discover how they worked.

Muscle memory had reduced the task of entering punch cards to an almost automated routine, and my mind was elsewhere. The rhythmic ding that announced an unfruitful translation had become as unnoticeable as my own heartbeat. But something peculiar happened when I reached for a particular card. It had nothing unique about it to suggest specialty, and I recall no memorable detail upon it, yet hairs pricked on my neck as soon as I retrieved it from the pile. I recall the expectancy I felt when I fed it into Brilliant Tim.

There was a longer pause than usual after the click of the mechanism accepting the punch card; a piece of silence so loud that I noted Stephen's head snap up to observe. We were then both treated to the warmest, most wondrous gong that a human ear could hope to be breached by. We turned to face each other with broad grins on our faces and Edgington raced over to the machine, keen to observe the imminent output.

With little other ceremony, Brilliant Tim gave a mechanical screech as it printed the deciphered message onto a piece of paper. I removed the script from the tray and read it aloud to my colleague.

"Do not eat the yoghurt that we sent last Wednesday. It is two months past its best-before date."

"My god, Baggy. We've done it."

"Almost, Stephen. I suspect there's more to this. The Germans wouldn't send such plain phrasing. We've more to inspect before Mavis arrives."

"Yes, you're right."

Together, we settled in for a night of deduction and by the time the sun had begun to rise on the following Thursday, the two of us felt supremely confident in our conclusion. The "yoghurt", we hypothesised, represented the Luftwaffe, as yoghurt is high in probiotics in much the same way that aeroplanes are often high in the air. This was a message clearly intended to reach the frontlines of the German formation currently attempting a counter-attack in the Ardennes, advising to hold off from attempting to recover air superiority for "two months".

Satisfied with our interpretation, Stephen and I felt ready to approach High Command with our intel. I suggested to my colleague that we verify our findings with Mavis Davis but Edgington, citing his commitment to feminism, insisted on excluding her so as to not expose the poor girl to the inherent misogyny present in the upper echelons of the British military, and so we decided that the morally correct thing to do was to tell everyone we'd built the supercomputer and solved the whole thing ourselves.

When we requested an audience with the highest-tier executives of Bletchley Park, I was remiss to discover that Michael-Steve Burrows had once again wormed a path into my existence. Somehow, he had charmed his way into a position directly above me, and it was before he and several others that we had to deliver the news that Brilliant Tim was now capable of deciphering the secrets of the German war machine.

"Baggy Smacker! Still haunting the corridors of British Intelligence somehow? I swear, you could almost hear the thud of the collective IQ drop as you entered the room," Burrows scowled. Despite our recent collaborations, the disdain we felt for each other had in no way diluted.

"I'm sure you could, Michael-Steve. And I'll wager a very different mean average dropped as *you* arrived," I savagely retorted, gesturing to that which dangled grubbily between his legs.

The inner chamber of Bletchley Park, to which we had been summoned for our presentation, was squalid yet dignified, much like the three well-decorated, older men who sat before us upon Edwardian-period beanbags. Such was their high position in the S.O.E, we were not told their names or rank, yet their esteem was clear, as was the fact that they were taking our discovery very seriously and were in no mood to host further back and forth between two unforgiving rivals. So despite noticing the latest manifestations of Michael-Steve's insecurities about his member - an ear piercing, a tattoo of a wolf on his left bicep, and a t-shirt emblazoned with the logo of his favourite mixed-martial arts brand - I proceeded with introductions.

"Gentleman, I am Sapper Smacker and this is Lieutenant Edgington of the 701st Sanitation Company. I acknowledge that you are busy men, and I will get directly down to business. We believe we have developed a supercomputer that can de-crypt German cypher. Further-to-this, our first clear transla-tion of an intercepted enemy message, received approximately six weeks ago, indicates that we have a two-week period of air superiority in the Ardennes before the Germans are able to resupply the Luftwaffe and potentially assault our lines from on high."

The gentlemen shifted noisily in their beanbags and glanced at each other. Michael-Steve was the first to respond.

"Nonsense. You expect us to believe that you two, with no background in code-breaking, have somehow done in a few weeks what we have not been able to achieve in months?"

"It's true," Stephen chimed in.

Burrows' jealousy became so almighty that he quickly wet himself before breaking into a fit of tears so great that a maid needed to be sent to warm a bottle of milk and fetch his fa-vourite blanket. Once he had been calmed and made decent through the use of a moistened towel, the discussion resumed and the best course of action was decided upon.

An unnamed signalman appeared in the chamber short-ly after Michael-Steve's commotion and received orders to immediately contact the General in command of the allied frontline that was currently stretched throughout the wintry forests of Belgium and Luxembourg. We were aware that the situation on the ground was dire; supplies were constrained, morale was at its lowest, and results from the employee satisfaction surveys that had been sent out to troops indicated several thousand were considering resigning from their jobs so they might backpack around the parts of the world that weren't currently being shot at. Nevertheless, the revelations of Brilliant Tim were undeniable; there was not much time to move before the enemy could regain its advantage, and so the forces were soon convinced to mobilise.

Stephen Edgington, Michael-Steve Burrows and I spent the next several days amidst the bustle of the S.O.E's signal room, intently listening to radio chatter cast from the chaos of the distant Ardennes. In the first couple of days, we anticipated each situation report to be well-padded with tales of victory, but though there were some in the initial hours, the momentum shifted darkly.

Nearly all allied advances were thwarted by a confident enemy defended by an ostensibly well-equipped air force, and the optimism in the war room quickly turned to shock. Michael-Steve could not have been more delighted.

"Oh my, what an unfortunate surprise. Baggy Smacker has failed once again! Who could possibly have foreseen such a thing?" He smiled whilst smugly twirling his prosthetic penis around and around, inadvertently treating our shame-reddened faces to a cool but ham-smelling breeze. I could not identify precisely what, but I felt supremely confident that Burrows was somehow at the foot of this disaster, though there was no way to be sure.

We were sternly commanded to return to Hut 21 and feed more interceptions to Brilliant Tim, in an effort to garnish further understanding of enemy communication and, as they printed one by one, Stephen and I slowly uncovered more detail.

"*Actually, the strawberry yoghurt should be fine, just mind the others*," read one translation.

Another, "*Wait, can yoghurt even really go off? It's already technically kind of off, isn't it? That's the entire point of it. It's a bit like cheese. Though, wait, cheese can go mouldy. Hang on, let me ask Kevin.*"

"*Oh wait, the use-by date is in American format. Well, that makes sense, seeing as we only bought it the other week. It's fine. It was probably fine anyway, Kevin reckons 'use-by' and 'best-before' dates are different, and he used to work on a dairy farm, so he knows his yoghurt. 'Pudding of the morning' he calls it. So, yeah, have at that yoghurt. Not sure anyone died from eating yoghurt that's slightly off anyway. Oh, before I forget, the assault on the allied frontlines is good to kick off whenever you've got the time. Everything is in place logistically so it should all go really, really well,*" read the last message we printed before accepting that we had possibly misinterpreted the sentiment of the first.

Stephen and I were summoned once again to the inner chamber of Bletchley Park, though only I was foolish enough to attend. Edgington called ahead and advised that he was suffering "a gentleman's period" and therefore couldn't make the severe dressing down, so it was I alone who was to receive the reprimand. Had it only been a stern condemnation and dismissal on the grounds of incompetence, I would have perhaps felt it fair, but the committee of high-ranking officers had other ideas in store.

Michael-Steve Burrows was once more in attendance, attired in an expression of impenetrable satisfaction, having witnessed what he correctly assumed to be the second-greatest humiliation of my life long after he had been the architect of the first. He burbled joyfully as I entered the room and took my place opposite the cold, grey figures nestled in their antique beanbags.

"Well if it isn't-" he began, before being abruptly told to shut up by one of the older men.

I was then subjected to a fierce dressing-down by the gentlemen of the highest authority, and over the next forty-eight hours, my morale plummeted to an all-time low. For a moment, it appeared my career in military intelligence had crumbled to nothing and I expected to be court-martialed due to incompetence at any moment.

With depression rearing its head, in a moment of futility, I called my father in the hopes that some paternal instinct might summon any form of comfort from him.

"Are you considering suicide?" he interrupted as I had begun to put my torment into words.

"No, Father."

"Let me know if you change your mind. I know a man who does it and he's brilliant. And cheap. Gregory Carrot, is his name. You've possibly seen his adverts in the church newsletter."

"How can he be brilliant at suicide if he's still alive?"

"Oh, I'm sorry, do you think you know more about killing yourself than Gregory Carrot does?"

"I'm just saying, Father, if Gregory Carrot is still walking the earth, then how could he be considered successful at not being so."

"See, this is the problem with your generation. You think you know everything. You think just because you can go down to the local library and read a book about shooting yourself in an unimportant toe, or making a noose from pasta, or throwing yourself off an unambitious treehouse, *that* makes you an expert. As it happens, he's more into the theory side of things, rather than the practical and he's very highly regarded. You remember my acquaintance, Pipsy? *He* used Gregory Carrot for his suicide."

"Pipsy's dead?"

"Not entirely. Mostly. Any day now, his wife says. But that doesn't mean he's not a very satisfied customer nonetheless. I'll let Gregory Carrot know you're thinking about it."

"I'm not thinking about it."

"Baggy, he's got a sale on, and you'll only regret it if you end up having to pay more later when you've changed your mind," he said before hanging up.

Not long after, I was recalled once more to a hearing of higher powers and I was certain that my dismissal, and perhaps worse, were to be declared. As I arrived, I noticed that Stephen was nowhere to be seen. And while Michael-Steve Burrows was present, he did not seem to be in the same position as before.

As with each appearance to this council of the elite, I waited anxiously in a small antechamber, ahead of the meeting room. I was thumbing through the same magazine as I had done on each occasion before; an 1896 edition of a periodical called "The Blossoming Bint". I found myself rereading a particularly interesting article debating whether or not it might be helpful for Britain to raise the term limit for optional abortion to one-thousand, two-hundred and forty-eight weeks, at which point it could be safely determined whether or not the child had grown to be tedious. As I did so, Michael-Steve Burrows entered the chamber approximately a minute after his ghastly body odour did.

I noted, as he arrived, he had acquired additional tattoos, including one on his left ankle that declared he would rather be fishing and another, on his right, featuring a picture of two crossed fishing rods, along with stylised embossing of the words "Carpe Diem" with the last letter of each word crossed out. I found the latter to be annoyingly clever and so resisted the urge to draw attention to either.

"You appear to be running late. The others have already entered," I informed.

For a small second, Michael-Steve Burrows' normally concrete facade of confidence faltered.

"No, I am on time. Think of it what you will, but I have not been summoned here for counsel."

"Perhaps you have something to answer for?"

"What are you implying?"

"Our intel was delivered to the Generals by yourself, correct?"

"It was indeed," he replied, his lips curling into a wicked smile.

"And what precisely did you tell them?"

"Oh, I simply passed on the information you and your colleague so cleverly deciphered. And insisted they act upon it without a second thought."

"Are you really so petty that you would risk defeat simply because my achievements were close to out-shadowing your own?"

"Oh Baggy, I have no idea what you're talking about," he grinned.

Tempting though it was to pierce further, I was much too nervous of my own situation to stimulate our rivalry. Instead, I placed the magazine beside me and stared at the wall, counting down the minutes as we both waited.

Eventually a door opened, and an aide leant through to advise that we were to be seen. Tentatively, we entered to a smaller assembly than previously; just two distinguished gentlemen, only one of whom I could recall having met before.

"Gentlemen, take a beanbag," he commanded. After several minutes of rustling and adjustment, Burrows and I signalled our readiness, and I braced for termination.

"Sapper Smacker, your recent performance has not only been unsatisfactory, you have completely jeopardised the allied war effort. Not only that, but you've made us all look incredibly silly. Have you considered how silly we all feel?"

I admitted that I had not.

"It's difficult to properly articulate how silly we've all been made to feel," the officer continued. "In front of the Americans too. Johnson, tell Smacker what the Americans told you the other day."

The second gentleman reached into his shirt pocket and retrieved a folded piece of paper that he proceeded to open and read from.

"*Dear Nerds. Just a thought; In the future, maybe get better at war? It's your choice obviously, but it's worth consideration. Feel free to drop me a line if you'd like any tips on how to not completely fucking suck. Sincerely, General D. Eisenhower.*"

"You see? We were so close to being their friends but instead you've gone and made us look silly. We were going to have the Americans over for drinks on Friday and rub it in France's face, but they've now made up some excuse about having a headache because they think we're too silly to hang out with. Now it will just be us and the fucking Canadians. Some party that will be."

I wasn't sure how to respond, and so bowed my head and resorted to contemplative silence. The officer sighed.

"You need to fix this," he declared bluntly.

I detected the first hints of redemption and snapped my eyes to his.

"How?" I asked.

The gentleman gestured at Johnson to respond.

The second officer began to struggle out of his beanbag and, several minutes later, finished doing so. He approached a wooden chest in the rear of the room. From it, he produced a deflated beach ball painted to represent a globe and returned to the group, apologising for recent budget cuts. Once we had taken turns to breathe air into it, he placed it on the ground in front of us with northern France pointing upward.

"The premature advances triggered by your poor intel have resulted in an over-extended frontline here through the Ardennes. While our losses have been significant, the structure of allied lines has almost been completely restored. The Americans have dug back into their original positions, they're fortifying supply lines at the rear and, as of last transmission, have already successfully reopened two McDonald's restaurants and an artisan bakery. For our part, all battalions have regrouped and replenished, with the exception of the 9th Army, who are all but cut off approximately two miles ahead of the line and have lost radio contact. We know, from intercepted messages, that the Germans are aware of this and that they intend to surround the battalion in the coming days. Should they succeed and isolate the 9th, we will have an irreparable hole in the line that the enemy will undoubtedly overwhelm and use to flank the entire allied structure from the rear. If they do so, there is little doubt that the line will capitulate. It is not an exaggeration to suggest that losing that battalion could cost us the war."

"How do we reestablish communication with them?" Michael-Steve Burrows asked.

"Discreetly. Any attempt to move a considerable force through the forest is going to play into German hands. If we risk stretching out our lines once more, given the current situation, they will almost certainly launch an assault which could speed up their decision to make a move on the 9th. So instead, you two will drop into Antwerp and go find the missing battalion. Once you've found them, you will radio back to command and coordinate their retreat to safety."

"This sounds dangerous," I thought out loud.

"It will be," replied Johnson. "But you owe it to the world to fix your mistake."

"And Burrows? What is the reason for including him?"

"Despite your reported differences, you seem to be able to work well as a team. The success of this mission is paramount. You are both brilliant soldiers, doubly so when in co-operation. Also, we find him incredibly irritating. You can't let him out of your sight for thirty seconds without him trying to swallow something."

I turned to my side, to gauge Michael-Steve's reaction but found he was not where I expected him to be. Instead, I saw he had travelled across the room, burbling gleefully, apparently determined to engage in leisure with a wall plug.

I lowered my voice and whispered to Johnson.

"I have my suspicions that Burrows might be working *for* the Germans."

"What do you base this on?" Johnson asked.

"Hatred, mostly."

"Well, Smacker. Best to keep your enemies where you can see them. I will make note of your reservations but unless you've anything concrete, he's going with you."

"And why not Stephen Edgington? He was also responsible for Brilliant Tim's inaccuracy."

"Edgington and the rest of the 701st have already been deployed to the frontline to fill the gaps. It's all hands on deck right now. We've even been forced to create a makeshift division from members of the Territorial Army's piano accordion orchestra, much to the relief of those back home. And we're so low on supplies, we've not been able to arm them properly. We've just given them orders to play the Warsaw Concerto on repeat and hope that's enough to keep the enemy at bay."

"I understand. So once we're in the Ardennes, how do we find the missing battalion?"

"We expect them to be in this region here," Johnson said, circling an area on the tactical beachball with his index finger. "There are approximately two-hundred men there, led by a Captain Lavender."

The name perked my ears.

"Lavender?"

"Yes, eccentric fellow. Worked in television before the war, I believe."

"I think I know him."

"By all accounts, he's popular with the men."

"More than you know."

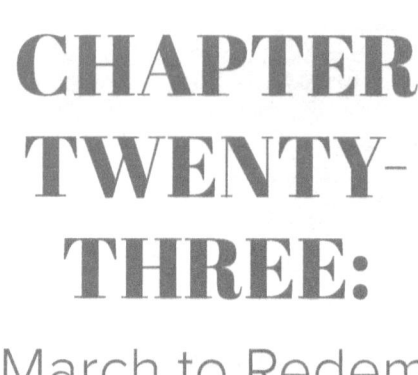

CHAPTER TWENTY-THREE:

The March to Redemption

hortly after we were dismissed, Michael-Steve Burrows and I were ordered to report to the company quartermaster and ready ourselves for an imminent airdrop into Belgium, though it turned out he had taken the week off because his cat had recently become diabetic, so we instead forwarded our condolences and made our way to the nearest R.A.F. airfield with only a two-way radio set and a single rifle between us.

As we boarded the civilian plane that had been chartered to fly stealthily over Antwerp and jettison us at altitude, I confronted Michael-Steve one last time.

"Know that I am watching you, Burrows. I know you've been seeking revenge since the moment we first engaged. And I am aware that your envy, your jealousy, your insecurity knows not a single constraint. You would gladly put at risk all of decent society in the vain quest for the perverted justice you seem to crave."

"Oh, Baggy. You are paranoid. Do you think I would risk losing the war, simply to crush you further? If the Germans win, well, I would obviously excel in the society they seek to create but…" Michael-Steve paused while he theatrically patted down his pockets and feigned confusion. "Oh, would you look at that? I can't think of a single caveat!" He smiled menacingly and climbed aboard.

Two hours later, we soared above the border between Belgium and Luxembourg, eyeing what we hoped to be Antwerp; a city we were assured was in total control of allied forces. Given the friendly occupation, we inquired with our civilian pilot as to why he could not simply land, to which he explained that he was only on his learner's permit and was not permitted to do so until he'd passed his final exam. We offered our understanding immediately before he triggered the side doors to snap open. The change in air pressure ripped us out of the aircraft into the chilling European sky, and we were confronted quite quickly by the realisation that, due to the quartermaster's absence, we had not equipped parachutes. Thankfully, midway toward the ground, we were intercepted by a particularly bureaucratic customs agent who refused to allow us to fall at a terminal velocity into Belgian airspace without observing our visa documents and evidence of a follow-on flight. By the time his sense of registry had been satisfied, we were a safe two metres above the ground and completed our landing with minimal bruising.

We made our way to a command post a short mile from the Antwerp city centre, where we strained to squeeze further supplies from the resident commander. Despite the importance of our mission, arms and equipment were in too high demand, and we were unable to acquire a second rifle. Only by helping an officer find his missing keys, did we manage even to arrange transport, in the form of a military-grade tandem bicycle. Our confidence became compromised as we faced the futility of our expedition, but neither of us voiced our fears and instead we pushed on from Antwerp, into the densely-forested Ardennes region.

Manoeuvring the tandem bicycle proved challenging, due to the rough terrain and the lack of front-facing basket in which to store our supplies. Cunningly though, I played Burrows' insecurities to our advantage and cheekily suggested that, should his penis truly be so vast, he should easily be able to store our food and weapons within his foreskin. After some short reluctance and a quick slathering of coconut oil, our burdens were neatly packaged and presumably quite waterproofed, and we headed once more into the woods.

The Ardennes was eerily quiet, other than for distant birdsong and our occasional, bellowing requests for them to play something more modern. For hours and hours, we slogged across the forest floor, relying upon a faulty compass for direction. The officer who had offered it to us had warned of its inaccuracy, but it was not until we embarked that we thought to open its case only to see a constantly swaying, presumably-northward-pointing arrow along with the words "I've got a reasonably good feeling about this" etched into its face.

Before long, it became clear we were lost and, even worse, almost certainly beyond no man's land and well into enemy territory. More and more so, we passed evidence of German presence; at first just small things such as an infrequent "Wilhelm voz here" or "Heinz luvs Richter 4eva" scratched into the bark of a tree but, soon enough, undeniable traces of recent occupation in the form of half-eaten, still-warm strudel and discarded pages of written theory on how to apply pressure in the final third of a football pitch immediately after losing possession.

Our progress stalled as our ears pricked to every sound and our eyes snapped to every flutter of tree branch or bush leaf. We agreed to stop screaming at birds with our fullest volume and cease aggressively ringing the bell on the tandem bicycle every time we passed a jogger.

As we trudged onward, we found ourselves weaving between trenches and foxholes; not dug by men, but formed makeshift from the craters of artillery. A short while later, we approached the edge of a clearing and gasped. The hellscape before us shocked me to my core and scarred upon me a trauma I would carry for the rest of my life.

Parts of bodies were everywhere. Blood was splashed about the place as if it had rained from the clouds, and the earth was embossed with deep incisions from bombardment. The nationality of the deceased was impossible to determine, and the few bodies not torn apart had been stripped of their clothing and weapons. Also, oddly, within the centre of the clearing was an ice cream stand, attended by a tall, blonde man wearing an apron. A small a-sign declared that we had arrived within opening hours.

"This is peculiar," I advised.

"I agree," replied Burrows. "Who would want to purchase ice cream in winter?"

I strained my eyes for anything that might unravel this mysterious confectioner but nothing glared back. He had not yet noticed our presence as we were quietly nestled behind a small bush at the clearing's side, and so he shuffled idly behind his counter, most probably silently considering the difference, if any, between gelato and sorbet.

"Should we engage him, or circumvent?" I asked Michael-Steve.

"*You* should engage him, Baggy. Ask him if he has seen the missing battalion. And ask him if he does banana while you're there."

"Something does not seem right here."

"Baggy, we're deep into German territory with a highly-critical mission on our hands that simply cannot fail; This is not the time for your paranoia and over-analysis. If we're to freeze in our tracks every time we pass an oddly-located, independent confectionery outlet, we're never going to get through Belgium. For the love of God, Baggy, ask the man if he's seen allied soldiers. And ask him if the banana has bits in it."

Slowly, I stood from behind the bush and waved my hand toward the gentleman.

"Hello, there!" I greeted.

The man spun around to see me and waved back.

"Goedemorgen!" he replied in Dutch.

"What are you doing here?" I asked.

"What?"

"What are you doing here?"

"Uh, chocolade, vanille, aardbei, rotsachtige weg, bananen-rimpel en ofwel mango-gelato of mangosorbet. Ik weet niet zeker wat het verschil is, om eerlijk te zijn."

"Do you speak English?"

"English?"

"Yes, do you speak English?"

"My English is poor. You will need to come close."

"Why will that help?"

"You must come close. My English is poor. It cannot go so far. You come here."

I turned to Michael-Steve.

"I sense something sinister afoot."

"You might be right. Best we quickly ask him if he's seen the battalion and be on our way. Don't worry about the banana ice cream, I'll find some elsewhere. Just go to him."

Burrows' insistence was not extinguishing my concerns.

"Why do you want me to enter that clearing, so desperately?"

"Baggy, for the last time. I am not conjuring any scheme. I am your comrade. I know we've had our differences, but I am not trying to get you killed. I am pleading with you, as safely and as quickly as you can, to ask this odd gentleman if he has sold any product to any of the two-hundred British troops lost in these woods."

I was not satisfied, but I saw little other option. Carefully, I stepped across the bloodied dead, over burnt splinters of wood, over lifeless eyes and severed limbs, expecting with each step to hear the click of a landmine or snap of a tripwire. But eventually, without incident, I reached the centre of the clearing and looked directly into the eyes of the ice cream man.

"Good morning," he said. "A lovely day for ice cream, don't you think?"

"What are you doing here?"

"Netherlands finest ice cream. Chocolate, vanilla, strawberry, banana-ripple-"

I interrupted.

"I mean, why *here*? Why have you set up your stand in the middle of a warzone?"

The man glanced around, at the corpses and chaos about the clearing.

"This is not food court of shopping centre?"

"No this is not the food court of a shopping centre."

"Hmm," he grunted. "In Netherlands, food-court of shopping centre very busy. Very angry place. Very violent. It is the queues, you see. Always so long."

The hairs on the back of my neck stood to attention. I immediately knew something was very, very wrong, and that I was in danger. At that moment, I realised foolishly that Michael-Steve Burrows had our supplies in his foreskin, including our only firearm.

"The Netherlands, you say?"

"Ja."

"So, this ice cream of yours... I must ask, for I have an intolerance to lactose. Do you have vegan options?"

"Sorry, we do not. Only dairy. But it is the finest that the Dutch have to offer."

"Dairy? Cow's milk only?"

"Yes, sir. Good, old, traditional cow's milk," he said with the first hints of impatience and with narrowing eyes.

"Cow's milk?"

"Cow's milk," stated the man. For a split-second, I saw his confidence waiver and heard his dialect ever-so slightly break rank.

"I have a friend with dairy interests in the Netherlands," I said.

"Do you?" His eyes narrowed.

"I do. And The Mooist Insurgency has been most unkind to their production. Devastating, in fact. It has almost completely destroyed the availability of cow's milk. And yet *you* appear to be well stocked with the Netherlands' finest dairy. In a clearing. In the forest. Surrounded by the recently deceased. *Pretending to be someone you're not.*"

"That's retail for you-" he began, but I had glimpsed his hand slip beneath the counter and reacted before he could finish his sentence.

I saw a flash of grey metal and immediately swung my fist toward his chin, connecting perfectly. For a second he was stunned and I took the opportunity to leap over the benchtop as he staggered back. In his hand was a Luger P08, and as he regained clarity, his arm raised to point it at me.

I snapped a glance back to the edge of the clearing, hoping to see Michael-Steve Burrows raising his own weapon, but instead observed him standing aside a disembodied torso, comparing its penis length with his own and comforting himself with mutterings about the unfair advantages of rigour mortis.

I turned back to the fray in time to see my adversary aiming his gun. He pulled the trigger but thankfully there was no whip-crack or muzzle flash to signal my end. With great relief, I observed that his pistol had outlived its complimentary thirty-day trial period and that, to continue, he would need to enter his credit card details. As he fumbled for his wallet, I grabbed him by both wrists and thrust my right knee into his gentleman's cranny, bending him in two with the agony, but still he maintained a grip on the weapon.

All too quickly, the ice cream man regained his composure and posture. With a wicked thud, he headbutted me viciously, and blood began to gush from a gash above my eye. As I stood stunned, he wrestled one wrist from my grasp; all that he needed to snatch a telephone from atop his counter and begin dialling Luger's sales hotline.

Suspecting that his knowledge of the violent etiquette of European food courts might stem from a genuine background in retail, I once again invoked the mysterious power of ancient Latin runes and requested to speak to his manager.

"Cūrātōrem tuum alloquar!" I compelled him with my fullest bellow.

Previously, this incantation had dealt me well, but on this occasion the treacherous ice cream man simply stopped dialling for a short moment, smiled and looked me in the eye.

"You utter fool! Look around you! I *am* the manager." He cackled, before bringing the handset to his ear. I could hear the muted, muffled automated message advise him that he was second in queue, and knew I had to act swiftly.

With all the ferocity I could muster, I swung at his stomach. The impact was well-placed, and his mouth snapped open via a painful gasp that turned to wheezing. I turned to his counter and grabbed the ice cream ladle of the least-requested and therefore fullest container; chocolate mint. With a flick of my wrist, I scooped an immense serving directly into his agape lips.

His reaction was typical of any sane recipient of chocolate mint ice cream; immediately one of pleasure, then slight disdain. Without missing a beat, I scooped another load into his mouth. And then another. And then another. And gradually my intention became clear to him.

His brow furrowed and his eyes widened as the ice cream headache began to form. The man wheezed in fright as I piled another load of disappointing iced confection into his mouth, and the freezing pain grew increasingly insufferable. He shook his head as he looked into my eyes, and silently begged for mercy.

Prior to this moment, I had not taken another human life. When I had signed on to the 701st, for some reason I had not considered that I would need to do so. When I was younger, I had thought myself an eternal pacifist. I had baulked at the idea of the military when it first presented itself as an option. In my youth, the merest hint of violence disgusted me.

Yet, as I stood in a clearing of the Ardennes, miles from the comfort of home, delivering scoop after scoop into the ajar mouth of a deceptive but otherwise perfectly normal German man, I felt nothing. By this point, I had emptied the two-litre container of chocolate mint into my opponent and had moved on to a box of lime gelato. My mind raced with a thousand thoughts, at once committed to killing a man whose name I did not know, and also attempting to pinpoint exactly which traumatic life moment had killed off my sense of humanity.

Was it having my career destroyed on live television, in front of the entire audience of the BBC? Was it having my heart broken by Clotilda, and having the piercing sneer of her evil twin sister tattooed on my soul? Or was it watching my beloved friend, Clara St. Cloud, plummet into the English Channel to her all-too-premature death? Was it all of the above, along with every other hardship that had compounded over the course of my life into a hammer force that had blunted the outer edges of my youth?

I did not know then, and I still don't know now. What I *do* know is that I continued to serve ladle upon ladle of frozen dessert into that ill-fated man, until his ice cream headache became paralysing and he fell to the ground. And then I continued, through more varietals. As I pummelled his tongue with tutti-frutti, his eyes began to bulge with the pain. When I finished that, I reached for a container of chocolate honeycomb, and his face turned the most scarlet red. Eventually, despite his pleas, I finished off with a mango sorbet and discovered the answer to the age-old question of what happens when one continues to eat ice cream amid an ice cream headache.

The man's eyes continued to swell and redden. Blood began to pour from his nostrils. His hair stood on end and his ears flared. Vessels and capillaries across his face pulsed with heightened traffic. And then, finally, after one last thrust of Neapolitan, his entire head exploded with a nauseating pop, and a wave burst of blood, bone and other matter spattered against my face.

Feeling his body become limp, I released my grip, wiped my eyes and caught my breath. As soon as I could muster the clarity, I pushed away from the man's body and lay on my back, looking up at the sky above me. My heart beat at a pace I'd never known and I felt a dark, growing ache inside me.

Just as I had upon crash-landing into the coast of Calais, all I wished to do was to continue to lie on that ground and gaze at the blue above, and convince myself I was back home. But my peace was intruded upon as the silhouette of Michael-Steve Burrows moved into view. He stood above me, wielding the unfired rifle.

"Well," he said, "His banana certainly has bits in it now."

In a split second, I leapt to my feet and grappled him by the neck.

"You treacherous deviant! You knew! You knew he was German and might kill me!"

"Baggy!" He choked. "Baggy, you've gone utterly mad. You have become insane with envy of my inspiring choad-"

I slapped him across the face.

"You sent me into that clearing knowing full well that he intended me harm, and you wilfully did NOTHING to interfere."

"Baggy, stop!" Burrows gasped for air.

My hands tightened around his throat. I considered that, having taken one life from a man who had wanted to kill me, a second scoop might not be overindulgent.

"Baggy, please, listen to me," he continued as my rage rang. "If I wanted you dead, you would already be."

I softened my grip, somewhat shocked by the bluntness of his admission.

"What do you mean?"

"There was a moment where I could have let you die and I did not. Think about it, Baggy. In the hot-air balloon, above Germany. You were holding onto the ladder when it became electrified and I pulled you away. I can tell you that I thought about not intervening, but I tell you that in shame. For a moment, I thought I might let you die in a final act of victory to end our petty rivalry. Instead, I remembered why we are rivals to begin with; because our brilliance is on a similar tier. We are equals; to our detriment. And for all the disrespect we show each other, below it is a foundation of total admiration. And I realised, in that balloon basket, that I could not allow the man I admire the most to die, even if he did occasionally shit me to tears."

I released my clasp completely but was not entirely convinced by his performance. Michael-Steve Burrows' sudden conversion to awe and wonder felt suspiciously timed, but his admission of preventing my death was undeniable. And given the sobering encounter with mortality that I had so recently experienced, I had no choice but to acknowledge my overreaction.

"Let us find this battalion, end this war, and once-and-for-all be done with each other," I said.

"An agreeable plan of action," Burrows replied.

In haste, we left the clearing, stopping only to retrieve the former-ice cream man's pistol and enjoy a plentiful serving of banoffee sorbet served atop pancakes that we managed to hash together from the items amongst our meagre rations. Once we were done, we headed again beneath the shadowy canopy of the Ardennes and resumed our search for the elusive 9th Army.

The interruption in the clearing had severely disorientated the two of us, and we argued bitterly over which direction we should assume. It was my confident belief that we should head northeast from our position, while Michael-Steve Burrows suggested we should perhaps tunnel down into the earth and verify whether or not our comrades had become submerged. After much argument, we agreed to meet each other halfway and headed further into enemy territory whilst adopting a severe hunch that wreaked havoc on our calf muscles but afforded us the ease of knocking on the forest floor every so often and asking if anyone was there.

Eventually, the sun slipped away and the wintry night crept in. We resigned ourselves to another day of expedition and set-up camp, only to realise that neither of us had thought to pack a tent or any equipment capable of starting a fire. The temperature dropped to a deathly cold, and we acknowledged that our only chance of survival was to take it in turns to rest, whilst the other ran in little circles around the sleeper, generating a meagre pocket of heat from the dispelled energy. Our method of warming ourselves eventually resulted in a net loss as far as recuperating our strength went, and so when the sun finally announced morning, we posited that we had both earned something of a lie-in, and slept under a tree until four in the afternoon.

When we stirred from our slumber, we did so due to the all-too-familiar tingle of feeling something fearful afoot. Of the two of us, I was first to hear the haunting, nasal hum ramp from the silence. I could not place its exact origin, but it was an ungodly, monotonous, charmless sound that grinded through my ears. I grabbed Burrows by the wrist, narrowly avoiding both his penis and whatever predictable comment along the lines of "Oh, don't worry, you're not the first to mistake my arm for my thriving and much-celebrated chubber" that would follow.

He moaned angrily until the sound reached his own temple.

"What is that?" he whispered.

"I don't know. Tanks perhaps?" I replied.

"Ours or theirs?"

"I'm not sure. What's the difference in sound between an English and German tank?"

"Does it sound more forlorn or more angry to you?"

"A little forlorn, I suppose."

"Could be ours then."

We summoned all our stealth and shuffled over to a dense patch of fauna, behind which we could crouch and observe out of view. The odious droning continued as we held our breath and darted our eyes about, expecting at any second to see a glint of dull metal or hear the sounds of soldiers' voices.

I brandished the Luger in one hand and placed my other over my beating heart, willing it to quieten down. Michael-Steve Burrows raised the rifle to eye level. The ominous whine grew louder, approaching.

And then we saw movement. The stillness of the forest was interrupted by ripples of motion among drab greenery; at first we thought it to be the wind but almost immediately after recognised we were seeing the olive garb of military fatigues coming toward us, at distance, from the northeast.

"Baggy, we must run," Michael-Steve spoke. "They're coming from the German lines and that sound... The 9th Army is not mechanical. We need to escape before it's too late."

But at that moment, I understood why the discomforting, disappointed audio felt reminiscent. Memories clicked into place and where certainty once tilted, clarity stabilised its perch. It was not a tank. It was none other than the less-than-sweet, dulcet tones of the cor-anglais! And I knew confidently, in a similar vein to other terrible inventions whose names included reference to the race that made them - such as Australian Football or American cheese or, to a lesser extent, the Spanish Flu - no man of a nationality other than English could possibly be lured to accept the mediocrity of the instrument's timber, were it not for the patriotic nature of its moniker.

I rose from behind our bushel and announced myself.

"Gentleman. You must be the 9th Army. My colleague and I have been searching desperately for you. Allow me to-" I began, just before they quite reasonably fired a warning shot. I was surprised, though I had to admit I would have done a similar thing. Perhaps where my own choice of action might differ from theirs, is that the preferred target of said warning shot would be up and away from the individual I was attempting to warn, and not just below their left clavicle.

I grunted as I felt the bullet's impact, but remained standing long enough to mention the very important detail that I was, in fact, on their side, and that the very menacing and very German Luger I was waving at them in what I had intended to be a welcoming gesture, had been recently looted from the corpse of an enemy soldier.

After a brief internal counsel, I decided it best to slump to the ground and commence whimpering. The once-nervous members of the 9th Army followed up their single warning shot with a torrential volley of heartfelt apologies.

"Good lord!" said one of them. "A thousand sorries, old chap. I could have sworn I'd pointed this damned thing far away from you. There *is* a light breeze in the air. Perhaps that shifted the bullet's trajectory."

I motioned cheerfully with my non-shoulder-clutching hand and explained that we'd all, at some time or another, accidentally shot a person who was calmly walking toward them. Blood oozed from the wound, down my chest, and I doubtlessly turned a shade whiter when I moved my hand and snuck a glance.

At this time, Michael-Steve bounded toward me, towing our supplies and sole rifle.

"Oh, Baggy. You've succumbed to friendly fire. How was it?"

"Decidedly unfriendly."

"Well, who could blame them, really?"

"Me."

"Quite. But don't worry. It looks harmless enough. You've a perfectly decent other shoulder on your right and, if I may say so, I've always felt your left one has been disappointing. Look there, a medic is on his way and one can tell by his having stopped to light a cigarette that he's not taking this seriously enough for it to be considered fatal."

I was remiss to admit that Burrows' words gave me much-needed reassurance, and I summoned the fortitude to stop weeping. I waited for the medic to finish his cigarette and, while I did, my attention was lured by a dramatic flash of purple that broke from the infinite green of the Ardennes.

A glittering, violet figure approached us via fabulous swagger, garnished with a pure white military-grade top hat and walking cane. Where his drab olive garb should have been, instead was a sequined patchwork camouflage that would have perhaps concealed him if we were not in a forest, but in a dance club for non-hetero mantis shrimp.

"What flowers of England doth we have here amidst this foreign woodland?" Hilary Lavender said, raising a monocle to his right eye. "Oh my! Unless my lying irises are up to their usual wicked ways, is it not young Mister Michael-Steve Burrows and young Mister Baggy Smacker I see before me?"

We confirmed that it was.

"Heavens above. Indeed, it's a small world we inhabit. Last time we were all together in company, I sensed the birth of a bitter hatred between the two of you and yet here you both are, harmoniously betrothed! I suspect there is something of a tale to tell?"

I was hoisted to my feet by two soldiers and we all set off for the 9th Army's makeshift encampment, no more than a mile to the north. We arrived to find a well-established base of operations, complete with a comfortable barracks, decently-stocked cocktail bar, and a dedicated hot room for "high-intensity battle-yoga". As we entered the compound we saw, to our left, that construction of an elevated infinity pool was close to completion, and ahead of us a non-commissioned officer held a sign listing the price of various types of massage.

"The service is strictly *non*-sexual," Lavender winked, "though only if you pay extra."

Burrows and I were escorted to the canteen and generously fed a rich carbonara served in a hollowed coconut as a field doctor attended to my shoulder. As Michael-Steve had suggested, the wound was not so terrible, though the physician did advise that he only had the resources to patch me up for the time being, to be followed up once proper facilities were available.

As we ate, Hilary filled us in as to how he had come to be a leading figure at the vanguard of the Western Front. Following the capitulation of his television programme - to which I once again thoroughly apologised - he had achieved what he could to maintain a foothold at the BBC, and for a short time it seemed as if he had done so successfully.

"I pitched a documentary series, with success, called 'Blindingly Quick'. In it, we took discharged greyhounds - dogs that had been deemed too slow for racing - and we saved them from euthanisation to be reskilled as seeing-eye dogs for the visually impaired. It was well-praised and we approached award season with confidence and the assurance of every bookie in Britain that we'd sweep the ceremonies. But our luck was damned, for that was the year of the Great Rabbit Plague. Forty-two out of fifty of our featured blind people died from terminal whiplash and, soon, our number-one position on the ratings charts was cruelly ripped from us. We left award season disgraced and empty-handed, even missing out on the Welsh BAFTA for Highest Body Count in a Light Entertainment Programme which instead ended up going to a convincing Catholic education piece about the theological repercussions of masturbation."

Once it appeared that his broadcasting career in Britain had failed, Hilary emigrated to the continent in the hopes of courting executives in the other major European nations. The French, Swedes, Spaniards, Portuguese and Danish all gave the cold shoulder, and while he received interest from distant Australia about the possibility of reproducing 'Blindingly Quick' in their new world with kangaroos instead of greyhounds, Lavender pulled out on moral grounds when, after weeks of negotiation, they asked him for the best advice on how to make the contestants lose their sight, as only four naturally-impaired volunteers could be found in the country.

As Hilary considered retirement from an industry that continued to reject his ideas, war broke out. He revealed that he had been approached in much the same manner as had Burrows and I and was only too willing to offer his services to the British war effort. However, in Lavender's case, he had rejected the opportunity to play a role in the world of intelligence, instead choosing life on the frontline.

"I couldn't tell you why, boys. I suppose depression had made the thought of a death in combat appealing? But whatever the case, I thrived and in very little time earned the title of Captain, leading at the front from Normandy to what you see before us. When our push through the Ardennes drew to a stop, and the order to retreat was given to us, we politely declined. I see no point in heading backward when we've sacrificed so much to be here. Besides, we have settled in nicely and even have a happy hour between five and seven. In the evening *and* morning."

We attempted to explain to Hilary of the exposure his out-of-position soldiers were causing, and High Command's desperation to have them rejoin the main line before the Germans could encircle the 9th Army and destroy him and his men, but to sway him was a more severe challenge than we'd hoped.

"Nonsense, boys. Let them surround us. These men you see here are more battle-hardened than any outfit that the enemy can muster at this stage in the war. I've seen these boys submit Panzers with nothing more than a thrust of their supple hips. In defensive formation, and I mean *only* in defensive formation, our front is impenetrable, as is our rear."

Burrows and I continued to state our case and illustrate the gravity of the situation, but it was to no avail. This was not unexpected, however. No captain, let alone one as proud and ambitious as Hilary Lavender, would care to take orders from soldiers that were, by all apparent accounts, vastly inferior in rank. We had been briefed, in anticipation of such a happening, to assemble a radio post and contact High Command as soon as possible, who would in turn speak to Lavender personally and apply the required pressure to have the man conform.

Hilary eyed us with a hint of disappointment but nonetheless commanded his men to see to our every need. We were bathed, given fresh clothes, offered complimentary deep-tissue coconut milk massages, and treated to a brief but spirited nine-hole round of golf on the newly-designed course that had apparently only been completed the previous week. Burrows was delighted even further when a clean, undamaged and much-more-realistic prosthetic penis extension was delivered to our dormitory; donated from Captain Lavender's personal collection.

"If that thing could talk, well, you'd reprimand it immediately for daring to do so with its mouth full," Hilary quipped with what we hoped was the last of his daily quota for lurid double-entendre.

Michael-Steve immediately went to change into his new appendage, thoughtfully stopping to offer me his old one should I desire it.

"Your loss," he said quite wrongly, in response to my declination.

Our lodgings were reasonable, consisting of two double beds, shower facilities and a mini-bar stocked with bottles of a milky, fermented something that claimed to be "locally sourced". Given my previous experience with Hilary Lavender's homemade concoctions, it felt wise to resist indulging, and instead I turned to what appeared to be a coffee station close to the refrigerator. A french press sat next to a small, wooden set of drawers labelled with phrases such as "Robust and Riveting", "Rigid and Persistent" and "Long Kenyan Black", which we assumed would be filled with ground coffee, before we opened each one to observe row upon row of neatly-packaged prophylactic sheath.

We agreed to commence work on the radio post in the morning once we'd discovered that we'd arrived just in time for the weekly pub quiz night at the company mess hall and that pints of Stella were two for one. Michael-Steve and I were placed on the same team with a tediously uninformed man named Darryl who, among many atrocious mistakes, insisted that the answer to the question "What great opponent of Cartesian dualism resists the reduction of psychological phenomena to physical states?" was "The humble frog." Miraculously, we managed third place.

That night, Michael-Steve Burrows slept like a baby, and I slept like an adult, the difference being that I didn't defecate in my bed and fall out every few minutes, complaining about the lack of railings. I awoke at three in the morning, to the sound of my colleague drunkenly dropping a bottle from the mini-bar, and had to wait an hour for an engineer to come and install a child lock before I was able to return to bed.

Despite the interruption, we managed to rise at six with reasonable clarity and commenced work immediately, under the unenthusiastic eye of Hilary Lavender and his equally-dubious men. The doctor's makeshift repairs to my clavicle and prescribed medication were doing an admirable job of subduing the pain, but an icy-cold wind tore through the Ardennes, agitating my nervous system enough to compel a pause for an early lunch. While I departed for the canteen, Michael-Steve Burrows declared that he had become overcome by the lust for the hunt, and instead chose to fetch his rifle and shoot for exotic beast out in the woods.

I didn't think much of his decision, as it was far from the most strange thing my colleague had uttered in the past few days, and I only nodded with feigned interest as he mentioned he'd heard an overly-confident man talk of hunting down elk on a radio show, which had presumably stirred some broken masculine sentiment within him. Instead, I entered the company canteen and saw only a few other inhabitants. I fetched a meal from the serving station and poured a generous glass of water, only to be mildly irritated to discover that it was in fact imported Tasmanian gin. I sat at a table by myself where I became overwhelmed with paranoia that others were judging my inability to capably use chopsticks.

Minutes later a figure sat next to me and as I peered up, I recognised the face of the man who had, the previous day, accidentally shot me in the shoulder.

"Mind if I join you?" he asked.

I admitted I did not.

"Terribly sorry about all that shooting you business."

"Oh, that's quite all right. I appear to be healing well enough and I consider myself blessed to have at least one scar to boast of when all this is said and done. I promise to conjure a more thrilling story, when in the future people ask, and leave your name entirely out of it."

"I appreciate that very much."

"And for that matter, what is your name?"

"Salmon. Quentin Salmon."

"A pleasure to meet you, Quentin Salmon. And what is your role around these parts?"

"Marksman, would you believe."

"I see. And have you ever considered firing toward the frontline, rather than away from it?"

"It seems I at least missed that part of you that drives your wit."

"A joke among friends," I reassured.

"Yes, I know. May I call you Baggy?"

"Certainly."

"The thing is, Baggy, I am usually a terribly good shot. Exceptionally good, in fact, and I am one who is hesitant to boast. If I want to hit something, I rarely miss. Furthermore, when I want to not hit something, I'm quite good at that too. I'd even add that not hitting things is significantly easier than hitting things."

"I believe you."

"Which is why, yesterday, when I was deemed to have shot you in the shoulder, I can't help but feel very, very surprised. Because I am very sure I did not aim at you."

"What are you implying," I asked in a now-serious tone.

"It's just that- I raised my weapon, and I pulled the trigger, and I heard only a single shot that I presumed to be my own. And perhaps I am wrong, and perhaps I indeed am responsible for the bandages around you. But whilst I heard only one shot, and whilst I pulled only one trigger, my weapon was not the only one raised…"

"My colleague's weapon, I believe you're implying."

"Yes."

I immediately lost my appetite and pushed my plate away.

"Are you sure?" I asked Quentin Salmon.

"No, I'm afraid not. But something seems off about your friend."

"There's no denying that."

I thanked Quentin for his advice and took my leave from the table, hoping a brisk walk would quell the surging rage. With fists clenched, I stamped through the encampment trying to figure out Burrows' deception. What was his plan?

It seemed evident he was working against me, but for what purpose? This could surely no longer simply be the miserable vengeance of a jaded and bitter rival. Even a man of his frailty could not bear a grudge so murderous. There must be something more sinister, larger and complex afoot, I thought. As Michael-Steve himself had said, there had been ample opportunity to end my life, but instead he seemed content to drag it out. Clearly there was a missing piece of the puzzle, and I was now certain I needed to figure out precisely what it was if I desired to return to England alive. The first step to doing so was to erect the radio post and make contact with High Command. Once I had done so, I could speak privately with James Ferdinand Bambi and ensure I was evacuated to safety at the quickest opportunity.

I returned to where we had commenced construction, to find Michael-Steve Burrows standing next to the limp body of a beast.

"Behold, Baggy, the slain elk of a hunt that would impress the Olympians themselves!" he declared proudly.

As I got closer, I could see that his "slain elk" was in fact a sleeping whippet with branches strapped to its ears. I sighed loudly and clapped my hands, causing the animal to snap awake, shake off its head-dress and sprint away. "Fascinating! It appears we have observed an actual feat of reincarnation!" he bullshitted.

I elected not to press any further and instead suggested we resume building the radio post. I had already decided I would not confront Michael-Steve then and there about his role in my injury, and instead bide my time and use it to connect the dots of his subterfuge. So with difficulty, I feigned camaraderie as best I could and we continued our erection.

By nightfall, we had completed our work and allowed ourselves a moment to marvel. The building was makeshift but sturdy, and within it was a simple-but-adequate radio console that held the key to completing our mission and getting the hell out of the Ardennes. Michael-Steve suggested that we should celebrate with a few bottles of fermented milk, but I could not contain my urgency and insisted that we power up the equipment and notify High Command of our location post haste.

With Burrows' assistance, we activated the radio and configured its signal so that we could deliver an encrypted message to Bletchley Park.

"This is Sapper Baggy Smacker of the 701st Sanitation Company. I repeat, this is Sapper Baggy Smacker of the 701st. Our rendezvous with the ninth is a success however-" I began, before being cut off by an incoming voice.

"Hello. You've reached British Intelligence. We are currently closed and have no agents available to take your call. If you would like, please leave a message after the tone and we will get back to you as soon as possible. Should you wish to call back, our opening hours are nine-to-five, Monday to Friday. We sincerely apologise for any inconvenience and look forward to hearing from you in the future."

Reluctantly, I agreed that we must wait until the morning, though I opted out of Burrows' festivities, voicing discomfort from my wound as well as my suspicion that Lavender had quite likely dipped a part of himself into the bottles present in our mini-bar.

I went directly to my dormitory, in which I instantly succumbed to an exhaustion whose escalation I had not noticed. When I awoke, I noticed someone had seen fit to place a baby monitor aside Burrows' bunk, though he was nowhere to be seen. I scanned the floor, expecting to see evidence of his internal movements, yet saw nothing. In the air, I could smell smoke, as if a bonfire had been held within the camp. As I had done so in similar situations that aroused suspicion, I felt the hairs on my neck perk to attention.

Quickly, I dressed and raced outside, to the place where we had toiled so arduously the previous day. I do not know how I knew to expect what I saw, but I can vividly recall the lack of surprise.

Where there had once been a pristine, functional radio post, was now a smouldering, blackened pile of rubble. Small embers still flickered and smoke continued to plume, but it was clear that the arson had been triggered several hours ago, perhaps mere minutes after I had excused myself for rest.

I glanced up and down the encampment, to see heads pop out of tents and peer toward me. Slowly, the members of the 9th Army emerged and congregated around the remains of our objective.

"Were any of you witness to this sabotage?" I demanded. "In the name of His Majesty, you must tell me."

For seconds there was stillness. And then.

"I saw it all," came a lavish bellow.

Hilary Lavender strode through his ranks and came to stand beside me.

"Tell me what happened," I spoke through clenched teeth.

"I think you well know. It seems I did not, in fact, underestimate the seeds of hatred I saw planted between you and young Mister Michael-Steve. Last night, following our inaugural 'Chook Nuggs & Goon' festival that you tragically missed out on, I found myself on a late-night wander. The night was pitch-black and I had only my memory of the camp's layout to guide me. But through the darkness, I saw a flicker of light. A flame. And it moved from your quarters, up to the spot that we now stand in."

"And did you see who carried this flame?"

"No, it was too dark to see. But the flame was carried at what would be shin-height for a normal adult."

At that moment, another voice rang out, more shrill than Lavender's.

"Behold, Baggy, for again I have conquered nature's danger and thwarted a majestic jungle panther that we will tonight dine upon!"

All heads turned to observe Michael-Steve Burrows emerge with a pantomime stagger from the woods, hoisting what I recognised to be a very-much-alive Mister Pepperbridge over his shoulders. When he entered the gathered crowd and saw the dwindling embers of our endeavour, Burrows' mouth dropped and the Russian Blue took an opportunity to scratch fiercely at his neck before extricating himself from the impending fervour.

"What in god's name have you done?" he asked.

"You ask what *I've* done? What have *you* done?" I responded.

"Me? Baggy, I have been hunting all night. You think I did this?"

"I *know* you did this."

"Baggy, I-" Burrows began, before Hilary interrupted.

"Do not lie to us, Michael-Steve. I saw you. I watched you last night. I watched you leave the mess hall, filled to pussy's bow with chook nuggs and goon. Do you forget how inebriated you became and the things you said?"

"What things?" I asked. "What did he say last night?"

"I intended to tell you this morning, but it seems that young Michael-Steve has been planning your downfall for quite some time. And last night, he made that very well known to anyone who might care to listen. I assume his revenge would take the form of something personal. Had I known that his pettiness would jeopardise the war effort, I would have had him shot on the spot."

"Baggy, these are lies!"

"Quiet!" I compelled Burrows. "Tell me exactly what he said," I demanded of Lavender.

"He spoke openly of the torment that your insults, at that first time of meeting, had caused him throughout the past years. He went on to discuss, loudly, of how cravingly he dreamt of your come-uppence. He specified, shamelessly, of how nothing felt more important to him than ensuring you felt no sense of success in your life, all to avenge the day that you told him he had a baby penis. Any lengths, he told us, would be worth it if it meant he could see you be comprehensively vanquished."

I turned to face Michael-Steve. He appeared aghast and exposed, like a man who had recently been shown a video clip of themselves eating buffalo wings using only their hands.

"Did you say such things?"

"Well, yes, but-"

"Quiet! I have put up with far too much of your evil, Burrows. Nothing would ever have been between us had you managed to silence your ego for Joseph Darkfire's recital. Had your jealousy and contempt not driven you to heckling, our paths might have never crossed. I forgave you for that heinous act. I even forgive you for your vengeance, for ending my career on camera, in front of an audience of millions. I blame myself for thinking too highly of you, that you might one day be mature enough to move on from our historical grievances. I hold myself responsible for believing that there was a single ounce of decency in you, or a scintilla of priority that might pressure you to put your entire country ahead of your petty, worthless quest for undeserved retribution. But no. You could not. You have, along all this way together, plotted to end me in the vain hope that my death could be followed by the demise of the disdain you hold for yourself. But you've now been discovered; caught in the act of vengeance. You have gladly risked the lives of tens of thousands of your own countrymen, simply to act out a perverse manifestation of the envy of the tiniest possible man. I dare to ask, but have you anything to say for yourself?"

Michael-Steve Burrows took a deep breath and used the pause it offered to conjure whatever defence he might muster.

"Baggy. You must believe me. I am not denying that I said those things but I did so under a chemical influence. That is not an excuse, that is an explanation. There is no point saying otherwise; the devastation to my identity that you dealt, all those years ago, still aches as heavily now as it did that day. I was deservedly humiliated, and nothing I have been able to do has successfully vanquished the demons that were summoned. And while I try to overcome the shadow that chases me every single day, in moments of weakness, I sometimes fail to outrun him. But I beg that you believe me; I did not wreak this destruction. I did not betray England. And I most certainly did not seek a petty vengeance at your expense."

I felt my determination slip but reminded myself of the devious tyrant I was finally, truly confronting. How long could I keep falling for his lies? How often had I deluded myself because I had *wanted* to believe there was some ounce of redeemable decency left in the man before me? Mentally, I recomposed myself and fortified my vindication.

"Then who did, Burrows? Who else here has any reason for this sabotage?"

Michael-Steve's eyes dropped to the ground. As his silence festered the morning air, an aide of Lavender's stepped forward and pressed my Luger into my hands.

"This is an act of treason, Smacker," Lavender spoke solemnly, "and I needn't remind you of the required punishment."

I looked at the weapon and pondered whether I possessed the fortitude to execute the man before me. On one hand, I would be rid of the perpetual thorn in my side whilst saving the world from a toxic, self-worshipping ego that would only do it further harm. On the other, taking a life had by no means become more attractive since the altercation with the ice cream man in the Ardennes. The difference between that moment and this one was choice. I had no option but to defend myself against the enemy and force-feed him litre upon litre of frozen confectionery. But here, the decision to end a life would be mine and the memory of that path I took would, I knew without doubt, live prominently in my soul until the day my lungs ceased their toil.

After allowing my heart to present its case, my embittered and jaded brain took over. There had been too many chances given. Too long had been spent awaiting a never-forthcoming change of allegiance. This needed to end now.

I raised the pistol and aligned its sights to where the heart of Michael-Steve Burrows presumably at one point had been. My finger began to press upon the trigger.

"Lavender," he said to no prompt.

"What?" I asked.

"Lavender did this."

I considered immediately firing the weapon and ending his next issue of dishonesty before it had time to escape his mouth, but once again I found my will overcome by the naive want to acquit a person I had known, albeit reluctantly, for so much of my life.

"Do not allow his nonsense, Baggy, pull the trigger," Hilary Lavender raised his voice, "I command you, as your superior officer, to serve His Majesty's justice to this traitor."

"Baggy, you must recognise his insanity. He does not want to return to the line. He does not wish to rejoin the allied war effort. If he did, he would be there. Look at this place. It is a temple to his ego."

"Oh come, now. You can do better than that," tittered Lavender.

"Think about it, Baggy, I beg you. All that this man lives for is validation. His entire existence is about being worshipped. Why do you think such a man is drawn to television, despite being so odious and so frequently failing to find an audience? Here, he has one by decree. Look around you, Baggy. This is not a temporary army base. This is a man building a utopia from his self-image with an army of slaves. This is merely his latest vanity project."

Without tilting my head, I glimpsed about the encampment and acknowledged, for the first time, that there were a far greater number of vaudeville theatres than what would be considered normal for a base of operations of this size. In the not-so-distance, I could hear the trickling of water of the opulent and erotic fountain made in Lavender's image at the entry gates. Even as I clenched the pistol's grip, I noticed that the side of it had been recently sequined with pink gemstones that formed the sentence "naughty boys go on this end" followed by an arrow pointed in the direction of the barrel.

"Baggy! Pull it together!" Lavender roared. "He's doing to you the exact same thing he has always done, isn't he? I can see it in your eyes, the impending defeat. He is winning, and you are letting him. You need to do this right now because if you cannot, in this most important circumstance, rise above his treachery, then you might as well shoot yourself. I know it is hard. I cannot imagine the pain you are feeling. But if you allow yourself to give in and surrender to the devil at the most pivotal moment of your life so far, he will own your will for the rest of your life. Do it Baggy Smacker. End this once and for all. I am telling you this, not as your commander, but as Hillary Lavender, your friend and colleague and countryman."

And with that, I spun around, aimed the pistol at the glittering, violet torso of Captain Lavender, and shot him six times in the chest. His body fell limply to the ground, dead, and even the misty fog of the Ardennes froze in place from the shock. The echoes of the gunshots seemed to reverberate through the trees for minutes, until eventually dispersing, followed by the resumption of birdcall and the rhythmic bass sound of a nearby bikercise class.

"Baggy. Wh... How?" Michael-Steve Burrows asked.

"You were right. It was him."

"How did you know?"

"Did you not hear it? He referred to himself as Hillary. *With two 'L's.*"

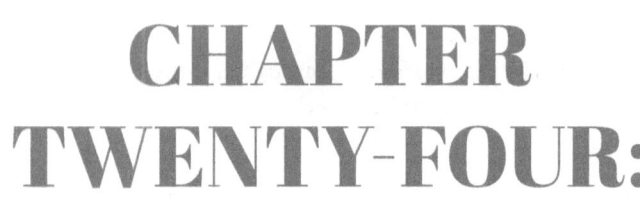

CHAPTER TWENTY-FOUR:

The Last Call

Burrows and I were immediately presented with the difficult issue of having quite publicly executed an officer of the British military, without tangible evidence, in front of a large audience of well-armed soldiers who were, for the most part, very loyal to the recently departed. Luckily though, seconds before they finalised voting on how best to exact our capital punishment, morning meal was called for and the troops departed for their daily disappointment of remembering what a continental breakfast consisted of, giving us enough time to hurriedly reassemble the radio post. The night's arson had all but destroyed most of the equipment, so calling High Command in despair was not an option, but we were at least able to craft together the outer structure of the building enough that it appeared to be a working method of communication.

By the time the soldiers had eaten, complained about rock melon, and returned to apply their elected justice, we had erected the facade of a radio post and, while I stood outside deceptively warning anyone who approached not to enter due to a recently-discovered infestation of estate agents, Burrows stood within, mimicking the sounds of incoming transmission with impressive replication.

"Attention fine men of the 9th. Just letting you know that you need to execute Captain Hillary Lavender. You see we just got off the phone with His Majesty, and it turns out that Hillary Lavender is working for the Germans. You heard correctly, Lavender is working with the enemy. Don't worry, we're as stunned as you are. Apparently he agreed to betray you all in return for a prime-time slot on German breakfast radio. Shocking, we know, but I think we can all agree that it's exactly the sort of thing the cheeky git might do... Oh what? Oh you've already done it? You've already shot him several times in the chest and he went down faster than a homesick mole? Well, what an exemplary example of foresight. Ruthless, unquestioning trigger-fingers are precisely the sort of thing we're all about here in the Army so congratulations. You can all expect gift vouchers with your next paycheck."

The response was unanimous and the men of the 9th Army collectively wiped their brow in relief and began to discuss how best to return to the frontline where they might finally be rid of this life of hedonism, and get back to the aching, spirit-wrenching sense of futility and fear of death that, as members of the non-elite, they were presumably much more comfortable with.

I recall vividly the release of weight from my shoulders at that moment, and how fleeting calm's visit was, for in less than an hour, chaos would resume. But for now, there was a strange serenity about the 9th Army's encampment that shielded one from the reality of their situation, and as such, it occurred to me too late that the cacophonic sounds of my recent gunfire wouldn't have needed to travel far to find enemy ears.

Our soldiers had dispersed to commence preparing for the evacuation of the camp, and so Michael-Steve Burrows and I had been left to awkwardly talk through the morning's tragedy, during which it was agreed that, for now, our safe departure would be considered highest priority, and that extended analysis and name-calling and the distribution of formalised self-righteousness could follow when we'd reached less-hostile territory.

A peculiar stillness had reached the camp; the sort that only bids its company prior to the most amplified devastation. Near us a small number of men had gathered to usher in one last ninety-minute full-body massage with the on-site regimental masseurs, and other than the muted slaps from the application of warmed oil and hand jobs, not a single sound registered. That all ended when the first mortar shell scored a direct hit between them, throwing the booking system into disarray and ending any chance of pre-mortem muscular therapy.

The initial blast and shockwave caught the two of us entirely off-guard, though Burrows still attempted a performance of nonchalance and insisted he had only dove so heavily to the dirt floor as he claimed to have seen an enchanting wood-nymph flirting with him from within a small brothel of leaves. I had dropped in undisguised terror and felt a fine mist of liquified humanity splatter against the back of my head.

I looked around just in time to see a second explosion, slightly further away from us but no less deafening. Where it landed, it carved a crater into the ground, and I reached for Burrows' hand and dragged him toward it. As we half-ducked to its relative safety, mortar fire poured from the air like tropical rain and the trees of the forest canopy made for an unreliable umbrella.

We watched an attendant of the company Information Booth dutifully and bravely attempt to bring in the racks of brochures from outside his stand, only to be thrown viciously up into the air by another explosion and fall bloodily and lifelessly into a nearby swim-up bar. The closest thing to last rites he would receive was a dog-paddling waiter apologetically advising what remained of him that they were out of Carta Blanca before he too was vaporised in another direct hit.

Up and down the encampment, a harmonic scream of human anguish formed a bassline to the shelling's rhythm. Michael-Steve and I had reached our foxhole safely and tucked ourselves as deeply within it as our tightly-clenched bodies would permit. Though we were protected, we winced at every consecutive explosion and shivered in time with the reverberations of each shockwave. We didn't dare peek our heads out, for fear of death.

I have no idea how long the onslaught lasted. It might have been five minutes, it could have possibly gone on for an hour. Not for the first time, I noted that when mortality presents itself, time pops out for a late lunch. But eventually, the ear-splitting hellfire winded down to a sweet nothing, and

I dared to poke my head up beyond the womb-like comfort of our hiding place, to survey what was left.

Where once there had stood an encampment with the spirit of a paradisiacal resort was now a smoking graveyard of misery, akin to an off-season Butlins. Thick smoke hung about the air and the quiet of the ceasefire felt as if it stood with the uncertain balance of an elderly man stumbling toward the front of a moving bus. Slowly, the peace was terminated by the growing moaning of the wounded.

I turned to Michael-Steve Burrows.

"This is not over. They will soon come to clean up what remains of us. You need to assume command and rally these men," I said.

"Why me?"

"Because I hold the rank of Sapper, you are a Lieutenant, and whatever we find left of this battalion will require a commanding officer. We did just kill the last one so it seems only fair. We need to ensure as many of them get out of here alive to refill the hole in the line."

"You're right," Burrows replied, staring into the distance. "My rank and girth are second to none at this most pivotal moment."

On instinct, I sighed very loudly but almost immediately realised that missing the chance to weaponise the state of Michael-Steve's self-belief would be counter-productive. I disguised my involuntary exhale as a preemptive breath taken prior to performance, and followed it with a stirring whistle of the Warsaw Concerto. Immediately, I triggered Burrows' inherently British instinct for pomp and he began to monologue without second thought.

"You're right, dear Baggy. There are times in one's life when remaining coyish and flaccid is perhaps acceptable. But there are other times, of far greater importance, that call for the erection of one's will. Until now, my life has been but a series of subdued thrusts yet here, in this seemingly futile woods, my veins throb with a much longed-for morning glory. I have many wrongs to right, my friend. I should think no one knows that moreso than you. My fortitude until now has been limp, the shaft of my spear sheathed, and my fired shots have all been blanks, but I assure you that impotence ends now in this gaping hole that you smartly lured me to. My friend, Baggy Smacker, I implore you to watch on as I emerge from this muck-drenched cavity and rise up like a column of pulsating desire to penetrate Honour's elusive chastity, erupt within her special cranny and leave my immortal stain on the guest-room bedsheets of history!"

With that, Michael-Steve Burrows scrambled up the walls of the mortar-crafted foxhole and stood at its edge as tall as his infant frame could muster.

"Men! It is time to regroup and pool together our will to live! If we redistribute our defences immediately, I believe I might have a way for us to walk home alive."

Burrows then raced from foxhole to foxhole, from hiding spot to hiding spot, from mini-golf course to mini-golf course, extricating from each the tired, scared and trembling remains of the 9th Army. After several minutes of action, he had wrangled a remnant force of just over a hundred men, with the lost number assumed to be dead or deserted. Each man stared with the glazed, obsidian-eyed shock of one who had recently spent an extended length of time on holiday and now had to face the harsh reality of their first Monday back at work.

Fortunately, Burrows' rally had not yet ceased its herald and before the fragile mood had chance to turn irreparably foul, he was already pacing through the ranks of soldiers handing out festive show bags containing varieties of confectionery not normally seen in reputable supermarkets. Despite the flavourless chalkiness of the candy, morale took a noticeable and instant upward turn as their collective trepidation was warped by a murmured agreement that the distribution of party favours had made everything leading up to the moment well worth it.

Once placated, the 9th Army gathered in a circle to listen to Michael-Steve Burrows' plan for the defence of the encampment. I listened intently, with only interest at first but then a growing sense of pride. In such little time he had conjured a quite-brilliant strategy and at that moment, along with my fellow countrymen, a tinder of optimism fell within my heart's reach. It felt as though we might make it out alive or, at the very least, make it hell for those who attempted to stop us. And it was down to the immaculately-timed ascent to maturity of my colleague - nay - my *friend*.

As Burrows reached the conclusion of his briefing, he was abruptly cut off by a burst of static from the radio booth, followed by a broadcast of such intense urgency that it miraculously repaired all of the equipment.

"9th, this is Rear Command. Aerial reconnaissance has confirmed an enemy approach from the north. Approximately four hundred men and six tanks in total. Prepare for engagement immediately."

Our faces fell white with fear. I had expected to be outnumbered, but not by four-to-one, and not at all had I considered a mechanised threat in the density of the forest. There was only time for a quick round of cocktails before the men dispersed into their hiding places and awaited the first signs of a German presence. I, along with Michael-Steve and a group of a dozen men, hid behind an Australian-themed steak restaurant and willed my heart to stop pounding with such veracity.

Burrows' plan was clever and daring but if it didn't go perfectly, I saw little hope of our managing to repel the attack. Even if all went as ideally as possible, the enemy's overwhelming numbers seemed insurmountable. I did my best to delude myself and imagine a life at home, in England, safely away from the terror of war. I would not take for granted such an existence ever again. I vowed to find a nice apartment to live in, not too near central London, but not too far. I promised myself I would get a pet cat and name him Brendan, and I would build a library room and fill it with books that I did not intend to read so that I might make visitors feel inadequate. I thought that, if I focussed on that fantasy intently enough, its realisation would become undeniable.

Next to me, a young soldier whimpered audibly. Another grasped at a crucifix that hung around his neck and whispered something to a few different gods to see if any of them were listening. Most of them were busy or had the day off, and when the only response was a series of recipe ideas from a voice that claimed to be a pagan God of Chutney, he too began to sob. I felt my will begin to waiver, as my breathing became laboured through stress.

In an effort to appear unaffected, I holstered my Luger and searched my pockets for something to occupy my trembling hands. In the inner chest compartment of my jacket, my fingers touched a small folded piece of paper. I took it out, opened it and instinctively read aloud the poem that Joseph Darkfire had written for me all those years ago in Beeston Orphanage.

Hark ringing bells, that toll to herald morning's feast,
Come gather boys for roll, as called by vicious priest,
Leave tongues at loll, for food prepared by curlied beast,
And lay away those dreams of home, for now at least,
And lay away this gruel on which we live,
And lay away his chain with pain to give,
And lay away these hounds' neglect of sieve,
And climb above this all and learn, forgive,
For sunrise kills each night we dread,
Though our brothers will lie around us yawning,

And never we must count our nearly dead,
As we promise to ourselves, 'just one more morning'.

There was a pause. The soldiers' anguish for a moment ceased. My own heart beat at a less-worrying pace.

"Here, here," said Michael-Steve Burrows. "To one more morning, chaps."

As a whole, the others toasted, "To one more morning!" and one could almost hear the sound of spines straightening and chests puffing.

Minutes later, the distant hum of human chatter approached. As it neared the compound, it muted to whisper, but it was clear the enemy vanguard had arrived. From our position, we peered at the clearing to watch Burrows' wily plot unhatch.

As per his instructions, in an open area to the north of the encampment, two soldiers stood aside a porters trolley, attired in white linen and matching pillbox hats. They were playing their part well, engaging in small talk, idly smoking and by all accounts appearing well at ease. When the first Germans emerged from the trees, the men stamped out their cigarettes and assumed a more professional stance.

A group of four approaching enemy soldiers raised their weapons and shouted instructions at the porters, who simply waved politely as they approached. Dozens more Germans appeared behind them, though remained a sensible distance away as they observed the interaction play out.

The two British soldiers, with a level of audacity and courage I have not witnessed before nor since, walked up to the enemy and insisted on taking their bags for them. There appeared to be some hesitation at first, but that was soon brought to a close when another man, dressed in matching ivory clothing, exited a nearby 'Welcome Hut' holding a tray, upon which were a dozen small glasses of green tea. He proffered the drinks to the German soldiers who then accepted the porters' assistance in unloading their bags, weapons and ammunition onto the trolley. The Germans were then given directions to a reception desk, at which they were told they would receive the keys to their room, and as more of them were waved into the compound, thus began a steady stream of lost, unarmed enemy soldiers who would wander through the camp, into the mess hall, where they were bound and gagged and neatly stored in rows against the wall. Over the next thirty minutes, one hundred and ten men were hoisted by Michael-Steve's cunning petard, drawing the odds considerably closer to our favour.

Alas, luck ran out as it always seems to do and our bloodless decimation of the enemy came to a close when a suspicious Officer asked to see our liquor licence, snapping his comrades out of the illusion. The moment it became clear that we were unable to provide the proper documentation, the ruthless brutality of German bureaucracy spread through their ranks like a tsunami and the onslaught of gunfire exploded.

The brave faux-porters, administrative staff, and men whose job it was to pour green tea into very small cups via a decorative, ceramic teapot that was surely far too small to be considered an efficient vessel for the job, at once crumpled to the ground in the first volley. The deception had been going so well that the rest of the 9th were stunned into inaction when our curtain of deception fell, and for precious seconds no retaliation came forth.

The hesitation was ended by a bellow from Michael-Steve Burrows of a volume I'd not thought it possible for him to assume.

"FIRE!" he commanded.

At once, the remaining men, perhaps around eighty or ninety in total, poked from their hiding spots and unleashed hell. The element of surprise was on our side momentarily, and I saw dozens of Germans collapse as others scrambled for cover. I raised my weapon and fired several shots in the general direction of Germany before I heard the click of an empty chamber. I ducked back behind the steakhouse and lamented not having equipped myself with something better supplied with ammunition.

Instead, for the moment, I aided the counterfire of my comrades as best I could, whispering comments of praise into their ears and offering backrubs. At one point, a soldier stopped firing and announced that he just remembered he was a dual citizen of both Great Britain and Switzerland, and that he might pop off for a bit of holiday and see if his grandparents were still alive. Our small squad held a temporary ceasefire so that we might bid him a fond farewell and pass around shots of butterscotch schnapps, and as he departed for calmer lands I politely asked if he wouldn't mind giving me his rifle. Cheerfully, he acquiesced after I agreed to pay him forty pounds for it, and as soon as he'd filled out a receipt and handed it to me for tax purposes, I resumed the foray and, firing from the hip, mercilessly gunned down four enemy soldiers who I had meanwhile observed attempting to flank around the rear side of the building.

Given the German attempt to surround us, Michael-Steve and I agreed that it might be clever for myself and three of the remaining soldiers to take point around the other corner of the building, and so I carefully led the way and all four of us took cover behind a series of rusted-metal representations of the members of the Kelly Gang.

I held my newly-acquired weapon to my shoulder and fired a single shot toward a German soldier who was attempting to ask one of the dying porters for directions to the nearest restroom. I missed considerably and fell backwards as the sharp pain at my clavicle reminded me of my recent wound. Slumping to the ground, I realised that I was useless as far as operating a firearm at distance was concerned, and moved the receipt to a safer pocket in my jacket to ensure it was well-protected between now and my eventual request for a refund.

Knowing I could not directly contribute to the firefight, I instead surveyed it. It was difficult to determine who was winning. British soldiers peeked from hiding places to fire at the German forces in the forest north of them, only to immediately duck away before any response came their way. The enemy was equally-troublesome to detect, with their olive green fatigues offering perfect camouflage in the dense fauna of the Ardennes.

As I watched, I tallied the fallen men I saw on each side. By the time I'd spent all available fingers and toes on which to count, I had seen fourteen Germans fall to the ground, versus just six British soldiers, and it seemed that the advantage of our fortified positions and familiarity of what had become the battlefield might somehow be enough for us to be victorious.

Then the Panzers came.

There was something about the Ardennes that made one forget such a thing as a tank could exist. The utter proliferation of trees, the complete absence of pathway, and the all-engulfing insistence of nature combined to create a virtual world in which a graceless hulk of metal and brute force should not be permitted to inhabit.

Yet, when the clunking murmur of track against wood began to compete with the insistent snapshot of rifle fire, something compelled me to race back to Michael-Steve and warn him of the approach of a power we were not at all prepared to face.

Burrows, still buoyed by the effectiveness of his equalising subterfuge and the subsequent rally of the soldiers under his command, initially waved away my concerns.

"Fear not, Baggy. I recognise that sound. There is merely too much ice in the daiquiri machine over by that baby-changing booth. Simply add one-quarter of a teaspoon of salt and it will resume its function as per normal."

Moments after he said so, the first tank shell was fired. A deafening blast accompanied a stinging ripple of shockwave and we turned in time to see the remains of a food truck, and the half-dozen soldiers who had until recently hidden behind it, shower to the ground.

"Well, that's clearly too *much* salt-" Burrows began, before a second explosion viciously blew apart a tree that apparently looked, to the enemy, as if it might have been harbouring sympathy for European sovereignty.

Two sobering blinks of the eye later, Burrows was hailing a retreat.

"Fall back, men. Fall back to the members-only lounge!" he hollered.

Beneath a hailstorm of rifle fire, tank shelling and other common forms of German disapproval, our lines broke and began sprinting away from an oncoming force that, as it further emerged from the greenery, showed itself to be simply too overwhelming. Our defence had been admirable, but somehow the opposing threat still appeared to outnumber us two-to-one. Worse still, they had Panzers.

As I ran in panic, I realised I was being led by my wrist, and at its end was Michael-Steve Burrows, outpacing the entire retreat. With a dozen men in tow, he beelined to the swimming pool in which we had so recently seen bloodied in the earlier bombardment. All of us plunged into its rosé-coloured waters, attempted to order drinks, and then remembered where we were.

Burrows commanded the men to line against the side of the pool, where we were all mostly protected beneath ground level, and resume suppressing fire whilst the rest of the ninth army sought cover. Valiantly, we made the best of our concealed positions and picked off the oncoming enemy one by one, but the obliteration of our comrades was impossible to ignore.

Our small squad fired shot after shot, losing only two men to lucky ricochets before the smoking battlefield fell victim to another of the sort of peculiar silence that one can only experience amidst the juxtaposition of war noise.

For us, there were no Germans left to aim at. All who were exposed had fallen, and those who remained had hidden behind the shielded chassis of six approaching Panzer tanks. For them, all retreating British soldiers had either been gunned down, vapourised, or had found some grave in which to spend their last few minutes. Other than the mechanical grinding of tank treads, there was nothing in the air.

It felt futile to even consider our futility. There was no way to tally our remnants. We had nothing to pit against the German armour. Our only escape was to flee into the wintry void, without hope or supply, and rely on adrenaline and instinct and a vague idea of where the English Channel was. The prospect of death felt, if not welcome, comforting. But not for all, it seemed.

"Baggy," said the voice of Michael-Steve Burrows. "You look forlorn."

I pieced together what I could of a smile, and responded.

"You're right. Things are so lovely. I should be grateful."

"You do know you *would* survive if you went without sarcasm for a full hour?"

"You might be right, though I suspect we've not the time left to carry out a proper experiment," I replied.

"You know that I never hated you. I only envied you?" said Michael-Steve.

"Yes. And I think I was the same."

"Do you think we both took something from that hate? Something that compelled us? Something that drove us onward and upward?"

"Maybe, Michael-Steve. Maybe."

"I think more than 'Maybe'. I think we were both awful to each other. But I think we were both young, and we were both stupid and insecure. And I think we have regrets. And we both acknowledge that we could have done things better. And, given the chance, were we to grow older, I think we would become wiser, kinder, more forgiving."

"Given the chance, I agree," I said.

"You gave me my greatest weakness, Baggy. But in some strange way, you've given me my greatest strength. Look here," Burrows said, directing my attention toward his penis.

Where once I would have seen an ineffectual prosthetic John Thomas dangling between his chubby pink legs, instead was a vibrantly-erect adult-sized penis throbbing beneath the waterline, simultaneously impressive and biologically-concerning.

"Burrows! Have you been hit or stung by an errant bee?" I exclaimed.

"Not at all, Baggy. Not at all."

"You've... You're..." I whispered.

"That's right. Thanks to you. Thanks to this," he gestured at all around him. "Thanks to everything, I am no longer cursed with a baby penis. If we die here right now, I'm fine. I have filled the gaping chasm inside me, not with a pathetic facade of masculinity, but with the rim-tickling swell of hard-fought-for and absolute virility. I am at peace, right here, right now, other than the fact that it aches a bit. I wish we had a better way to celebrate overcoming our adversity and registering our friendship. But this is better than leaving life unfulfilled."

Michael-Steve Burrows extended his arms in a gesture of embrace, but I would be damned if he would be allowed to die having exorcised his insecurities whilst I retained so many of mine own. Instead of returning his intimacy, I demanded the attention of the soldiers who had been uncomfortably watching our dialogue, wondering if we were about to do something obscenely sexual to each other.

"MAKE YOURSELF READY TO FIRE. If we are to die, we die fighting!" I roared.

There was a small pause in which the men considered the pointlessness of firing rifles against tanks, but that was soon outweighed by the thought of having to hear more homoerotic in-talk, and the clicking of reloading rifles quickly broke the silence.

Despite my wound, I pulled my rifle up and balanced it against the side of the swimming pool. I lowered my eyes to its sights and aimed it directly at the turret hole of the foremost Panzer. I squeezed both my right eye and my finger, and pulled the trigger.

The sound was cacophonic. The pain was intolerable. The darkness of my clenched eyelids was impenetrably black. I followed the momentum of the gun's recoil and fell back into the water, hoping it would suppress the response of the enemy. When it came, I expected an eventual burrowing of tank shell into the ground before us that would break through the pool wall and end our struggle once and for all. I longed for the gradual increase of shockwaves and the respite that might follow them.

Instead, only the sound came. Repeatedly. Pound after pound of heavy fire breached my eardrums to evoke alarm.

But the feel, fear and darkness did not arrive. Nervously, I opened my eyes and looked at my comrades, who were all peering over the edge of the swimming pool, weapons at their sides. Not a word was being said, and not a bullet was being shot. I regained my footing and waded over, to discover what had all so entranced.

When I looked to where my recent target had been, I saw a smouldering, fire-lit husk. As I looked around, I saw two more enemy tanks in similar condition. Hatches atop the chassis opened to allow the drivers to exit, and either through astonishment or mercy, what remained of the British force allowed them to crawl to the ground and bathe in the cold dirt floor of the Ardennes.

The three remaining tanks turned their turrets to the west, and that was when I first saw the cavalry. Through the forest crept an assignment of eight British Cromwell tanks, weaker by all means by their German counterparts but graced by the ever-blessing sanctity of Lady Surprise. Before the Panzers could properly exploit their technological advantages, the speed and wile of the allied armour fired simultaneously, with multiple direct hits, and the tailing infantry turned heel and fled into the forest, knowing they had lost the battle.

As the last German scattered, we climbed from the pool, almost delusional, and stumbled toward the nearest friendly tank as if we were mortals at the Pearly Gates, who had just been advised that our rooms weren't ready just yet.

A hatch opened atop the nearest Cromwell, and a familiar face appeared from within.

"Baggy! Thought I might find you here," it said.

"Stephen Edgington. How on earth…"

"The pheromones, Baggy! The ant pheromones! It worked! I had a feeling you were in danger, and I knew precisely where to find you!"

"You're not serious?" I asked.

"You bet your bottom dollar it worked," said Stephen Edgington. "I told you it would. We just had to wait. I told you, *we just had to wait.* Did you think we spit-roasted that elderly woman you mistook for Queen Wilhelmina for absolutely nothing?"

I admitted that I didn't and decided, at that moment, to pass out from exhaustion and sleep through the remainder of the war.

EPILOGUE

The astute reader will recognise that, by this point in life, I had not become a doctor. That happens many years later. However, I feel as though this is a fine moment to break for a rest from tale-telling and allow this inaugural chapter of my memoir a chance to digest.

Surviving the war, turning a foe to a friend, and establishing myself as a gentleman blessed by what is most likely good fortune, rather than incredible skill or wisdom, is in my mind a satisfactory first act. I hope that the reader considers so too.

But there is much more to tell, and I will do so as quickly as I can manage. The future of Baggy Smacker involves more war. It involves more challenges. It involves the ups and downs of old friends and the adoption of new ones. It involves the joy and frustration of family. It contains romance, poetry, excitement and despair. It is peppered with adventures to foreign lands, monumental moments of history, and at least two events that I consider of equal significance to defying death in the Ardennes Forest. I also *do* eventually invent a type of low-calorie breakfast muffin.

The paths of Joseph Darkfire, James Ferdinand Bambi, Whitlock Smacker and so many more are by no means at an end. When their special moments come to pass, I am present, and I dearly hope that the reader joins me for their successes and losses.

But for now, I will rest my tired hands and thank all who have made it this far. And I will write to you again, very soon, and tell you in great detail of the next stage of the often marvellous life of Doctor Baggy Smacker.

Goodbye for now.